THE CARGO FROM NEIRA

THE CARGO FROM NEIRA

Alys Clare

**SEVERN
HOUSE**

First world edition published in Great Britain and the USA in 2023
by Severn House, an imprint of Canongate Books Ltd,
14 High Street, Edinburgh EH1 1TE.

Trade paperback edition first published in Great Britain and the USA in 2024
by Severn House, an imprint of Canongate Books Ltd.

severnhouse.com

British Library Cataloguing-in-Publication Data
A CIP catalogue record for this title is available from the British Library.

ISBN-13: 978-0-7278-2302-1 (cased)
ISBN-13: 978-1-4483-1281-8 (trade paper)
ISBN-13: 978-1-4483-1067-8 (e-book)

Typeset by Palimpsest Book Production Ltd., Falkirk, Stirlingshire, Scotland.

for Richard,
companion on the Island (and everywhere else);
with love, as always.

ONE

February 1605

'**D**octor. *Doctor*!'

The words were barely audible, the second one a mere hiss. I realized it was the voice of my housekeeper, Sallie. This was no reflection on the accuracy of my hearing, however, since she was the only person likely to be up and about in the house.

It was a raw, bitter morning in early February. January had given us a full month of this weather, with more snow than we were used to and an unrelenting cold that had meant the land was permanently white. I had been kept so busy that a whole night's undisturbed sleep was a rarity, and Christmas – which had been a particularly jolly season when even my solitary brother Nathaniel had deigned to join us – was now a faint memory.

I had been called out not long after midnight to attend a child in a desperate state. He had a congestion of the lungs, and consequently his breathing was so difficult that fear had spilled into panic, making matters far worse. His mother and I had sat him up, rubbed, patted and hit his back repeatedly, and the action had at last yielded the desired result: the little boy finally managed to cough up a good deal of thick phlegm.

Meanwhile the father had boiled a pan of water and, on my instruction, dropped into it a few drops of a strongly-smelling substance that Black Carlotta had given me in a small bottle made of dark glass. As the aroma filled the little room, it seemed to me that all four of us breathed more easily. The fact that whatever was in those drops also tended to make the eyes water copiously seemed a small price to pay.

Black Carlotta is, for want of a better term, our local wise woman. It may appear strange, or even inappropriate, for a modern man of science to have any dealings at all with such

a person, never mind doling out her remedies, but in the years
I have known her I have learned to trust and admire her. The
knowledge she shares with me comes from decades – centuries,
probably – of experience, handed down by word of mouth
through generations of women, and it is every bit as precious
as book learning.

I had been home for under an hour: time for little more
than a quick wash before diving into my bed and falling at
once into deep sleep.

And now here was Sallie, waking me up by hissing at me
in a manner that told me she wasn't going to stop until I
responded.

I opened my eyes and turned over to face the door.

'What is it, Sallie?'

She darted a glance back along the corridor as if checking
for eavesdroppers. Since at this hour on an icy winter morning
my sister Celia was undoubtedly tucked up warmly in her bed
at the far end of the house and still fast asleep, Sallie's caution
seemed unnecessary.

'Someone wants to see you,' she whispered.

'Yes?'

Another glance. 'It's that man. The coroner's man. *Sssshhh!*'
she added anxiously, even though I hadn't said anything.

I guessed who she meant, but before I could say his
name, she produced it. She didn't speak it, even in a whisper,
but simply mouthed *Jarman Hodge*.

I was already throwing back the covers and getting out of
bed. If Sallie was going to be quite so cautious, it would
take far too long to establish why Jarman Hodge wanted me,
and, more intriguingly, why it apparently had to be in secret.
'Give him a hot drink and tell him I'll be down directly,' I
said.

She nodded, closed the door with exaggerated caution and
was gone.

I took a long, last glance at my bed, then found clean
linen, dressed in my warmest garments and followed her
downstairs.

She was hovering at the foot of the stairs, and, catching my
eye, she jerked her head in the direction of the parlour.

'Library,' she whispered. Then she scurried into the kitchen and closed the door firmly behind her.

With a quick nod I strode through the parlour and into the library. The sky was barely light, and its weak rays did little to illuminate the room. The fine set of matching chairs were pushed under the heavy oak table, Celia's and my more comfortable chairs stood in their usual places either side of the hearth, and a fine layer of dust covered the polished wood: Sallie had not yet attended to the room this morning. The cold ashes of last night's fire added to the cheerless air, and in my sour, sleep-deprived mood I reflected dejectedly on the depressing fact that a place that was so warm, welcoming, secure and pleasing to all the senses in the evening felt so miserably cold and uninviting only a few hours later.

To add to my growing irritation, Jarman wasn't there.

I cursed under my breath, and was on the point of going to look for Sallie to demand why on earth she had misled me when a very soft voice whispered, 'Down here, Doctor.'

And Jarman Hodge crawled out from under the table.

I watched in silence as he stood up and straightened his garments. He held his cap in his hands, and he was twisting it nervously.

Of all this morning's disconcerting events, this disturbed me most. I did not think I had ever before seen Jarman Hodge show the least sign of anxiety.

A dreadful thought stuck me. 'Theo?' I said urgently. Theo Davey is our local coroner, and Jarman's superior.

His frown lifted in instant comprehension, and he looked contrite.

'No, no, Master Davey and his family are all safe and well, or they were last night.' Reading my expression, he added, 'Sorry, Doctor. I should have said.'

Just as Sallie had done earlier, he glanced round to check we were alone.

'For God's sake, what is it, then?' I demanded, and it was quite an effort not to yell at him.

'Is anybody about?' he asked.

'Just Sallie, and she's shut herself up in the kitchen.'

He hesitated. 'Er – Mistress Palfrey?'

My sister had been a widow for nearly two years, and hearing her referred to by her married name struck a discordant note. 'Celia is still in her own quarters.'

Jarman nodded.

'Why the extreme caution, Jarman?' I asked quietly. 'Whatever you said to Sallie put the fear of God into her, and now I find you hiding under my library table and scared out of your wits.'

He shook his head. 'I'm not scared for me, Doctor, nor for you and your household – there's no danger to you, or least-ways not yet, or at least I don't think so . . .' Now the anxious look was back.

I took his arm and led him over to the fireplace, then pushed him down into Celia's chair, sitting down to face him. 'What's the matter, Jarman?'

He swallowed a couple of times, then said in a low rush, 'I've just found a body. In the river. Upstream a way from where it joins the Tamar, on that bit of shingle that forms a little beach.'

I knew the spot. Some eddy in the current meant that river detritus often washed up there. 'You've informed Master Davey, I take it, and now he's sent you to fetch me. Fine, I'll—'

But as I began to stand up, Jarman said, 'No.'

He'd only recently found this body. And I remembered that he'd just told me he hadn't seen Theo since last night.

'You haven't informed the coroner?' I asked softly. He shook his head. 'Why in heaven's name not, Jarman? It's the first duty of anyone who discovers a dead body, and you of all people know that!'

He came forward out of his chair, right up to me until he was kneeling in front of me. Then he stretched up and whispered right in my ear, 'It's a suicide. Stones wrapped in a length of cloth tied round the waist.'

Then he resumed his seat and simply sat staring at me.

A suicide.

I thought for a few moments, then said, 'I know the laws pertaining to suicides are harsh, Jarman, but we have no choice. You are a coroner's officer; I am a doctor. We must comply with them.'

'But the church says it's the work of the devil and the unforgivable sin, and people who kill themselves are cursed by God and damned for ever!' Jarman said in an agonised whisper. 'And all their goods are forfeit, so their kin and that must suffer along with them.' He paused, his face contorted with deep anxiety, and added, 'It's perilous even to be *talking* about such things, and I don't want anyone knowing I'm here!'

That explained the hiding under the table. But he was quite right, and perhaps *harsh* hadn't been a strong enough word, I reflected sadly. 'I know,' I said, 'but what can we do?'

He looked at me, his eyes fixed on mine. As the silence extended, I realized that there *was* something we could do, and here he was asking me to do it.

'You wish me to perpetrate an untruth,' I said slowly. 'You are asking me to view this body and somehow hide the fact that the dead man perished by his own hand. Then, presumably, report this lie to my good friend Theo Davey, who happens to be the coroner and your employer, and who in addition is a fine and decent man to whom we both, for our own reasons, owe allegiance and the *truth*.' The last word emerged more forcefully that I had intended, and once again Jarman gave that nervous glance towards the door.

He went to speak, then stopped. He sat for a few moments, lips moving as if he was preparing his words. Then he looked straight at me and said, 'It's exactly what I'm asking, Doctor. I realize how it sounds, and I don't think I can explain why.' He paused, then said, 'Come with me? Come and see for yourself?'

I knew it was the wrong thing to do. What I should do was go straight to Theo and tell him what Jarman had just told me. If I did what Jarman was asking of me, I was going to have to answer for it, sooner or later, not only to the authority invested in the ancient office of coroner but also to myself.

But there was something in Jarman Hodge's expression that made these considerations irrelevant. I stood up and said, 'I'll fetch my bag and meet you in the yard.'

We took the familiar track that leads steeply down from Rosewyke to the river Tavy. A path ran along at the foot of the bank; it was quite often impassible after heavy rain, but today the ground was hard with the winter cold, and Jarman and I rode swiftly. He was in the lead as we reached the short stretch of shingle, and as we dismounted and tethered the horses I was already looking beyond him to the still shape lying just above the water line.

We approached together.

The dead man lay on his front and he was entirely covered by a heavy cloak, its hood drawn up over his head and face. I wondered if that was how he had washed up, or whether Jarman had spread the cloak out of respect for the dead. As if he read my thoughts, Jarman said softly, 'Thought it best to make sure prying eyes didn't see.'

I nodded.

'You mentioned stones, tied in a length of cloth?'

'Yes.' He shot me a swift look. 'I removed them.'

He had already taken the decision to cover up this crime, then, otherwise he'd have left those damning stones where they were and let Theo draw his own conclusions.

'Show me,' I said.

He grinned, very briefly. 'Hard to do, Doctor, since I've put them back in the place they most likely came from.' He pointed to where a tumble of stones ranging in size from a clenched fist to a large boulder were scattered to the rear of the little beach.

'And the cloth?'

'Tucked it away under the cloak. Along with that.' He reached down and briefly raised the edge of the cloak, revealing a small bag made of coarse cloth. 'It was left on the shore, well above the water.'

Jarman had been thorough. What he had done for this dead man had removed the evidence that he had killed himself, that was for sure, but what still concerned me was why Jarman had acted as he had done.

'You – you don't *know* this man, do you?' I asked. 'Is that it? Did you do this great kindness for him so that he would not suffer the suicide's fate, and to save his family from ruin?'

But Jarman was shaking his head. 'No, that's not it, Doctor.'

Then he knelt down beside the corpse and with gentle hands

turned back the hood. Even as the surprise shot through me
he continued, drawing the heavy, soaked cloth away until the
body was fully revealed.

I thought perhaps I was beginning to understand Jarman's
actions.

The corpse wasn't that of a man. It was a woman's.

Her face was colourless, and the smooth skin had a trans-
lucent look. Automatically I put my fingers to the base of
the throat, but there was no heartbeat. The flesh was icy to the
touch. Her closed eyes were heavily fringed with dark lashes,
the brows well shaped, and there was a pleasing symmetry to
her face. Her hair appeared to be very dark brown or black,
although it was still soaking wet and could have been a lighter
shade when dry. She was dressed in a gown of good wool,
and even in death it was apparent that she had had a fine
figure: full, deep bust, shapely waist and hips, long legs, small
feet in leather slippers that were totally inadequate for a
riverbank in February and now thickly caked with mud.

I stared for some moments at the front of her body. I might
have been mistaken, but I didn't think so. The belt around her
waist looked to have been raised an inch or two, and beneath
it there was a definite bulge in her belly.

She had been pregnant.

And, glancing at her left hand, I didn't see a wedding ring.

My eyes returned to her face, and now that my quick
inspection of the rest of her was done, I could admit the power
of my first impression: the dead woman had been very
beautiful.

I glanced at Jarman, who stood beside me staring down at
the dead woman as intently as I had just been doing. I hadn't
previously thought of him as a man susceptible to female
beauty – if I'd ever thought about it, I'd have said he was too
practical, too efficient, too detached. Yet here he was, guilty
of covering up evidence of suicide because the victim was a
beautiful woman.

'Is that it, Jarman?' I asked.

He turned to stare at me. 'Hmm?'

'Is the reason you're doing this simply because she's very
lovely?'

He looked down at his feet, scuffing at the sandy ground. 'Had to work on a suicide once, with Master Davey. This was some years ago, before you came here, Doctor. It was hard,' he went on with sudden vehemence, 'cruel hard. That was a woman, too, younger than this one, I reckon. The coroner reported her to the priests – as was his duty, I know that, he had no choice and I always reckoned he didn't like it any more than I did – but the consequences were terrible.' He paused, his eyes staring out over the fast-moving water. 'Suicide's the result of extreme despair, according to the church's teachings, and it's a mortal sin. From what I picked up, it seems it's a gross defiance of the Almighty to take your death into your own hands, because it's an insult to God to see yourself as beyond forgiveness and redemption. Or something like that,' he added with sudden angry impatience, 'which I reckon was pretty harsh for someone like this poor dead young girl I'm speaking of, pregnant because some bastard of a man raped her, then thrown out of her home, no money, nobody to help her, so starved you could count every one of her bones. You'd expect maybe a modicum of pity, perhaps, but what did the priests do? I'll tell you, Doctor. They punished that poor girl's corpse like they were executing the worst of murderers, mutilating her limbs like it was a quartering and then hammering a stake through her heart once she lay in the ground. And not consecrated ground either, they made sure of that. They shoved her in a ditch beside the foulest midden.'

A disturbing coincidence, I reflected, that the girl whose death had so affected Jarman Hodge had been beset by the same misfortune as the woman who lay dead at our feet. But then I thought that this was probably the reason behind the suicides of most young women who found themselves in despair: it was so easy for a man to impregnate a woman and take no interest in the consequences. Such irresponsibility was quite impossible for the woman.

Jarman had spoken with passion, his pain and anger very evident as he recalled this earlier, unknown young woman's awful fate. I wondered if his deep emotion justified what he had done – what he had involved me in doing with him – and in that moment I believed that it did.

After a pause I said, 'Had you thought what we should do next, Jarman?'

He picked up the fact that I had said *we* and he shot me a brief and very grateful smile. 'I reckoned maybe take her to your house, Doctor, to Rosewyke, and make out that you'd been at home when I arrived with the body, and judged that she'd drowned.'

I nodded. 'Well, at least that part is true, I imagine.' But something was troubling me. 'Jarman, why did you not do that anyway?'

He looked questioningly at me. 'Do what?'

'Bring the body to me and say you'd found her drowned on the bank?'

Surprise crossed his face, then a faint smile. 'I couldn't have done that, Doctor. I'd be involving you in a crime—' he paused '—I *am* involving you in a crime, and I'd never have done that without asking.'

Involving me in a crime.

Yes, I realized, feeling cold suddenly. That was exactly what he'd done; what I had willingly taken on.

We weren't achieving anything by standing there mooning over the woman's body; it was time we were gone. I fetched my horse, and Hal stood obediently still while I mounted and reached down to take the body out of Jarman's arms. Free of his burden, Jarman bent down and picked up the length of cloth and the small canvas pack, both of which had fallen out of the folds of the cloak. I set off along the bank, and Jarman mounted up and followed. I had arranged the corpse face down across my saddle bow, and as I rode I found myself patting and rubbing her back, as if somehow she could still feel the comfort of human touch.

We came to the steep track leading up to Rosewyke, Hal shortened his stride and I leaned forward, adjusting my weight.

I realized afterwards that it was probably the increased pressure of my body on hers that made it happen. At the time, however, the exhalation and the tiny gasp for air that imme-diately followed it shocked me so deeply that I shouted out and Hal started, all but losing his footing and plunging all three of us off the path to tumble down the rocky slope. Jarman, riding just behind, wasted no time but was instantly off his own horse and at Hal's head, holding on to his bridle.

When Hal was calm once more, Jarman looked up at me, his face full of fear. 'What's happened?' he asked worriedly. 'Why did you yell like that?'

But I was wresting Hal's bridle out of his hands, urging the big horse on up the slope, for now the need to reach home and warmth was suddenly very urgent.

Because the woman was still alive.

In the flurry of racing up to the house, yelling for Samuel and Tock to tend the horses, dismounting and taking the woman down and into my arms – carefully now, so very carefully – one thought kept battering at me, furiously and insistently.

Jarman had found a woman lying insensible by the river, the body weighted with stones. Both of us had taken the decision to disguise the fact that it was a suicide. An *attempted* suicide: we had removed the body, only to find she was not dead after all.

If I managed to save her life – and it was by no means certain that I would – just how grateful was she likely to be? Not only had she tried to kill herself, which was murder in the eyes of the church and probably according to the law of the land as well, but if she was indeed pregnant, she would also be accused of trying to murder her own child.

I didn't know what the penalty for this attempted double murder would be, but I was in no doubt that it would be terrible and probably agonizing. And in addition, she would still have to bear the burden of whatever tragedy or disaster had driven her to try to kill herself.

As I carried the unknown woman inside the house, I wondered if I'd have done better to leave her for dead on the riverbank.

TWO

S allie came hurrying to the door to meet us, and behind her I spotted Celia, dressed in one of her warmest gowns and wrapped in a heavy woollen shawl. Cutting short their concerned enquiries, I said, 'Jarman found a woman by the river. He thought she was dead, but she still has breath in her. She needs—'

But my sister and my housekeeper were accustomed to life in the household of a physician and knew full well what was needed for someone fresh out of the river on a cold February morning. Sallie spun round and headed across the kitchen and into the hall, opening the door to the little morning parlour. 'In here,' she said over her shoulder. 'The fire's going well, she'll soon warm up in here, the poor soul. There's a kettle on the hearth, and I'll put broth on to heat.'

Celia had delved into the big chest in the hall and was hauling out towels, blankets, cushions and a thin rolled-up mattress. As I bore the woman into the morning parlour, she edged past me and swiftly arranged a makeshift bed in front of the fire. Then, standing up, she said, 'I'll help you undress her, Gabe. If we lay her down as she is, she'll rapidly soak the bedding and she'll never get warm. We may have to cut the strings of her corset – they're impossible to untie when they're wet.'

We put the still body on the floor and between us removed the cloak, gown and undergarments. I took off the inadequate shoes, discovering too late that they were full of water. I noticed Celia taking in the details: she was the expert, but even I could see that the clothes had originally been of good quality but now were heavily worn, torn here and there and very dirty.

Celia and I each took a towel, drying the icy flesh and rubbing the long hair. Celia dressed the woman in a clean nightgown – it was one of her thin summer ones – and we wrapped her in thick blankets. Without her clothes, it had been even more apparent that the woman was pregnant, by as much as perhaps six months. I had no doubt that Celia noticed this, too, but I knew she would not mention it, even to me.

For some time we were fully occupied in restoring our patient. Soon after tucking her up she had a violent and prolonged fit of coughing, and she also retched up quite a lot of foul-smelling river water. Her distress was pathetic to watch, for she seemed to be worrying more about having soiled the blankets than her own suffering. My kind-hearted Sallie, who happened to be kneeling at her head at the time, wiped her mouth and face with a cloth wrung out in hot water as tenderly as a mother with a newborn and infinitely fragile baby, and I heard her say softly, 'Don't you worry yourself, my lovely, we'll soon have this neat and tidy again.'

I took a moment while both Celia and Sallie were with the woman to slip out of the room and find Jarman Hodge. He was in the kitchen, a mug of what looked and smelt suspiciously like mulled ale in his hand, his back to the fireplace to warm his buttocks, and he started guiltily as I came into the room.

'I'll have some of that,' I said, indicating the ale, and he bent down to pick up the jug and pour out a mug for me. It tasted as good as it smelt.

'She's alive?' Jarman muttered after a moment.

'Yes.'

'Will she live?'

'I expect her to, yes.'

After quite a long pause, he asked very quietly, 'What are we going to do, Doctor?'

I had my response ready; delivering it to Jarman was the reason I had sought him out.

'I shall look after her until she is fit to go on her way. That is my job. You will seek out Theo and inform him that you found a woman on the riverbank early this morning, summoned me, and that we brought her here to Rosewyke. That is *your* job.'

'But—'

I didn't let him make the protest I knew was coming. 'Jarman, there is no evidence,' I said, leaning close to him and speaking in a low whisper. 'Our story is true, as far as it goes.'

He gave me a long look. 'As far as it goes,' he echoed dully.

I had the strong sense that he was judging me. Even though it was he who had brought this dilemma about, his steady gaze seemed to reprove me for the lie of omission; for proposing that we did not tell the coroner – Jarman's superior and my very good friend – that there was more to this tale.

Another thought struck me, if anything even more uncomfortable: that this lie of omission would have to be repeated to Jonathan Carew.

Jonathan is our vicar. He is a man of the highest moral strength, and I was coming to look upon him as a brother. He was also becoming very close to my sister, but that's another story. The thought of telling him about the half-drowned woman and not revealing that she had tried to kill herself was all but intolerable.

Jarman was clearly expecting me to say something. I couldn't think of anything, so I lamely muttered, 'Let's see how it goes, eh?'

It was obviously as unsatisfactory to him as it was to me. Shaking his head as if I'd disappointed him – well, I had – he said, 'We might keep the finer details to ourselves, Doctor, but what about her? Supposing she wakes up, realizes with dismay she's still in the land of the living and starts howling that she wants to die, that we should have left her in the water and let the stones do their work?'

It was a frightful thought. I muttered an oath under my breath, and said aloud, 'Well, let's just wait and see if the care and kindness that my sister, my housekeeper and I are going to give her can change her mind.'

He started to say something about blind optimism not being much to hang your hopes on, but I'd had enough. 'Oh, for God's sake, bugger off back to Theo, Jarman!' I said in a furious whisper. 'Stop making me feel guilty – this is all *your* doing!'

With a look of deep affront, he put down his empty mug and strode out of the kitchen.

I went back to my patient.

From being so cold that her flesh felt like marble, as the hours went by the woman began to feel hot to the touch, and finally she was burning. She slept for much of the time, but it was a restless sleep that kept her twisting and turning in the makeshift bed, throwing off the covers one moment and huddling beneath them the next.

Remembering that surge of foul water as her body voided itself, I was very afraid she had picked up one of the terrible waterborne sicknesses that all too often drive a dark swathe of death through riverside populations. There wasn't much I could do for her other than sponge the sweat from her poor body and try to force her to drink good, pure water to replace all that she was losing. My awareness of others in urgent need of my help gnawed at me, and my sister clearly noticed.

'Go, Gabe,' she said. 'There's nothing you're doing that Sallie and I can't manage.'

She was right. The strong light outside told me that it was late morning, and I had been shut away here for too long. I gave Celia a grateful smile and was about to issue careful instructions for our patient's care when my sister said, with only the lightest irony, 'I don't think I shall have any difficulty in continuing to do what I've been doing all morning, thank you, Gabe.'

I bent to drop a kiss on top of her bright, smooth hair and left.

As I rode out of the yard I had it in mind to find the time to call in on Theo at some point in the day. I'm not sure I got as far as formulating what I would say to him, bearing in mind the heavy secret that Jarman and I shared, but in the end it didn't matter because I never made it to his office anyway.

I have come to understand that some sort of highly efficient communication system operates in the rural landscape where I practise my profession. Somehow it becomes known that I am in attendance – even in the wildest, most out-of-the-way hovel, cottage or smallholding – and even before I have finished with my patient, someone else comes to wait silently outside, to say quietly as I'm leaving, 'While you're in the vicinity, Doctor, I wondered if you'd have a look at my wife/mother/father/child?' (On one occasion a very old man asked if I'd advise him on how to treat a cow with persistent foot rot.) In this way, what starts as a day with five or six calls ends up with getting on for twice as many.

Thus it was on the day we found the body.

The weeks since Christmas having delivered so much cold-related sickness, I hadn't of late had a day that didn't end long after dark, and this was no exception. As at long last I rode into the yard, I was so tired that it was only Hal's need to get back to his feed and his stable that had brought me home safely.

Samuel and Tock were waiting in the yard. Samuel acknowledged my thanks with a nod. 'We'll look after Hal,' he said as I went to unbuckle the girths. 'You get along inside, Doctor.'

I didn't need to be asked again. I must have looked even worse than I felt, because Tock tried to take my bag from me to carry into the house.

The kitchen was empty, the door to the hall standing open. I went on past Sallie's little room, which opens off the kitchen, and down the short passage into the morning parlour. Sallie sat beside the woman, and hearing me come in, she looked up and put her finger to her lips.

'She's fast asleep, Doctor,' she said very softly. 'Got off about an hour ago.' She glanced down at the woman. 'Much to her and everyone else's relief, I might add.'

'Really? Why is that?' I crouched beside her, feeling both my knees protesting.

Sallie folded her lips. 'I know she wasn't herself – Miss Celia said she was raving, and it was because of the fever – but language! I never heard the like.' She frowned. 'Well, I did, else I wouldn't have known them for bad words, but I never expected to hear them under *this* roof!'

'I'm sorry if you were offended, Sallie,' I said.

A guilty look crossed her face. 'I should have more charity, given what the poor soul's been through.'

I patted her hand. 'You have plenty of charity, dear Sallie. It's been a very long day, we're all tired, and that nibbles away at our forbearance.'

She studied my face, frowning. 'Dear me, but you look done in, Doctor!' she exclaimed, struggling to her feet. 'Go through into the library – Miss Celia's in there, and there's a good fire going – and I'll bring you hot food and strong drink to fortify you. We'll soon have you to rights!'

She hurried out of the room, and I followed more slowly, crossing the hall and going through the parlour into the library. The fire was as good as Sallie had promised, and Celia sat in her chair, her feet up on a footstool and her head back. Her eyes were closed – she too looked worn out – but they flickered open as I sat down opposite her.

'Gabe,' she said with a smile. 'Goodness, you're late.'

I nodded. 'It seems to be becoming a habit.'

She sat up. 'You must be ravenous, I'll—'

'Stay where you are. Sallie's fetching me something.'

She sat back again. 'You've seen our mystery woman, then.'

'I have. Sallie reports that she finally went to sleep after quite a lot of raving.'

'She was clearly delirious,' Celia said. 'And, oh, Gabe, it was awful to hear, because she's clearly dreadfully unhappy, and worried about someone who seems to be called Ned, and also—' Abruptly she stopped.

'Also what?'

She shook her head. 'Never mind. It's Sallie's turn to watch her,' she hurried on, 'and I shall take over later in the night, but honestly, Gabe, by the look of you, you are not going to be much use to anyone tomorrow unless you go to bed and have a decent, long sleep.'

She was right, but I couldn't let her take on what was my burden. 'I'll have my supper, then go and sleep, but only for a while,' I replied.

'But you can't—'

'Then I'll relieve you and make up a second bed in the

morning parlour,' I went on. 'I'll be able to sleep, but I'll wake if she's restless.'

My sister gave me a look she's been giving me since childhood, and which says as clearly as words, *That's what you say, but I know you too well to believe you.* And as if she wasn't confident that I'd got the message, she said, 'You won't sleep. You'll be watching and listening.'

I suppressed a huge yawn. She was right.

Sallie came in bearing a large tray, and laid out a bowl of thick, fragrant soup, a platter of cold meats and pieces of cheese, some chunks of warm bread wrapped in a napkin and a dish of butter, as well as a tankard of hot, spiced ale. 'I've more of everything in the kitchen,' she said, 'but this'll do to be going on with.'

I thanked her – I could tell by the wonderful smell that the soup was pea and ham, one of my favourites – and fell on the food before she was even out of the room.

Later, Celia and I were back in our chairs either side of the fire. I was trying to suppress yet another belch. I'd gulped down the food and the ale, and my stomach was protesting. I didn't think Celia had noticed, but presently she got up, went over to the board and brought back a bottle of brandy and two glasses. She poured generous measures, handing one to me.

'You never know,' she said as she sat down again, 'brandy might prove to be a previously unsuspected remedy for wind.'

'Oh. You heard.'

She grinned. 'I might be tired, Gabe, but I haven't been struck deaf.'

We sat in silence for some time, sipping the fine brandy. Her eyelids were drooping, and I thought she was falling asleep. I was about to suggest we went up to our beds – we'd both be well advised to catch up on sleep while we could – but then her eyes opened again and she looked straight at me.

She said very quietly, 'What is it you haven't told me, Gabe?'

'What do you mean?'

She tutted in irritation. 'If that is a means of affording yourself a little thinking time, it doesn't work. I *mean*—' her repetition of the word had an edge of sarcasm in it '—that this morning Jarman Hodge came to see you and did his utmost to keep the visit a secret, which was pretty silly because for one thing, Sallie told me as soon as I came down, and for another, I heard horses and looked out of my window as the pair of you hurried away.'

'Oh.'

'Oh indeed.' She paused, but she had by no means finished. 'You come back with a woman found in the river, she's in a state of extreme distress, and when she recovers sufficiently to speak, she starts shouting about terrible danger and she's clearly scared out of her wits, and then she seems totally amazed to find herself lying there in the morning parlour and not at the bottom of the river, and she starts sobbing about the stones, the big heavy stones, and why didn't they work, and she hurls out accusations that we've interfered when we should have left well alone because now everything is ten times worse.'

'Oh.'

'Good Lord above, Gabe, is that all you can say?' Celia's eyes sparkled with annoyance. 'When she says *we* interfered, and *we* should have left well alone, I'm guessing she means you and Jarman, because the first I knew of her was when you carried her dripping into the little parlour, and all I've done for her is try to look after her!'

I wondered how much to tell her. Or, rather, I wondered how little I could get away with. 'Jarman pulled her out of the water,' I began, 'and came to fetch me to look after her.'

One look at my sister's face told me it was no good.

Which was actually a great relief; I really didn't want to lie to her.

'Shall I tell you what really happened?' she asked quietly. I didn't reply, but she carried on anyway. 'Jarman did indeed find her, but he thought she was dead. Drowned. He's not stupid, and if there had been any life in her – or, rather, if he had detected any life in her – he wouldn't have left her by the river and come for you, he'd have loaded her up on his horse and brought her to you as fast as he could. And there would have been no need to keep her presence a secret, since he'd be doing what every Christian soul ought to do for someone in distress, which is to help them.'

'Yes,' I said.

She gave an ironic grin. 'Marginally better than *oh*,' she remarked. 'And then,' she added, lowering her voice, 'we come to the matter of the stones.'

I looked at her, straight into her eyes.

'Stones in conjunction with a body in the river can surely only mean one thing,' Celia said. 'When Jarman found this woman, she had somehow contrived to weight herself with stones in order to drown herself. Jarman, believing her to have succeeded, also knew that the very charitable and compassionate laws of the land and, more crucially, of the church, lay down that suicides are criminals and mortal sinners. The woman is pregnant, so I imagine that she would also be deemed guilty of killing her unborn child as well as herself. Her body would have been buried in unhallowed ground, probably staked down, and her belongings would become the property of the Crown.' I tried to speak but she didn't let me. 'And *this* explains Jarman's extreme caution: he thought she was a suicide, he saw that she was very lovely, his heart went out to her and he made up his mind to dispose of the evidence. Then he came to find you, believing that, unless you acted completely out of character and instantly decided to denounce both the apparent suicide and Jarman, you would help him. Which, of course, you did.' She looked at me, frowning, 'Have I the whole tale?'

I nodded. 'You have.'

She was quiet for some time, which was a blessing as I was desperately trying to work out whether it mattered that she knew what had happened, and whether this knowledge could be a risk to her, while understanding miserably that I was far too tired for my mind to work properly.

Then Celia said, 'Of course, she isn't dead.'

I looked up at her and said dully, 'Is that important?'

She gave me a pitying smile. 'Dear me, Gabe, you *are* exhausted, aren't you? Yes, it's important. You can only be guilty of a crime if you manage to carry it out, or so I believe. I could sit here and decide I was going to go and punch Tock because he always lets his mouth hang open and his teeth aren't a pretty sight – I wouldn't dream of doing so, by the way, Tock can't help it and he has a very kind and gentle heart – but I'm not guilty of assault unless I actually *do* it. So if someone tries to drown herself by tying stones round her body and wading into the river but then someone pulls her out and throws away the stones, then firstly, she hasn't committed the crime, and secondly, nobody knows that she even tried. Well, you and Jarman know, I know, and I'm sure Sallie has guessed too. But unless we tell anyone else, this is simply a matter of a woman falling in the river, Jarman rescuing her, and you, Sallie and me nursing her back to health. Isn't it?' she demanded when I didn't instantly answer.

'Er—' There had to be a flaw in her argument and I was pretty sure there was such a crime as attempted murder.

But she ploughed on, not waiting for my reply, and I saw from the change in her demeanour that something was deeply troubling her.

'This,' she said, so softly that I strained to hear, 'is the problem: this matter of our not telling anyone else.'

I knew what she was going to say, but I let her speak.

'All this time that I have been sitting beside the woman, puzzling it all out, my thoughts have kept turning to the one person I really want to share it with, because he understands both church law and, I have no doubt, common law as well, or at least a great deal better than I do.' She hesitated, and I thought I saw a sudden, faint colour in her cheeks. 'He is also a deeply compassionate man, and another reason why I have longed to talk to him is because I care for him.'

She was speaking of Jonathan Carew.

I waited, for I knew there was more.

'Gabe, I don't think I can lie to him,' she said. 'I don't know about you – and I suspect you feel the same – but Jonathan will soon hear about Jarman and the woman in the river, because these things are never secret for long, whatever Jarman may think. Then he'll come to see us – Jonathan, that is – and offer his help, and although I've tried to see myself not telling him the whole story, I'm afraid I can't do it.'

There was pain in her face, and I caught the glint of tears in her eyes. I knew that she and Jonathan had grown close, but I don't think I had understood until that moment *how* close. Here was my dear sister, imagining herself implying a lie to a man she cared about, and the very thought of it was enough to move her so profoundly that it brought tears to her eyes.

I let myself fall forwards out of my chair and, kneeling in front of her, took her hands.

'It's all right, Celia,' I said gently. 'I can't do it either.'

THREE

T he intense radiance of the light through the bedchamber window next morning informed me there had been more snow during the night. I lay thinking about that, and remembering how my sister and I had made sleds out of old planks and stamped down the snow on a nastily steep incline at our childhood home, enabling us to shoot repeatedly down the increasingly perilous slope until Celia overshot and landed on the pond. It was frozen hard, thankfully, but the bruise on her bottom was so huge that my mother forbade any more sledding. It didn't stop us, of course; we merely found somewhere out of her sight.

I was still half asleep, dream images mixing pleasantly with reality, and then it struck me that if it was full daylight, the morning must be quite advanced. Then immediately I wondered why Celia hadn't summoned me for my turn watching over the mystery woman. Hurriedly getting out of bed, I noticed a ewer of steaming water just inside the door, and guessed that this had been Sallie's diplomatic way of waking me and telling me it was time to be about the day's business.

The appetising smell of bacon was coming from the kitchen as I came down into the hall. Ignoring it, I went on into the morning parlour. Celia was sitting in a chair, calmly stitching a piece of very bright silk with even brighter thread – it seemed to be a pattern of flowers – and the patient was propped up on several pillows and apparently asleep. There were two patches of hectic red in her cheeks, and I could hear the rasp of her breathing.

'You didn't wake me,' I said to my sister.

'No,' she agreed. 'Sallie and I decided we could cope between us, we both managed more sleep than you might imagine, and you needed the rest.' She stared at me critically. 'You look a great deal better.'

'I feel it. Thank you,' I added.

I knelt before the woman, and Celia came to crouch beside me. 'She has been feverish throughout the night,' she said softly, 'and Sallie and I have bathed her repeatedly with cool water. She was crying out in her sleep again – she seemed to be having a nightmare, because she was ranting about a leopard, I think, although the word was distorted and sounded more like *luipaard*, and she muttered the name Ned more than once.' She shook her head. 'Nothing, really, that makes any sense.'

I nodded. I put my hand on the woman's forehead, then bent over her and listened to her chest. 'Any more vomiting?'

'No, thankfully. That one episode yesterday morning seems to have cleared whatever it was out of her.'

I glanced at Celia. There had been a great change in her over the past two years, and it seemed to me she had grown from a headstrong and somewhat self-absorbed girl into a mature and responsible woman. Her marriage and how it had ended surely had much to do with that; very few people know exactly what happened,[1] and those of us who do keep it to ourselves. Although I feared very much for my sister at the time, her natural resilience and her undoubted strength of character seemed to have brought her through. As for the fast-developing sense of responsibility for others, I suspected her growing feelings for our vicar might have something to do with it.

'Go and have your breakfast, Gabe,' Celia said, returning to her embroidery. 'Sallie and I will continue to keep watch, so you can proceed with your day once you've eaten.'

As well as becoming more mature and responsible, I should add that Celia was also considerably more bossy.

I sat finishing the last of a very generous breakfast, Sallie hovering to make quite sure I couldn't eat another morsel, and thinking about how best to plan my day. There were calls to make, and I knew I should make time to seek out Jarman Hodge, not only to give him news of the mystery woman but also to find out how he was feeling about what he – we – had done.

---

[1] see A Rustle of Silk

I stood up, thanked Sallie for my breakfast and also my restorative night of undisturbed sleep, and was about to set off when I heard the sound of hooves outside, swiftly followed by a heavy thumping on the front door.

'Oh, Lord, that sounds urgent,' Sallie muttered, already wiping her hands on her apron and turning towards the door.

'It does,' I agreed. 'Stay here, Sallie, I'll see who it is.'

I hurried across the hall into the little entry porch and opened the door. Theo Davey stood there, so heavily muffled against the cold that it was largely by his height and bulk that I recognized him.

My instant response was deep guilt. And I hadn't even told him a lie yet, even one of omission.

With what sounded even to me like very suspicious over-enthusiasm, I said, 'Theo! Good to see you! Come in and warm yourself, you look half-frozen, and—'

'I won't stop,' he said through several layers of wool wound round his lower face. I took in, belatedly, the fact that he still held the reins of his heavyset mare. 'There's a body. I need you to come with me. I've told your Samuel to prepare your horse, so fetch your bag and a warm cloak and we'll be off.'

He was clearly in no mood for argument. I turned back into the house, collected my heaviest winter cloak and my bag, called out to Sallie and Celia that it was Theo at the door and he needed my presence, and was back outside as Samuel brought Hal round from the yard.

We rode in silence for a while, then when we were out on the wider road leading down to Plymouth and able to ride two abreast, I said, 'Where is this body?'

'Down by the port. In a narrow little passage behind that filthy clutch of cheap boarding houses and rough inns at the far end of the quay. Shoved in a ditch and blocking the flow to the cesspit, which was what alerted the locals to its presence. *His* presence,' he corrected.

Oh, good, I thought. Out to look at a dead body in the rougher end of Plymouth on a freezing cold morning, and to make it even worse, the corpse would be covered in shit.

Silence again, but as if Theo picked up my lack of

enthusiasm, he said presently, 'You might be intrigued when you see how he died, however.'

'Might I?' Despite the circumstances, my curiosity stirred.

'Yes. And don't worry about the contents of the cesspit. The corpse has already been extracted and I've detailed a pair of fellows to hose it down.'

We rode on. Something had struck me, and I saw no reason not to ask. 'Why did you come to fetch me? You usually send Jarman or one of the others.'

Theo grunted. 'No alternative. The others are all busy and Jarman's off on one of his missions.'

I wondered if this mission, whatever it was, had been a welcome excuse for Jarman to make himself scarce. Or whether in fact he was simply lying low.

There was a pungent odour of human waste and rotting things as we made our way through the dark, tiny passages to where the dead man had been found. We'd left our horses in the care of an ostler at one of the many quayside taverns, which meant we had to paddle through quite a lot of substances we'd much rather have avoided.

I saw daylight at the end of the passage, over Theo's shoulder. We emerged into a small open space between the lean-tos of a couple of ramshackle hovels, made even smaller by the pair of coroner's officers and the dead man presently occupying it. The cesspit was at the further end, and the channel leading into it ran right across the little yard. It was narrow and clearly well used, and it was apparent that a large human body thrown into it would have a detrimental and instant effect on the area's plumbing. The stream of ordure and general filth was flowing again now, and the stench was awful.

I bent over the corpse. There was no question of kneeling down: as it was, my boots would take a lot of cleaning. One of Theo's men started to speak but, turning to him with an apologetic smile, I said, 'Not just now, Matthew, if you don't mind – I prefer to form my own impressions.'

'Sorry, Doctor T,' the man muttered.

I returned to the body. He was lying on his face, and I took hold of his shoulder – still wet from the hosing-down – and shoved until he fell on to his back.

The first quick look had revealed no obvious bloodstains on the coat, shirt or hose, and he hadn't been strangled or had his throat cut. His eyes were wide and staring, and as I bent closer I thought I could make out something in his mouth. I reached inside my tunic and took out my pen knife, opening the smallest blade and digging at whatever it was protruding from the man's wide-gaping lips.

It wasn't one thing, it was several. Hard, round spheres, or so it seemed, each about the size of my thumbnail. I raised him so that his head hung down and thumped him on the upper back, and several more of the little spheres fell out of him; I guessed they had been lodged in his windpipe, and were possibly what had killed him.

Abruptly I stood up. This was a foul place, and the sooner we got the corpse and ourselves out of it, the better.

'We'll take him to that crypt you use for bodies, Theo,' I said, 'and I'll have a proper look at him.' Turning to the other two men, I said, 'I'm sorry to ask you, and you did a good job with the initial hosing, but if you could throw a few more buckets of water over him before you take him down and put him on the trestle table, I'd be very grateful.'

The men knew from experience that my gratitude habitually expressed itself in a few coins for an ale or two, which was probably why they didn't look too unhappy about the task.

They certainly earned their beer money, as I discovered when I began my proper inspection of the body. The garments were now saturated, and removing them made my hands so cold that it took some time to thaw them out. But it was important that it was I who took off the clothes in the case of a suspicious death; sometimes they contain clues to the manner of death, such as the way in which a sword or knife thrust lines up with a rent in the shirt or tunic revealing whether the blow had been delivered from above or below.

I was wasting my time in this case, however. Even a quick inspection of each item as it came off, plus a much more thorough inspection of the flesh below, revealed nothing other

than that the man's clothes were flashy but probably hadn't
cost all that much, being of poor quality, that he had walked
a long way in his boots and that he wasn't in the habit of
frequently changing his underlinen: even after the hosing and
the buckets of water, his shirt stank of old sweat, its underarms
yellow and stiff with it. With some relief, I wrapped it up
inside the rest of the garments, took the whole bundle up the
stone steps and chucked it outside.

Now the naked body lay stretched on the trestle before me.

He was around forty or forty-five years old, not tall – shorter
than me by a head and shoulders, I judged – and heavyset,
with an accumulation of fat around his lower belly (I had
noticed before I unclothed him that he wore his wide leather
belt below the big bulging stomach). He was long in the body,
short in the arms and legs, and thick with muscle; despite the
fat, he'd have been a strong man, and, I'd have thought, well
able to defend himself. In addition, it might have been as a
result of his violent death, but I thought I detected an angry
belligerence in his face. Still, I reasoned, even the strongest
will fall if enough men assail him.

I went over every inch of him, looking for a fatal wound.
There were bruises, grazes, old scars and signs of broken bones
that had not set quite straight; whoever he was, he'd had a
very active life, to say the least. But my initial impression
back beside the cesspit appeared to have been right: he hadn't
died by the blade.

Next I examined the head to see if he had been stunned, or
even killed, by a blow to the skull, and this time I did find
something. His dark hair was long and very thick, dirty and
tacky with grease, and I had to thrust my fingers right through
it to the bones of him, but after feeling all over the head I
found a lump, and soon after that, a shallow dent.

The bump was on the back of the head, and I thought it
had probably been the first blow. Although I couldn't be sure,
I doubted if it had been enough to kill him: this man's bones
were sturdy, and I guessed his skull was thick. But whoever
had killed him seemed to have had some knowledge of the
anatomy of the head, for the second blow – the one that had
caused the dent – had been to the left temple. As a physician

who nowadays sees more than his share of murder victims, I have reason to be glad that not too many people are aware that, in even a heavily-boned man with a hard skull, this is a place of weakness.

I stood back from the body, thinking, trying to put together a possible sequence of events. It was unlikely the man had been killed in the tiny yard where he was found, for whatever reason did anyone have to visit a cesspit unless he was paid to do so? Assailed nearby, then, in one of that maze of dark passages, and then dumped in the cesspit ditch. The attack would have had to be in reasonably open space, because whatever he'd been hit with would have been swung in a wide arc. A blow to the back of the head to stun him; then, perhaps even as he slumped and fell, a second, more forceful swing to the side of the head. The left side, I remembered, so probably a right-handed assailant.

Then what? He – they – dragged the dead or dying man to the stinking court and threw him in the channel feeding into the cesspit; perhaps in eloquent expression of their opinion of him?

And just when had someone taken the time to shove those odd little spheres into his mouth and down his throat? Even if he had survived the blow to the temple, which I doubted, he'd have died as soon as that was done to him. It had to have been important, because it wouldn't have been achieved in an instant, and it was logical to assume most people who have just killed someone would feel the strong urge to disappear as soon as they could.

I had no idea what the spheres were made of. Back where the dead man had been found, one of Theo's men had held open a small cloth bag and I had dropped them into it, and it had accompanied the corpse down here into the crypt. Now, together with the rest of the effects, it was on the wide board beneath the one high window where I put the lanterns and the candles. I picked it up, opened the drawstrings and tipped one of the spheres into my hand.

It was very hard; like a nut, or perhaps a large seed.

I looked at it for some time, rolling it between my fingers and thumb. Then I put my hand up to my face and sniffed.

There was a faint aroma, only just detectable. Or perhaps, I thought with a smile, my sense of smell had been temporarily affected by everything I'd put it through today.

I replaced the little ball in the bag and tied the strings. I'd had a suspicion that I knew what the unusual items were that had been thrust so forcefully into the dead man's mouth, and now it looked as if it had been confirmed.

I believed they were nutmegs.

I hurried the short distance up the road and found Theo in his office. As usual, he looked as if he was doing the work of three men, the big desk covered with scrolls, bound documents and stray papers, a severe frown on his face as he glared up to see who was disturbing him. '*What?*' he demanded. 'Oh, it's you, Gabe. Sit down.' He waved a hand at the two chairs set back against the wall, but they too were covered in documents.

'I won't, Theo, I'm not staying,' I replied. 'I just called in to report on the body.'

Whatever was engaging all his formidable powers of concentration just then clearly wasn't the corpse from the drainage channel, and it took him a moment to remember. 'Yes,' he said. 'What did you find?'

'One blow from behind with something heavy and blunt to stun him, a second to the temple which almost certainly killed him, then he was thrown in the channel.'

Theo's bright blue eyes were fixed on mine. 'And what about those little balls?'

I'd been hoping he would have forgotten, because I couldn't be entirely sure they were nutmegs until I checked a reference among my papers, but of course he hadn't. I muttered something about needing to do some research.

'Tell me when you've done so,' Theo ordered.

'Of course. Any idea who he is?'

'None of my men recognized him. And the one man who appears to know everyone in Plymouth and most of the county by sight isn't here.'

Jarman hadn't come back, then.

I bade Theo a swift good day and left him to his work.

*　　*　　*

It was approaching noon as I rode home. I called in to check on a couple of my more seriously ill cases, but I was well aware that their households would be busy preparing food for the midday meal and that if I was there, they would feel obliged to share the food with me, so I kept the visits brief. Many of my patients have little or nothing to spare, but the ancient customs of hospitality mean that they couldn't leave a caller unfed when they themselves were eating. I had recently mentioned this to Celia – who appears to have been making more calls on the poorer members of the parish of late – and she replied that many cultures shared this sense of responsibility, and that the ancient Greeks believed you must not be forgetful to entertain strangers because you might unwittingly be entertaining the gods. There was a myth on the subject, which she repeated to me. I wondered if this was another example of our grandmother's teachings; Celia had been extensively tutored by Grandmother Oldreive when she was a girl, which I am certain was largely what turned Celia into the clever, knowledgeable and perpetually inquisitive woman she is now.

I finally reached Rosewyke with my stomach growling with hunger; I'd just made a final unplanned call on my little boy with the congested chest, to find him a great deal perkier and about to tuck into a bowl of broth that smelled utterly delicious. As I walked into the kitchen, Sallie – who I sometimes suspect of being a mind reader – gave me a quick assessing glance and said, 'You'll be off up to your study, I dare say, Doctor, so I'll bring you up a tray.'

I could have kissed her.

But first I must check on the mystery woman. 'How is the patient?' I asked Sallie as she moved with practised ease around the kitchen preparing my food. 'Celia's with her now, I assume?'

Sallie gave me a swift look. 'Miss Celia and I sat with her most of the morning, taking it in turns, but she's fast asleep now and we reckoned it was all right to leave her awhile. Miss Celia's gone out for a ride – needed the good fresh air, bless her, after all those hours watching the patient. I've kept the doors open so I'll hear the woman if she calls out, but seems to me the fever's abating somewhat. But of course, Doctor, you'll need to judge for yourself,' she added, clearly abashed that she'd spoken out of turn on what was a medical matter.

'I will look in on her, but not to verify what you've just told me, Sallie,' I said. 'I don't suppose she's said anything?'

'No, Doctor, just ramblings and ravings that make no sense. She's still far, far away from us.' Sallie paused, a worried look on her kindly face. 'I wish we had the poor soul's name, but she hasn't even told us that!' she exclaimed. 'Doesn't seem right, not calling her anything.'

I murmured an agreement, then went to look at the woman. She was, as Sallie had said, soundly asleep, and the fever had indeed lessened. I straightened the bedding, noticing as I did so that the woman had somehow managed to get hold of the canvas bag that Jarman had brought back from the river. She was clutching it in both hands, holding it tightly to her breast.

It seemed that our mystery patient might not be quite as far away from us as Sallie believed.

As Sallie placed the food and ale on my desk, I was already flipping through the pages of my beautiful old botany book. It had been printed in Italy almost a century ago, and the illustrations were like miniature renaissance paintings. Finding the right page, I stared at it. My Italian was not sufficient to translate the finer details of the text, but the image was enough: the hard little spheres in the dead man's mouth and throat were indeed nutmegs.

My study is somewhat better organised than Theo's desk, but all the same it took me a while to find the other document I was looking for. I pounced on it with a smile of satisfaction, and sat down at my desk to read it again.

It was a paper written by one of the other physicians who make up the group which we named, in a moment of self-congratulation, the Symposium. The other members and I met when we were studying, and recognized in each other the common bond of an enquiring mind willing to question the old ways of thinking that dominate so overwhelmingly in our field. We had started as a larger group, but one by one the

members had lost their enthusiasm for going against established tradition. I didn't blame them; it's easier to risk your
good reputation when you don't have a wife and children to
support, and many of my fellow students were now married
men. The hard core of the Symposium consisted of just the
three of us: Jasper Hart, who lived in London; Gawen Mills,
who had settled in Bristol; and me, here in Devon.

We had contrived to convene a meeting towards the middle
of December. Jasper Hart had been unwell and gone to stay
with relations in Exeter to recuperate, and my Bristol friend
and I went there to join him. We spent a very happy three
days congratulating Jasper on having evaded the recent wide-
spread outbreak of plague. He had remained in the city, and
although he didn't say as much, it was clear to us that his
profound dedication to his profession was the reason he had
been unwell: he had worn himself out. He gave the clear
impression that he was sick and tired of London and was
thinking of a change, but Gawen and I put that down to fatigue
and the residue of long weeks and months striving to stay free
of infection.

It was hardly surprising that the paper Jasper presented to
the Symposium concerned methods of treating the plague. I
had been intrigued at what he'd had to say, as well as distressed
and angered by the vast number of quack remedies he listed.
Some of their advocates were probably sincere in the belief
that the remedies could help, despite the usually ghastly side
effects. Some, for example, worked on the theory that the
poisons in the buboes could be defeated by other poisons, such
as hellebore, viper flesh, arsenic and mercury, adding to a
patient's misery by violent vomiting and diarrhoea. Others
believed that smoke and vapours cleared the foul air, and
advised the burning of brimstone and the wafting of the stench
from various bodily waste substances, the more noisome the
better, as well as the copious smoking of tobacco. Some stead-
fastly followed the wisdom of earlier physicians, relying on
blood letting and the application of leeches as well as clysters
and emetics, and, verging towards the less creditable, putting
a puppy on the stomach in the hope that the disease would
pass to the animal so that it died and the patient got better.

The sick were even told to bathe in urine, or rub their boils with a chicken's anus.

But also there were the straightforward fraudsters; those whose main aim was the making of money from the misery of others. They did not even pretend that there was an iota of scientific theory behind their remedies, merely plying their bottles of foul-tasting water and unguents made of vividly-dyed goose grease to the increasingly terrified and desperate who believed those heartless pedlars who solemnly swore that they would help.

I don't know why I was so disgusted by the self-serving and callous behaviour of my fellow men; it was hardly a surprise to learn what people were capable of, even in the midst of a ghastly epidemic with the dead piling up in heaps and grieving mothers, fathers, spouses and children everywhere you looked.

The reason for digging out Jasper's paper now was that he had mentioned nutmeg.

I sat back in my chair, dipping a chunk of bread into Sallie's thick and delicious soup, my friend's paper in my free hand, and read right through the relevant section.

The nutmeg plant only grew, apparently, in a group of islands that were thousands of miles away to the east, in the seas of Indonesia. Perhaps its rarity added to the mystique, but, according to Jasper anyway, traders in India and the East had become fascinated, if not obsessed, with this spice from the earliest times, moving it via the most complex routes over land and sea all the way from Banda Neira to the markets hungry for it in the west. (The likelihood that this obsession was to a great extent due to the colossal profits that a canny trader could make was pointed out by the paper's author in a footnote.) Stories and myths had spread about its powers: according to an early Arabic writer, the profits made from the spice had created an impossibly luxurious and wealthy empire whose army was both enormous and invincible, and although the writer did not actually say so, it was implied that the invincibility might well be the result of nutmeg consumption.

As enterprising traders gradually extended the spread of the spice into the west, it found its way into the late Queen's England. Its price made it the preserve of the very, very rich; Jasper opined that grinding it and adding it to meat greatly enhanced the flavour, although he didn't say if he was speaking from personal experience of this costly luxury. I remembered remarking when he'd told us this that any additive which succeeded in covering up the taste and smell of meat on the turn was worth its weight in gold, to which Jasper had replied that nutmeg cost much more than gold.

The problem, apart from traders' greed, was that a cargo of the spice had such a long way to come and passed through so many pairs of hands: the people who grew it, the local men who bought it from them, those in the larger ports who purchased it from them and in turn took it further on its long journey, often trading it with the Chinese for their beautiful porcelain. Then thousands of miles on to India, north and west to the Red Sea and the Arabic Sea, from where the spice would now continue overland on camel trains over the endless sands until they reached the ports that traded with Europe.

And then, Jasper's paper had said, as if the price of nutmeg was not exorbitant enough already, someone had the bright idea of proposing it as a cure for the plague, and in a matter of weeks, if not days, the price shot up again.

The first questions that Gawen and I had asked Jasper were, of course, just how was the spice employed and did it work. He replied that physicians in pestilence-stricken London had taken to wearing pouches containing nutmeg round their necks, and sometimes it was ground and put inside the long beaks of the plague masks that covered the nose and mouth. Having had occasion to dress myself up in garments designed to protect against the plague only recently[2], I was particularly interested in this aspect. As to the efficacy of the spice, Jasper could only shake his head.

'I do not know. It has a strong smell,' I recall him saying. 'Perhaps it clears the foul miasmas in the air, if their presence is indeed the cause of this terrible scourge. Perhaps it deters the blood-sucking parasitic insects that some believe spread

[2] see Magic in the Weave

it so inexorably from person to person.' Then he had shrugged, eloquently indicating that our guess was as good as his.

I had long mopped up the last of the soup, and now I sat back in my chair, sipping my mug of ale and thinking. When people believe they or their family are going to die, they will do pretty much anything to save themselves and those they love. The rich had the money to spend on very costly remedies; a wealthy man might well reason, I mused, that even if this remedy's efficacy was not proven, his money was of no further use to him if he was dead, so why not try anyway?

No wonder the price of nutmeg was now astronomical.

I lit a pipe of tobacco, my thoughts racing on.

And for the life of me I couldn't think why several whole nutmegs had been shoved down the throat of the man found this morning behind a cheap and seedy Plymouth tavern.

FOUR

Celia's grey mare was pretending she had never seen snow before and wasn't sure she liked it, and consequently it took most of Celia's concentration to get them both safely down the long track from Rosewyke to the lane. The snow lay deep, and the prints made earlier by Gabe and Hal were now only the faintest dents in the unbroken surface.

The going was better in the lane, and better still once they were on the main Tavistock to Plymouth road. People didn't abandon their day's business for a snowfall, even quite a heavy one, and the passage of feet, hooves and wheels had packed the snow down into a hard, if slippery, surface. The mare was eager now, and Celia kicked her into a canter.

She had always loved to ride, and back when she had first become a married woman she had taken the firm decision to ride astride. Jeromy hadn't appeared to notice, Gabe thought it was a good idea since it was undoubtedly safer, and the objections of her father could safely be ignored since she no longer lived beneath his roof and he wouldn't find out anyway.

Smiling to herself, Celia was remembering her very first mount: a hobby horse she had named Gubbly Gee. Gabe had poured a lot of scorn on this name, but, although Celia had only been three years old, she was used to scorn from that quarter. She was also becoming adept at slipping in a sly punch, and when Gabe, forgetting he was her restrained and responsible older brother, had been driven to take his revenge, she had found that the best way to deter his strong attacking hands was to bite him.

For some reason she had never yet fathomed, her parents had been far more shocked by her infant tooth marks on Gabe's upper arm than by his twisting of her wrist that had driven her to defend herself. Still, she reflected now, it had been an early lesson in the undoubted fact that men ruled the world and a woman had to use every ounce of her intelligence and her courage to survive, never mind live happily, in it.

And Gabe had long ago grown out of such behaviour.

Gabe. She sighed, cross with herself for letting her preoccupations break into her memories. This ride was meant to be a break from the disturbing emotions within the house, and here she was returning to them. She had very much wanted to talk to Gabe, but whatever had summoned him from home so early this morning had kept him busy, until finally her patience was all used up and she'd had to get out.

The first thing she'd needed to discuss with Gabe was the mystery woman's state. Watching her closely, Celia had come to suspect that she wasn't as profoundly asleep, or unconscious, as she would have them believe. A couple of times, Celia had shot a quick glance at the patient and was almost sure she'd caught the woman staring at her between her heavily-lashed lids: there had been a definite glitter of dark eyes, she'd have sworn to it.

And there was the matter of the bag.

Jarman Hodge had brought the woman's paltry belongings, amounting to merely a length of inferior wool – a shawl, perhaps – much darned and with the fringes worn to almost nothing, and a small canvas pack with a leather strap and a buckle to fasten it. Marks on the canvas suggested there had originally been two buckled straps, although one had gone. Celia had subsequently spread the shawl out to dry before the kitchen hearth, but out of respect for the woman she hadn't touched the canvas pack, other than to place it beside the bed within the woman's reach when she awoke.

There had come a short time when both Celia and Sallie were out of the room. And when Celia went back to resume her watch, the pack had disappeared. Since neither she nor Sallie had moved it, that left only one person: Celia was quite sure the pack was now tucked away beneath the bedclothes.

So that was one thing that troubled her.

The other was rather more serious: what Jonathan was going to say when he found out she and Gabe were sheltering someone who had tried to kill both herself and the child she was carrying. She was almost sure he would understand, but he was answerable to a higher authority that might well take a different view.

'I don't *know*,' she exclaimed aloud, her sudden angry utterance making the grey mare flick her ears.

The obvious solution – and one her straightforward nature was forcefully suggesting – was to go directly to Jonathan, tell him what had happened and what they had done and were now doing. But to do so would involve Gabe, Sallie and Jarman Hodge in the matter, and Celia didn't feel she had the right to do this until they had agreed.

Which meant she couldn't go to Jonathan at all; for now, he was closed off to her, because she knew full well she wouldn't be able to talk to him about everyday matters, or indulge in the fascinating discussions on a wide range of matters they had both come to enjoy so much, with this wretched business of the mystery woman hanging between them like a dark cloud that only Celia would be aware of.

'Oh, curse the woman,' she muttered, instantly regretting the words because whatever distress she was causing Celia was surely nothing when compared with whatever terrible event in the woman's life had led her to try to end it. By walking into a freezing cold and fast-moving river with stones tied round her body. In a bitter February with snow on the ground.

Celia was filled with pity for the woman. But it didn't blot out her dismay at being kept from Jonathan.

She knew now that she was starting to care for him deeply. She was fairly sure he felt the same. Neither of them had spoken of their feelings, but she saw the same lightening of the expression in him when she approached that she knew to be happening on her own face.

The Christmas season had been a delight. It was quite a surprise to both Gabe and herself when their parents had accepted the invitation to come to stay at Rosewyke; Benedict Taverner was renowned as a man whose preference for sleeping in his own bed meant he very rarely slept anywhere else, and Celia's mother Frances had been forced to employ all her powers of persuasion to make him agree. Gabe and Celia's brother Nathaniel had refused to stay; he had the unarguable excuse of the farmer, that he couldn't possibly leave his livestock for more than a few hours, but he had grudgingly attended the church service at St Luke's and then joined the party for the Christmas feast.

And it had indeed been a party. Jonathan had attended; a smiling presence in their midst and still full of joy after celebrating the Lord's birth in his lovely church, and their midwife friend Judyth Penwarden had joined them. Celia had picked up a certain new note in the exchanges between Judyth and Gabe, and she had an idea that their friendship might be deepening into something more.

Celia's mother had been too busy watching her daughter and the vicar to spot what was so obvious to Celia. Fearing that she was going to have to endure some quite penetrating questions and probably a lengthy lecture, Celia had done her best to avoid being alone with her mother.

But Frances Taverner was as determined as her daughter, and had cornered Celia in her bedchamber when she went to fetch a fresh handkerchief after they had finally finished the meal and risen from the table.

'Your vicar gave a fine sermon,' she observed, settling herself in the comfortable chair in the anteroom to Celia's bedchamber. 'I liked the emphasis on love and joy. Our own priest does tend to remind us of Our Lord's great sacrifice and his tragic end in the Christmas address, which of course is never to be forgotten, but all the same it was a pleasant change to be encouraged towards undiluted happiness, even if just for one day.' She eyed Celia closely. 'Jonathan Carew is, I believe, a good man.'

Celia took a breath, then said calmly, 'Yes, he is. The parish is lucky to have him.'

'I'm told he was once destined for a greater position,' Frances went on.

Careful, Celia warned herself. 'He studied at Cambridge. He–Gabe says he was once involved in work of a sensitive nature, with some of the great names of the late Queen's reign.' She stopped.

Back in the autumn there had been a moment – just one moment – when she had felt Jonathan was about to reveal something of what had happened during that time of his life.

But the moment had been driven away[3]; crushed by imminent danger. So far it hadn't recurred.

'And he ends up down here,' Frances murmured. 'In a region which, even though its inhabitants appreciate everything it has to offer, one must admit is rather a backwater.'

'Jonathan doesn't think it's a backwater,' Celia began hotly, 'he—' Then abruptly she shut her mouth.

Too late, for her mother had noticed and was smiling. 'If a highly intelligent and sophisticated man such as he has found happiness here, then I can think of one very good reason for it.' The smile deepened, and Celia, dismayed, thought it meant her mother was congratulating herself on having accurately judged Celia's feelings for Jonathan and was about to embark on the expected lecture and it would all become so embarrassing and make Celia angry because her mother was interfering and . . .

And then she understood.

Her mother wasn't crowing in triumph at her own perspicacity. There was a suggestion of tears in her eyes as she looked at her daughter, and, *oh goodness*, Celia realized, *she's not going to reprimand me and tell me I mustn't risk my happiness again, she's glad for me!*

She and her mother held each other's eyes for a moment, then Frances beckoned and said, 'Come here, my lovely girl,' and Celia obeyed, sitting on the floor at her mother's feet.

She felt her mother's hand on her head, gently smoothing her hair. 'We never speak of the past,' Frances said, 'and I shall not do so now. You are not that wilful girl any more, Celia. I would rather you still were,' she added vehemently, 'than that you had to endure what you did in order to become the woman you now are. But I cannot change the past, and so I shall simply rejoice in the result.'

Celia waited a moment, then said, 'Thank you, Mother.'

They had sat in silence for a while. Then, with a final pat on Celia's head, Frances had stood up and suggested they return to the menfolk.

*   *   *

[3] Magic in the Weave

The short daylight was fading as finally I left my study and went downstairs. I strolled into the kitchen, but it was empty. I went on to the little parlour, and found Sallie sitting beside the sleeping patient. Sallie looked up, caught my eye and jerked her head towards the hall. I nodded my understanding and retraced my steps, crossing the hall and going on into the library. The fire had been laid but not lit, so I bent down and, striking a spark with flint and stone, lit a taper and set it to the kindling.

Behind me, Sallie said quietly, 'She's shamming.'

I looked up at her.

'Yes, I think so too.'

Sallie's face showed her surprise. 'Do you?'

'Yes. When I checked on her earlier, the canvas pack that was beside the bed had somehow got itself into her grasp, and she was hugging it close to her.'

'So *that's* where it went!' Sallie exclaimed. 'I wondered if Miss Celia had taken it, perhaps to dry it out like she did that tatty old shawl. The woman picked it up!' Her eyes were round with wonder, but even as I watched, I thought I saw an edge of anger, that this mystery woman we had brought into the house and were tending so assiduously should be deceiving us.

'She may have her reasons, Sallie,' I pointed out. 'She has surely been through some terrible experience, and until she can recover her senses sufficiently to talk to us – if she chooses to do so – she can have no idea if we are friends or foes.'

'But we've been looking after her!' Sallie protested. 'Even though she—' Abruptly she stopped. 'Well, never mind,' she muttered. She frowned, clearly thinking, then said, 'Yes, Doctor. I see what you mean. Until she knows what we're planning to do with what we know about her, she's going to keep up the pretence that she's still too sick to wake up, and keep whatever's in that pack to herself.' She smiled grimly. 'Reckon I'd probably do the same.'

Remembering her initial remark, I said, 'What did *you* see that makes you think she's pretending, Sallie?'

'Oh, that's easy,' she replied. 'Caught her looking at me, didn't I?'

I was just reflecting that not a great deal escaped my canny housekeeper when there was a sudden blast of cold air and the noise of footsteps stomping across the hall in boots, and I spun round to see Celia hurrying into the library.

'Oh, you're back,' she said to me. 'Where have you been?'

Briefly I told her about Theo summoning me to attend the dead man hidden behind the tavern on the quay. She nodded, not appearing particularly interested.

'It's snowing again, coming down really hard,' she said, sidestepping round Sallie and me to get to the fire, 'and there was someone, or maybe more than one person, lurking at the end of the track as I approached.' She bent down, taking off her heavy gloves and holding her hands to the flames. Her fingers were white to the knuckles.

'You stayed out too long, Miss Celia,' Sallie said. There was a note of disapproval in her voice. 'I'll go and warm up some broth.'

'Thank you,' Celia said absently. She was frowning into the fire. 'Oh, Sallie?' she called.

Sallie turned back. 'Yes?'

'Could you warm up a good quantity, please? Jarman Hodge followed me up the track, and I'm pretty sure Judyth is with him.'

Sallie managed to hold back whatever remark was undoubtedly hovering on her lips. With a curt nod, she left the room.

'Did you mean it was Jarman and Judyth at the end of the track?' I demanded, going to sit in my chair beside Celia, still crouched on the hearth.

'No. Didn't I make it clear?' she replied impatiently. 'I saw the man, or men, as I was riding up, but I assume they saw me and they hurried away.' The frown was back. 'Well, that's not right— I didn't actually see them go, it was more as if they were there one moment and gone the next.'

'Oh, good Lord, you're not suggesting they magically disappeared?'

She grinned. 'Of course not. Merely that they're well practised in the art of concealment.'

The suggestion that the men had been spying on the house

was disconcerting, in view of the fact that we had a mysterious woman under our roof.

'And then, once I was almost up at the house,' Celia was saying, 'I heard riders behind me and saw Jarman and Judyth. I'd have stopped to greet them only I thought it better to come on in and set Sallie to preparing something hot to welcome them with. And,' she added disarmingly. 'I didn't think I could go on being so cold any longer.'

Smiling, I got up and went through to the yard door to meet them.

Jarman caught hold of my arm and held me back as Judyth went on inside. 'I fetched her,' he muttered, 'because of the woman in there.' He jerked his head towards the house.

'Yes, so I assumed,' I replied. He still had hold of my arm, and I guessed he was intending to speak to me in confidence; I pointed out that if he was trying to be discreet for the sake of the mystery woman, there was no need because all of us in the household already knew about her. 'And I assume you've told Judyth,' I added. The woman was pregnant, Judyth is a midwife, Jarman had gone to fetch her, so it was a logical supposition.

He nodded. 'Reckoned it'd be all right,' he muttered. 'You and her being friends.'

Friends.

We had always been that. But I had been attracted to her since we met, and I believed I had reason to think this attraction was reciprocated. We had spent little time alone – convention and our busy lives saw to that – but late last year we had shared a quiet supper together in her sweet-smelling little house above the river. We had talked, revealing much about ourselves that had previously been left unsaid. I had held her hand. As I left, I bent to kiss her cheek. She had reached up to take my face in her hands and very firmly kissed me on the mouth.

I had no idea what she had meant by that intimacy, if it meant anything. She had withdrawn into her professional self – approachable, generous, spicing our conversations with her accustomed teasing remarks – but she hadn't kissed me again.

Friends . . .

Hoping very much that Judyth would feel we were more than that, I went into the library to greet her.

She had her heavy fur-lined cloak on, and was unfastening the hood to throw it back. 'Good evening, Gabe,' she said.

'I'm glad to see you, Judyth. Our patient is perhaps six months pregnant—' I hurried on; Judyth's lip turned down in an ironic smile as I dived straight into speaking professionally rather than anything more intimate '—and Jarman here will no doubt have told you about her being in the water. Since then she has suffered from an episode of violent vomiting, followed by a high fever. She is still giving the appearance of being deeply asleep, but Sallie and I both think she's more aware than she makes out.'

'I think so too,' Celia added. 'In fact I know she is.'

Judyth had now removed her cloak, and she threw it over a chair. She wore her big leather satchel across her body. 'I'll go and see her,' she said calmly.

I stayed where I was.

I only realized I was staring after her when Jarman gave a slightly awkward cough and said, 'I'll be off back home, then, Doctor. Snow's getting worse and we're in for a blizzard, like as not.'

I went out to the yard with him, and Samuel emerged from the stable buildings with his horse. A large, low, black shape came with him: my dog, Flynn, had seen me, and I bent to rub him behind the ears as he pressed against my legs.

'You've said nothing yet to Master Davey?' I asked Jarman softly.

'Haven't seen him.' Jarman's tone was curt, and he didn't meet my eyes. I reckoned he didn't like the subterfuge at all.

Sick of it myself, I said, 'Tomorrow, Jarman, we tell both Master Davey and Jonathan Carew. We have done nothing wrong,' I went on before he could speak, 'and since the woman didn't succeed in what she attempted to do, it's quite possible she hasn't either.'

'But—' he began.

'Go home, Jarman,' I said firmly.

He mounted up and rode away.

Samuel stood beside me, and I was sure he was as keen to get back to his hearth as I was to mine. 'Will Mistress Penwarden be needing her horse?' he asked.

I had no idea what Judyth's plans were once she had seen the mystery woman, but the snow was falling heavily now and I was prepared to do whatever I could to persuade her to remain at Rosewyke overnight.

'Let's assume not, Samuel,' I said.

He gave me a knowing look. 'I'll see to the gelding then, Doctor, and then Tock and me'll turn in.'

I went back into the house, and Flynn came with me.

Judyth spent a long time with the woman.

Celia and I decided not to wait to eat – the aroma of Sallie's broth was just too tempting – and we consumed our food sitting in our chairs either side of the library fire.

'Sallie says you were out for a long time today,' I said, once we had taken the edge off our appetites.

Celia muttered something that sounded like *Sallie should mind her own business*.

'She worries about you,' I said gently. 'She still thinks you're—' I hesitated, searching for a description that would be both accurate and not offensive to my sister.

'Delicate? Fragile? Weak?' Celia suggested, each word uttered with increasing vehemence.

'None of those, since you're very obviously not any of them,' I returned. 'I believe she sees you as restless, and I think she worries that, not having enough to occupy you here, you'll leave us.'

I was probably transferring my own worry to Sallie.

She paused, spoon on its way to her mouth, and stared at me.

'It's true I often used to feel I'd scream out loud if I had to spend another afternoon sewing pretty but trivial little nonsenses,' she said slowly. 'But of late I have come to find rather more purpose in my life.'

'You mean you—'

'Don't interrogate me, Gabe,' she said very firmly. 'When I'm ready to speak to you, I will.'

Both of us, I'm sure, knew exactly what we would be talking about.

There was a rather tense silence.

I probably should have gone on to make any remark other than the one I actually did, but unfortunately I was still thinking about what we *hadn't* just said.

'Did you call in on Jonathan?'

The words hung in the air. Celia gave me a long, hard look, then went back to her soup.

'No,' she said after an uncomfortable pause. 'He was the one person I *did* want to see, because I feel strongly that one of us ought to find out exactly where we all stand concerning sheltering and aiding an attempted suicide. I'm not saying I regret what we've done because I don't, but until we decide to share our secret outside this house – which, incidentally, Jarman Hodge has apparently just done – Jonathan's counsel is shut off to us.'

I sensed a strong note of reproof in her tone.

'I've just told Jarman that tomorrow both Jonathan and Theo must be told about our woman,' I said. 'Celia, we have to put our faith in them. We know full well that neither of them is the sort of man to condemn someone out of hand, and—'

I stopped, for she was now smiling at me, shaking her head in exasperation.

'*What*?' I demanded.

'You don't have to convince me, Gabe,' she said, still grinning. 'I was all for seeking the pair of them out yesterday.'

When Judyth finally joined us, the wind was hurling the snow against the windows with increasing fury, and it was already drifting deeply either side of the track down to the lane. She went over and looked out through the gap in the curtains.

'May I stay, please?' she asked, turning back to us as I stood up to welcome her.

'Of course,' Celia said. 'I'll make up a bed for you in my workroom. We'll be glad to have you,' she added.

Judyth smiled. 'Thank you. I wasn't looking forward to setting out in that—' she indicated the wildly-swirling snow '—

and I truly think I ought to stay. Your patient—' she turned to me '—is not at all well.'

'The fever has dropped,' I said quickly, 'and she—'

'You're right, she's recovering adequately in herself, considering the ordeal she has suffered. The members of your household take good care of the sick, Gabe, as I have good reason to know.'

I muttered a thank you, but she ignored it.

'It's the child she carries,' Judyth went on. 'Or, more specifically, what she has to say about it.'

'She was talking to you?' I asked.

'Yes. You were quite right when you said she'd been awake and aware for some time. She confessed to the subterfuge because she's very frightened, and she didn't know what you were going to do to her.'

'We weren't going to do *anything* to her, if by that you mean shout out to the world that Jarman Hodge fished a would-be suicide out of the Tavy and that we've all been trying to help her!' Celia said in a sort of suppressed shout.

Judyth turned to her. 'I know that, Celia. But then I have the great benefit of knowing what sort of people you are, and she doesn't.'

'What about the baby?' I asked. I had an idea what Judyth was going to tell us, and I was hoping I was wrong.

Judyth sank down into my fireside chair, briefly closing her eyes. 'The child is, I fear, one of the reasons why she felt she could not go on living,' she said very softly. 'She doesn't want it. She is alone, there is no husband, she is homeless and hungry. Destitute, in fact.'

'Where has she come from?' Celia asked. 'She's not local, is she?'

'No, I don't think so. I have no idea, however, where her home is nor how she came to be here. She won't reveal anything, save that she was in Plymouth and something frightened her very badly, and she hurried out of the town and followed the road along the Tamar estuary, then turned down on to the track by the Tavy. Her terror did not abate, and finally she made her way down to the water's edge and walked right in.'

'But she won't say what frightened her so badly?' Was it, I wondered, something she saw in Plymouth? Some*one* she saw?

'No. She has refused to say another word, and she hasn't even told me her name.'

Judyth lay back in the chair, and I saw she was exhausted. 'Let Celia make up the bed for you straight away,' I said. 'We should all try to sleep while this storm rages, for nobody's going to be leaving the house until it passes.'

Even, I might have added, a desperate woman who has just tried to kill herself and is carrying a child she would rather did not exist.

Nobody inside the house attempted to leave during the night.

But somebody tried to break in.

I was in bed and deeply asleep and, contrary to the usual house rules, Flynn had crept up with me and was curled up in front of the fire. I was very glad he was, for his sharp ears picked up the soft sounds that should not have been there long before mine did.

It was his low, continuous growl that woke me. It isn't a sound he often has cause to make, but when he does, it is so reminiscent of his wild forebears that it makes the hairs on the back of my neck rise up.

He had come over to the bed, and I put my hand down to him. He was stiff with tension, and abruptly he broke away from me and hurled himself at the door. Now the growl had turned into furious barking, and he was saying as clearly as he could *let me get at them!*

I got up, flung on my tunic and opened the door. Flynn raced out, along the passage and down the stairs, and I was close behind. I was aware of Celia and Judyth, running towards the stairs from Celia's end of the passage, and I yelled, 'Stay back! Someone's trying to get in!'

I might have known it was pointless, for women like Judyth and my sister don't take kindly to being told what to do, even when it's for their own safety.

'We know, Gabe, we heard someone trying to break the

library window!' Celia cried. She had a cudgel in her hand and Judyth was carrying a heavy pottery jug.

I jumped the last few stairs into the hall, the pair of them right behind me, and darted across to the main door to pick up my sword.

Someone was screaming, the sound vibrant with panic.

'Sallie! *Sallie!*' I shouted over the screams, all too aware that she too was probably bracing herself to fight off the intruder and undoubtedly armed with something even more unwieldy than a jug.

'I'm here!' she called out, and, turning, I saw her coming out of the morning parlour. 'Oh, Doctor, she's terrified!' she exclaimed, shooting a glance back in the direction of the sick woman, 'she's sobbing, crying out that she's going to die, and she's trying to bury herself under the covers!'

Flynn had disappeared through the door into the main parlour and in the direction of the library, and I ran after him. I flung back the thick curtains, and just for an instant I had the impression of a face pressed hard against the diamond panes of glass. The lower half of the face was black with a heavy beard, and one hand was poised and holding what looked like a rock. Flynn saw it too, and let loose a violent and extremely loud cannonade of barks. He must have been an impressive sight from the other side of the window, jaws wide open, red throat gaping between a lot of sharp teeth, and even as I unlatched the window and flung it open, the bearded face fell away. I heard the sound of scrabbling feet and I made out a powerful, stocky figure running hard away from the house.

Then it – he – disappeared into the darkness.

I held on tight to Flynn's collar.

I could feel his furious desire to give chase, and it was tempting to let him loose.

Flynn is a large and heavy dog, he has an intrepid heart and he is fiercely protective. I did not welcome the prospect of explaining to Theo why I had a dead man outside my house whose throat had been torn out, and so I closed the window.

I crouched down to Flynn. 'I'm sorry,' I muttered in his ear, 'I know you'd have caught him. But you heard him, and you raised the alarm, and that was enough.'

Flynn gave a huff, which I took to indicate that he didn't agree with me. He was trembling with tension.

I stood up and went out into the hall to reassure the rest of my household.

The woman's screaming had thankfully stopped, and now she was huddled in the blankets with Sallie's arms round her. Sallie was whispering a constant stream of quiet reassurances, one hand gently stroking the woman's thin back. She glanced up and met my eyes, pausing the quiet flow of words to mouth, 'I'll stay with her.' I mouthed back 'Thank you.'

Celia, Judyth and I stood in the hall. Flynn had gone on a circuit of the ground-floor rooms, and I guessed it would take him some time to calm down. Just as well, perhaps, since a highly alert dog would hear any further approach long before any of us did.

'And who, do you think, was *that*?' Celia asked. She was pale, but her eyes were glittering. And she still gripped her cudgel.

'Do we, do you think, surmise that he was looking for our patient?' Judyth added.

'I imagine we do,' I agreed. 'But who he was, and what he wants with her, we have yet to find out. I'll—'

But Celia didn't let me finish. 'We cannot keep this to ourselves, Gabe,' she said firmly.

'We are not going to,' I replied.

FIVE

I was up early the next morning. I knew Judyth would not linger, and I wanted to speak to her before she left. She was putting on her cloak as I went down the stairs; I had almost missed her. She gave me a quick, involuntary smile but then quickly her expression straightened. 'I must be about my day's work,' she said firmly, as if I had been trying to detain her.

I went out into the yard to see her on her way. I'd thought perhaps to have some quiet moments with her, but both Samuel and Tock were lurking, and – understandably, I grudgingly admitted to myself – Samuel insisted on telling me every last detail of the arrangements the pair of them had made to protect the household. Samuel was still feeling guilty because neither he nor Tock had heard anything until Flynn started barking, although I reckoned they had more than made up for it subsequently, each of them arming himself with a stout length of timber and embarking on so thorough a patrol that now there was a hard-trodden icy path all around the house.

As Judyth mounted up and rode off, promising to visit the patient later, Tock closed and barred the yard gates.

I regretted turning Rosewyke into a fortress: the front and yard doors were also bolted and the windows shut fast, but I accepted it was necessary.

Samuel and I watched Tock as he carefully slotted the bars into their iron brackets either side of the gates. 'Is he all right?' I asked. 'Not scared by the intruder?'

'He'll do,' Samuel replied. He is a man of few words. He has been with my family for years, moving from my parents' house, Fernycombe, to Rosewyke when I set up home here. Tock was taken in by my blacksmith grandfather when he was a young boy – he is limited, our Tock, but what he can do he does thoroughly and diligently – and Samuel, it seemed to me, looked on him as a son.

Judyth was a distant figure far down the track now. I nodded to Samuel and went back inside.

I set out shortly afterwards. The blizzard had stopped some time around dawn, and no more snow had fallen. The skies had cleared to a pale blue, and there was no sinister gathering of dark clouds. Hal picked a careful way through the deep snow on the track leading down from the house, unbroken save for the prints of Judyth's gelding, and before too long we were on the wider road heading for Plymouth.

I very much wanted to talk to Jonathan. My conscience troubled me that I hadn't sought him out as soon as we had brought the woman to Rosewyke, for he was perhaps the one person who could have helped someone in such despair. However, I had decided to visit Theo first; I needed to find out, for my household's sake and my own, if helping and tending a would-be suicide was an offence, and I knew he would undoubtedly tell me.

I had made no arrangement to met Jarman Hodge this morning, but as I turned my horse into the road that led to Theo's house, he was waiting for me.

'How long have you been here?' I asked.

He smiled grimly. 'Not too long, Doctor. I can still feel my feet.'

'We'll talk to him together, shall we?'

He didn't reply, except to nod.

Theo was already hard at work. Looking up, he frowned as he saw us. 'So you've turned up at last?' he said to Jarman. 'Care to tell me where you've been for the past two days? Good morning, Gabe,' he added.

I was about to start on the tale but Jarman forestalled me. 'I found a body in the river, day before yesterday, early,' he said tonelessly. 'In the shallows, rolling over and over in an eddy, and I fetched a long branch and pulled it out. It was heavy, and I thought it was on account of the waterlogged clothes, especially the travelling cloak, but it wasn't. There were stones, a lot of them, wound up in a cloth and tied round the waist.'

'A suicide,' Theo murmured. 'Poor man. Go on.'

Jarman took a breath. Then: 'It was a woman. Young, dark-haired. There was this little pack on the shore.' His voice shook, and he paused briefly. 'I untied the cloth and threw the stones away, then tucked the cloth and the pack under the cloak and went to fetch Doctor Taverner.'

Theo was watching him steadily but he did not speak.

'I know suicide's a sin and a crime, just like murder, but I also know what we do to suicides, how the law has the power to take away all their goods and their property and leave their families in penury, and then there's the burial, that's brutal, and—' He stopped.

'So you didn't come straight to me but instead sought out Gabe and involved him in your deception,' Theo said.

'He didn't deceive me!' I protested. 'He told me what he'd found and what he'd done, and I went with him willingly.'

Theo nodded, then turned his bright gaze back to Jarman.

'We went back to the river and Doctor T loaded the body up on his horse,' Jarman hurried on. He shot a quick, nervous glance at me. 'But as we approach Rosewyke, turns out she's not dead after all. So we take her inside, and the Doctor and his womenfolk have been tending her.'

'She is with child,' I said.

Theo turned back to me. 'So I dare say someone has summoned Judyth Penwarden to attend her.'

'That was me,' Jarman mumbled.

'And how is she?' Theo asked.

'She's recovering,' I replied.

There was a long and increasingly awkward silence. My patience ran out before Jarman's, and I said, 'What do you think, Theo? Did we do wrong?'

Theo made us wait a few moments more, then said, 'If the woman had succeeded in her desire to end her life – and that of her child – then the covering-up of what you rightly refer to as a capital offence would indeed have been a crime. The corpse would have been handed over for burial in uncon-secrated ground, although it is possible that in these more enlightened times, the stake through the heart might have been dispensed with. And as His Majesty's coroner, it would indeed have been my right to confiscate the woman's property, assuming she had any.' He stared at Jarman, then at me. 'However, she did not succeed. You have just revealed to me that suicide was quite clearly her intention, but there is no dead body.'

This time the silence seemed interminable. Finally Jarman said, 'Am I in trouble, Master Davey?'

'No, Jarman,' Theo replied. 'You acted out of compassion, and I dare say I might have done the same.' Jarman's expression lifted and he was just starting to smile in relief when Theo added, 'But seeing that you have two days' work to make up, you can start right now. Yesterday a body was found in a dark little passage off the quayside – ask Matthew, he'll tell you about it. We don't know who he was, so you can go and find out. And don't come back till you've done so,' he added as Jarman scuttled away.

As the outer door banged shut behind him, Theo looked up at me. 'Why didn't you come and tell me straight away?' he asked. 'Jarman's reluctance I can understand, since he works for me and he knew he was doing wrong. But you, Gabe – did you truly believe I'd be so lacking in compassion that I'd take this poor woman to task for what she tried to do?'

I shook my head. 'No.'

He still looked hurt. 'And Jonathan? No doubt you told him all about your unexpected patient, even though suicide's a mortal sin and—' But he was still watching me closely, and he must have read my expression. 'You didn't tell him either.'

'No, and I still haven't. He's my next call today.'

Now Theo smiled. 'Then no doubt you're impatient to be on your way.'

'I am, but there's something more.' I told him about the would-be intruder at Rosewyke.

'You think this man was looking for your woman?'

'She's very frightened. She's obviously hiding something, and she's been pretending to be unconscious so that we haven't been able to question her. It's logical, surely, to assume our night snooper was after her.'

'Did you drive him off?'

'Yes.' I didn't see any need to tell him I'd stopped Flynn from hunting him down.

Theo was looking thoughtfully at me. 'A desperate woman with a secret, a dead man in a drainage ditch behind a cheap inn, a dark figure at the window in the night.'

'You think the three are connected?'

'I do. Given your dark figure got away, I also think there's worse to come.'

As I set off for Tavy St Luke's, I was hoping Theo was wrong, but depressingly sure he was probably right. I tried and failed to see what might link the woman, the dead man and the face at the window. The one faint note of optimism was that Jarman Hodge was now busy trying to discover the dead man's identity. Assuming he was successful – and Jarman was very good at this sort of work – then that would almost certainly help.

I tethered Hal in the lean-to behind the Priest's House in the little village, then went round to the front and tapped on the door. It opened almost immediately, and Jonathan greeted me with a smile.

'Gabriel! Good to see you. I meant to come up to Rosewyke yesterday to see how the snow was affecting you, but the day took on its own momentum and then the blizzard began, and after that—'

'I have something to confess, Jonathan,' I interrupted, not really taking in what he was saying.

His expression changed. 'Shall we go across to the church?' he asked quietly.

'No, that's not what I mean. It's a matter of—'

He was already ushering me inside, to a chair by the hearth in his dark little room. He sat down opposite me, and waited.

I gave him pretty much the same account that Jarman had just given to Theo.

He was quiet for some time when I was done.

Then he said thoughtfully, 'Catholic theology views suicide as a mortal sin because it is murder, but also because, as a deliberate act, it is the result of a despair so profound that the perpetrator believes he – or she – is beyond God's help and God's mercy. Moreover, as St Thomas Aquinas opined, to take one's own life trespasses on the province of God, as well as being utterly at odds with man's natural instinct for self love.'

He paused, a distant look in his eyes. 'It is a sin that is whispered about, forbidden, feared, and association with it is deeply shameful. This was not the attitude of the ancient world, interestingly. Marcus Aurelius says in his Meditations that the power to withdraw from life – I believe I have the wording correctly – is in our own hands.'

I had momentarily forgotten that Jonathan was a scholar.

I gave him a few moments to finish his inner musings on this Marcus Aurelius, then said, 'Did we do wrong, Jonathan?'

His strange green eyes turned to me. 'Wrong, Gabe? You took this woman in, you and your household are caring for her, no doubt devotedly.'

The silence extended. 'But she tried to kill herself, and she'd have taken the unborn child with her, and that's both a crime and a mortal sin.'

'But she isn't dead,' Jonathan said softly.

It was just what Celia had said the day before yesterday.

Presently Jonathan spoke again. 'Do you think your patient would like to see a priest?' he suggested tentatively. 'It seems she believes herself to be far from God at present. Perhaps I could reassure her.'

'She's terrified of something,' I replied. 'For all I know, it may be God's wrath.' Remembering the pale face at the window, however, I was fairly certain it was something of rather more earthly origin.

'I don't propose to tell her she is doomed to the eternal fires,' Jonathan said gently. 'Rather that there is a path back, and the door is always open.'

I looked at him, his lean face filled with a sort of glow, as if he was already imagining his conversation with my mystery woman. 'I think she would at first resist seeing you,' I said candidly. 'But then when you'd begun to talk to her, she'd be very glad you were there.'

He stood up. 'Then let's be on our way.'

Tock was on lookout as Jonathan and I rode up to the house, and he had the gates open as we approached the yard. Samuel reported that there had been no sign of any unwanted visitors – no visitors at all, in fact – and also that Tock had tried to follow the tracks left by the intruder as he fled, but lost them once the man had broken out of the cover of the trees, where they had been covered up by the subsequent snow.

Thanking them both for their diligence, I led the way inside.

Sallie was in the kitchen, from which appetizing smells were emanating. The resulting complaint from my stomach informed me that the day was well advanced now, and yet again I seemed to have missed every opportunity for grabbing something to eat. We went on into the morning parlour, and found Celia sitting beside the bed. The woman was awake, alert, propped up on pillows and holding my sister's hand.

Celia turned towards us as we came into the room, and her face lit up when she saw Jonathan. But she didn't pause to greet either of us; instead she said, 'Our guest and I have been talking. Let me present Artemis Brownyng. Artemis—' she turned to the woman '—this is my brother the doctor, Gabriel Taverner, and this is our vicar, Jonathan Carew.'

The woman had been looking up at us with a tentative smile until Celia introduced Jonathan. Now the smile was replaced by a deep frown, and, shaking her head, she muttered, 'No, no, I can't—'

Jonathan stepped forward. Without a word Celia gave up her seat beside the woman, coming to stand beside me. We heard Jonathan's opening words – kind words, uttered in a voice of compassion – and then Celia nudged me, quite hard. I took the hint and left the room, Celia just behind me, and she closed the door.

'Come over to the library,' she commanded, leading the way across the hall, 'I have quite a lot to tell you.'

Sallie, bless her, had set a tray of bread and cold meats on the table, with a jug of ale and mugs. I glanced at Celia, but she said shortly, 'I've eaten – Sallie brought us food.' So I helped myself, and Celia and I settled by the fire in our habitual chairs. As I started on the food, she began to speak.

'She is entirely alone,' she said. 'She's not local and I don't know where she's from, but wherever it is, there's no home there any more because both her parents are dead. Her father was a scholar and a lover of the classical writers, as you'll have surmised by her given name, and it appears he was a confirmed bachelor until some instant of madness prompted him to marry his housekeeper. Artemis was the sole result of their unlikely union. Artemis didn't call it that,' she added, 'I'm adding my own interpretation. Anyway, Artemis seems to have spent a lonely childhood, with a distant father absorbed in his studies and a mother who appears to have been relegated to her subservient role soon after Artemis was born. Bearing all that in mind, it's very understandable that when she finally met someone – and she must have thought she was never going to because she was no young girl, from what I gather she must have been more than twenty years old – she should fall in love as deeply as she appears to have done.' She shot a glance at me, and I saw she was blushing faintly; I wondered if she was embarrassed by her moment of sentimentality. 'I *believe*,' Celia went on, considerably more briskly, 'the man's name is Edwyn, Edwyn Warham, although she muttered it softly, half under her breath, and I can't be sure. It would make sense for him to be called Edwyn, of course,' she went on, more to herself, 'because she was crying out for someone called Ned when the fever had her in its grip.'

'Go on,' I prompted, as she sat frowning in thought.

'Oh. Yes. It seems this Edwyn is ambitious, and wants to make his fortune before he takes Artemis to wife, and he's gone off on a voyage, which seems very callous, and I think it's quite possible that he might just have been making up a story to get away from her, and perhaps he was weary of her devotion and her expectations . . . Furthermore,' she added before I could comment, 'he wouldn't tell Artemis where he was bound or how long he would be, and that was some time ago now, at least—'

'At least six months,' I supplied.

She shot me an irritated look. 'How did you know that? Oh, of course – because she's six months pregnant. Well, she didn't talk about either the baby or its conception, and *I* certainly didn't mention it, not when it seemed she was starting to trust us enough to open up a little, although I quite agree with Judyth that she is aghast to find herself with child.'

'But you just said she didn't talk about the baby!'

Celia sighed. 'Oh, Gabe. People don't have to put something

into words in order for others to know what they are feeling, especially when it's an antipathy as strong as the one Artemis has for the child in her belly!'

She looked at me expectantly, as if she thought I was suddenly going to understand exactly what she meant and divulge it to her with total accuracy. I wasn't.

'You'll have to tell me,' I said.

'Well, I have spent a lot more time with her than you have,' she remarked charitably, 'although I have always considered you to be slightly more perceptive than most of your sex.' She shot me a swift, mischievous grin. Then her face straightened and she said, 'You know how most pregnant women are? Their hands seem to move to their bellies almost by themselves, and they cradle the growing child inside them as if already imagining the baby in their arms.'

She was right, although I wasn't sure I'd ever remarked on it until now. 'Yes,' I agreed.

'Well, far from stroking her stomach, Artemis won't even *look* at it,' Celia said sadly. 'Of course, she knows she's pregnant. She must do. I think her back hurts her, for frequently she shifts around on the bed as if she can't get comfortable. But she takes great pains to keep her body covered all the time, and once when she was changing her position and the blankets slipped off her, she saw that she was only wearing that flimsy nightgown of mine with which we replaced her wet clothes, and she looked in horror at her belly and her face went quite white.'

'She must realize we know she's pregnant,' I said. 'Jarman brought a midwife to see her yesterday, after all.'

Celia was frowning, chewing her lip. 'Yes, of course,' she replied. 'That's what I'm trying to say – it's not us knowing about the child that so distresses her; it's that *she* knows, and she's all alone, unmarried, her man gone six months with not a word, and she hasn't the first idea what on earth she's going to do.'

Not having anything to add to Celia's disturbing observation, I didn't speak, and the two of us were still sitting there in silence when Jonathan came into the library some time later.

He looked first at the big windows, a surprised expression crossing his face as he noticed the light already fading. 'It is later than I thought,' he muttered.

'Will you have something to eat, Jonathan?' Celia asked.

'Oh—' He stared at the food, and I sensed the desire to accept was fighting with the urge to speak to us concerning the woman and then hurry away. Hunger won: he smiled gratefully at Celia and said, 'Yes, please.'

We left him to eat in peace – not that it took long – and then I said, 'I realize you cannot tell us very much, Jonathan, but were you able to assuage her anxieties?'

'No,' he replied baldly. 'She is truly in torment. She is very afraid, yet will not explain what so terrifies her. She is unwell and in pain, but will not discuss the source of the symptoms. She is grieving, yet will not say for whom, other than that his name is Edwyn, and he has been gone more than six months, and she is sure he is dead.'

'We already knew his name, or at least the shortening she used,' Celia said when he did not go on. 'She – Artemis – cried out for him in her fever.'

'Yes,' Jonathan said. 'She is profoundly disturbed concerning what else she may have revealed. I tried to convince her that in my experience people deep in delirium make little if any sense, but I doubt whether I succeeded.'

Celia got up and drew the heavy curtains. Glancing up, I noticed that the sky had grown much darker, and it looked as if more snow was on the way. Jonathan noticed too, and with a muttered exclamation, got to his feet. 'I must go,' he said.

I got up too. 'We can help our patient with one of her worries, at least,' I said. 'This house's defences are strong, and after the face at the window last night, we are alert to anything untoward.'

Jonathan looked doubtful. 'I'm sure you'll be on your guard, Gabriel, and that the details of the extra precautions would sound very reassuring, but I don't believe poor Artemis Brownyng is open to a reasoned argument just at present.' He turned to Celia, and they exchanged a smile. Then he strode out, and I went to see him off.

'I'll return tomorrow,' he said as he turned his bay cob's head towards the gates, nodding his thanks to Samuel.

I was looking up at the sky. 'If the snow permits it,' I said lugubriously.

He grinned. 'Ever the optimist, Gabe.' Then he nudged the bay into a trot, then a canter, and was away down the track.

I returned to the library. Celia was standing at the window, gazing out through a gap between the curtains. She turned as I sat down, pulling the curtains together again with a sharp, impatient gesture.

'What should we do next?' she asked as she sat down again. 'We do not appear to have made any advance at all in the mystery that has landed in our laps, or offered very much help to the woman who so desperately needs it.'

'Well, there is some small hope of progress to come,' I replied, and I told her about my visit to Theo, and Theo's conviction that the dead man dumped behind the inn on the quay, our would-be intruder and our uninvited and terrified house guest must surely be connected.

'But if as you say nobody knows the dead man's identity, how can that aid our understanding?' she demanded crossly.

I had an idea as to the cause of her ill temper. But her feelings for Jonathan were her own business, and I knew better than to make even the most obscure reference to them. 'Theo has set Jarman Hodge to finding out who he was,' I said instead, 'and I have no doubt he won't return until he has done so.'

She stood up, then reached down for her sewing bag, sighing deeply. 'I'm going back to sit with Artemis,' she said. 'She ought not to be—'

We both heard the wild flurry of hooves beating hard on the track, and she only reached the window before I did because she was already on her feet.

The light had faded almost entirely now, and the clouds crouched so low that it was as if a black curtain had been drawn across the sky. But it was possible to make out the horse that was fast approaching, the wide blaze on the nose bright in the darkness. Even as we watched, the rider drew his mount to a standstill and almost fell out of the saddle, stumbling towards the front door.

Celia and I knew who he was.

Side by side we raced out of the library and across the hall, and I flung back the bolts as Celia turned the iron handle. We heaved the heavy door open even as Jonathan raised a hand to knock.

The smell of blood hit us like a fist.

I heard Celia's horrified gasp. She flung her arms around him, and as he lurched forward into the light I saw that his face was ashen and the front of his black robe was soaked in blood.

'Dear Lord, Jonathan, let me look, I'll—' I began.

'*NO*,' he cried.

'But you're badly hurt, you're bleeding, let him attend you!' Celia pleaded, her voice shaking with emotion.

He reached out his hand and, with a gesture of infinite tenderness, briefly put it against her cheek. 'It is not my blood,' he said gently.

I felt the relief flood her as if it was tangible.

But that sweet instant of relief – and I felt it too – was swiftly followed by a more urgent thought. 'Where?' I demanded.

'End of the track,' Jonathan replied. 'Under the tree to the right of the gate.'

I turned, reaching down for the bag I keep inside the door, but Jonathan put out a hand to stop me. 'You can't do anything for him, Gabe,' he said.

'You don't know that!' I shouted. 'Let me at least try!' I shoved his hand away.

'I *do* know,' he countered. 'He hasn't—' He glanced at Celia, as if reluctant to speak in front of her. But I was trying to push past him, my bag in my hand, and I didn't really leave him much choice.

'Truly, Gabe, the man is beyond help,' he insisted. 'He no longer has a head.'

SIX

Jonathan and I rode back down the track like the Knights Templar of old, two brother knights mounted on one horse. Their doubling up was because of the vow of poverty and the bonds of brotherly love, no doubt; ours was for expediency.

Jonathan had wanted to take me straight to the dead man. Celia had insisted he first exchange his blood-soaked cassock for a borrowed garment of mine. Thankfully Celia prevailed.

I was mounted behind Jonathan, and I carried a pair of lanterns and an old blanket.

The bay gelding smelt the dead man when we were still some way from the end of the track. Jonathan spoke quietly to him, and he walked on. We stopped some ten paces from the gate, and Jonathan tethered the horse to a tree.

As we walked towards the dark shape lying under the right-hand tree beside the gate, he said quietly 'We should keep to the left, for I am sure I saw the tracks of at least one pair of feet on the right.'

The last of the day had faded rapidly, however, since Jonathan had hurried away, and now we were glad of the lantern light. He was right: on the edge of the track I could make out two sets of footprints, and, judging by the length of the strides, both men – assuming they were men – had been running fast. The first man had been lighter on his feet, and in places his imprints had not deeply dented the snow. His pursuer – if I had it right – was heavier, and ran on flat feet.

We walked up to the body.

The man lay on his front. He was slimly built, long-limbed, and had probably been tall. The neck ended in a stump; the head lay perhaps half a hand's breadth apart. The face was turned towards us: a man in his thirties, I thought, light brown hair, gingery at the temples, cheeks clean-shaven.

'Was this how you found him?' I asked Jonathan, keeping my voice low.

'No,' he replied. 'He–the head was further away. There.'
He pointed to the ridge in the snow that marked the track's
grass verge.

'You replaced it,' I said.

'I did.'

'You didn't think to—' I stopped.

'To revive him? No, of course not.' Jonathan paused, then
added quietly, 'I knelt beside him and prayed for him, Gabriel.
That is, I imagine, how my cassock became soaked in his
blood. It seemed utterly wrong to pray over a body without a
head.'

I nodded. Without the head a body is largely anonymous:
except to those who know us very well, it is our face, our
features, that identify us. 'I understand,' I muttered.

Jonathan looked at me briefly. 'I believe you do,' he murmured.

We stood side by side looking down at the man. Then I
crouched beside him and, holding up my lantern while Jonathan
moved his closer, I examined the wound.

It looked like a clean cut, suggesting a very sharp blade
swung with both skill and force. Few people would be able
to behead someone quickly and neatly; it was a craft that had
to be learned. Most of us, I reflected as I stared at the wound,
were only too familiar with the much-advertised mercy of
Henry VIII, who sent for a French swordsman for Anne Boleyn
to spare her the more haphazard hacking that far too many
suffered whose heads were severed from their bodies with the
axe.

A professional killer, then. And my house, containing as it
did my sister, my servants and a woman called Artemis
Brownyng for whose well-being I had willingly taken on
responsibility, was close by . . .

I managed to put aside that worrying thought and returned
to the body.

From which direction had that swinging blade come? I
peered more closely, and there was a possible clue in the fact
that the throat edge of the cut was cleaner than the rear one.
I would not be able to say for certain, however, until I inspected
the body more thoroughly in Theo's crypt in the morning.

Jonathan, it seemed, had seen what I had seen.

'Could he have been attacked from the front?' he asked. 'One man pursuing him while a second lay in wait under the tree, sword raised?'

'Hmmm.' I was trying to visualize the scene. 'If it happened like that, the swordsman was either highly proficient or very lucky.'

I inspected the rest of the body. It was very dark now, however, and the snow was beginning again, and soon I decided I was wasting my time. I stood up. 'We'll move him to the side of the track,' I announced, 'and cover him with his cloak, and in the morning I will report the death to Theo and have the body moved to the crypt.'

Jonathan bent to help me.

We moved the body first, then the head. We united the two parts of the body as closely as we could, then brought up the edges of his cloak and wrapped them tightly around him. I covered the head and shoulders with the blanket, tucking the ends in underneath. Feeling the severed head move independently of the rest of him felt utterly repellent; catching sight of Jonathan's face as we worked side by side, I was sure he was suffering the same sense of a profound wrong.

We stood over the dead man for a few moments. Jonathan, I surmised, was praying. Then we walked the few paces back to his horse.

'You will not come back to the house?' I asked.

'No, but thank you.' He paused. 'I need—'

He didn't finish, but he didn't have to. He needed, I was sure, to be in his church.

I touched his arm. 'Tomorrow?' I said as he mounted.

He nodded. Then he kicked the gelding and rode away.

I ran back to the house; all at once I very much needed to be there, and I would keep my sword close. I rapped on the door, glad that Celia had remembered to lock and bolt it, and Sallie let me in.

'Miss Celia's in the scullery,' she hissed as I shot the bolts again. 'She's *washing* it!' she added, indignation vivid in her voice. 'Been rinsing it in cold water to get the worst of the blood out and stop it fixing, and now she's scrubbing it in the hot! I told her it wasn't her job and I'd happily see to it, but she'd have none of it! Quite sharp, she was,' she added, and she sounded hurt.

I rested a consoling hand on Sallie's shoulder, and strode through the kitchen into the back scullery. Celia – or Sallie – had heated water, and Celia was bent over the sink, sleeves rolled up, working on Jonathan's cassock. She shot me a quick look, frowning, and shouted, 'Don't *you* start too!'

I raised my hands in surrender and left her to it.

Some time later she came into the library to join me. 'Sorry,' she said. 'I've apologised to Sallie too. This, all of this, is so horrible, I just had to *do* something.'

'Yes, I see that,' I replied.

She sank into her chair, rolling her sleeves down again. Her hands were scarlet from the hot water. Presently she said, 'Did you recognize the man?'

'No.'

'It–he wasn't . . .' She hesitated.

Then I thought I understood. 'He wasn't the man from last night,' I said. 'When I saw the face at the window, I had a clear impression of a pale oval with a thick black beard covering the lower half. This man had light brown hair and was clean-shaven.'

I saw again the detached head. Saw the smooth cheeks and the firm jaw, hair neatly trimmed. Thought of the man, perhaps attending to his grooming only that morning. And now he was dead.

I reached for the brandy decanter and the glasses and poured two very generous measures.

I was awake early the next morning. As soon as I was dressed I went to see Artemis Brownyng. Celia had sat with her for some time last night, and, although she insisted she had made no mention of the dead man, when I checked on our guest before going to bed I thought she seemed agitated. It was as Jonathan had said: she was very frightened.

This morning she was sleeping deeply. I rested my hand very gently on her forehead, relieved to find that the fever had all but passed. Not that it meant she had recovered; absence of fever in the morning does not mean it will not reappear by evening.

I would have liked to wait until she woke so that I could talk to her. But there were more urgent matters I must attend to.

I sent Samuel down to Theo's office to report the discovery of the body. Calculating how long it would take for the message to be delivered and the men to return with the cart, my horse and I were waiting by the gates when Samuel rode up. The cart was not far behind.

I watched the men load the corpse and its severed head, then rode with them and watched again as they unloaded it and took it down to the crypt. Their work done, they left me to it, one of them – Tomas – saying he'd tell Master Davey I was making a start.

I lit the lanterns, the lamps and the candles and, removing the concealing blanket, set to work.

The torso and legs were on the trestle, the head in its anatomically correct place but set apart by a space about the length of my forearm.

I spent many years as a ship's surgeon and I saw many truly horrible examples of devastating damage to the human body, some of which put the victim beyond my aid, some that I could patch up adequately for him to have more years of life, although not often an active life. This was, however, the first time I'd stood over a man whose head had been cut off.

I would have put a decent wager on there being nothing left in the way of catastrophic injuries that could make me feel faint. As I stared down at that stump of neck, silently naming the bones, blood vessels and muscles to myself, I realized I was wrong. I suddenly had the strange sensation that my knees had gone missing, and knew I had to sit down before I fell.

I stumbled to the narrow bench set against the end wall, crouching over so that my head was between my knees. Then slowly I straightened up, drawing a few deep breaths. The dizziness eased, I could see properly again and cautiously I stood up.

Then I went back to the corpse.

Making myself concentrate only on the task in hand, I
removed his clothing. Cloak, tunic, shirt, undershirt, belt, boots,
hose. Everything was of good quality, and the hose and boots
looked new. The belt had a pouch slung on it, and the pouch
felt heavy. I put the lot on the bench beneath the high window
and went back to the body that lay naked before me.

He had been approximately in his mid-thirties, tall, long-
limbed and strongly-built, the muscles well defined. The
hands were reasonably clean, in that there was not the
deeply-ingrained dirt you find on the hands of a labourer,
nor the specific pattern of marks and scarring that is to be
found on an artisan such as a blacksmith or a carpenter.
These hands showed only everyday filth; I thought the dead
man had probably lived by his wits rather than the sweat of
hard physical work. There were a few bruises on the lower
legs and a huge but fading one on the thigh, but nothing
that couldn't be found on most active people's bodies. I
continued my inspection, front and back, and concluded that
there was nothing else on the corpse that had any bearing
on the man's death.

Then I looked at the head.

Dark blond hair, worn short, the coarser, ginger areas at the
temples indicating the colour that his beard would have grown.
I peeled back the eyelids and saw that the eyes had been very
pale grey-blue. Regular features, wide mouth; he'd been a
good-looking man. Something occurred to me, and I wondered
if it was merely an illusion, something to do with the head
having been detached: gently moving it so that it joined on to
the neck, I looked again.

No, it wasn't an illusion. This man had had a long neck,
and the neat, well-shaped head was quite small in relation to
the strong body.

With the gap between torso and head now closed, the corpse
looked less disturbing. However, the joining-up meant I could
now study the fatal cut in its entirety, looking at both edges
together. I examined it for some time, bringing a lantern up
close and thinking about what a very sharp sword could do
to tissue and bone. Finally straightening up again, I decided
that I'd seen nothing to contradict the initial opinion I'd formed

last night: that this man had been assailed from the front, and, judging by those fast-running footsteps in the snow, he'd raced unaware to meet his death and probably would have known little about what was happening to him.

So I hoped, anyway.

I rested my hand on his shoulder for a moment in farewell, then unfolded the large sheet of coarse linen set ready at the foot of the trestle and spread it over him.

Then I set about a more thorough inspection of his garments and possessions.

There was nothing much to arouse interest until I began on the shirt. I'd only touched it briefly as I removed it; it was heavily bloodstained, and that was what I'd noticed most. Now I folded the soiled areas inside the remainder and had a proper look at the fabric. It was white, fine, soft and had a sort of sheen; it would, I thought, have been very comfortable next to the skin. It wasn't silk, and it wasn't thin wool. I wasn't sure what it was, and I decided that once I'd washed off the blood, I'd show it to Celia and see what she thought.

Finally I picked up the pouch and took it off the belt. Both items were made of very good leather, chestnut-coloured, strong and supple, with the deep gloss of long use. I held the purse, turning it over once or twice. It was as wide as the length of my hand, and roughly two-thirds as deep, and two stout leather loops extended from the top to hang it on the belt. The flap was as deep as the pouch itself, and fastened with a strap and a buckle. The pouch was very elegant: the bottom edge curved up slightly, and the stitched edges of the leather had somehow been pressed, or crimped, into a pleasing pattern. I unfastened the strap and opened it.

The interior was lined in very soft, fine leather of a paler shade of tan, and divided into three sections. The front section contained a folded document of some sort, wrapped in oilskin. In the rear pocket there was a small leather-bound notebook, and over half of the pages had diagrams and lettering on them. The middle section was bursting with coins. Most of them were small and made of silver, the images worn and many of the edges clipped, but a dozen or so were larger, heavier, and at least half of these were gold.

I tried to make out the images, the letters and the figures stamped on them, but the light wasn't good enough for such very fine details. On one of the gold coins, however, I managed to make out the letters CBVR, then a symbol, then ET.BRA, followed by a crown under a hand and then ARCH.AVST, and something I couldn't read. The design was of two crossed branches, or perhaps torches, with a four-legged animal suspended from the crossing point. On either side of this cross was the date 1600.

The reverse side showed an elaborate crest under the same crown, and more letters. It was tempting to try to make these out, too, but there wasn't a lot of point because I knew virtually nothing about coinage so I would be wasting my time. I put the coins back in the pouch and fastened it, then replaced the remaining items in a neat stack on the bench, took one last look at the corpse, extinguished the lamps and the lanterns, then, clutching the pouch, went to find Theo.

It very soon became apparent that Theo's knowledge of foreign coins was little better than mine. I'd summarised my findings on the decapitated man fairly quickly, then proceeded to hand him the pouch.

Now he was still sitting behind his desk, examining the clutch of coins, and he had yet to pass any comment.

'Do you know where they're from?' I asked, my patience finally giving out.

'No.'

The curt response appeared to verify my assumption.

'One of the big gold ones has quite clear markings,' I pointed out.

He sighed. 'Yes, Gabe, so I noticed.'

What sunshine there was that overcast morning was streaming in through the window, so I picked up one of the silver coins and went to look at it in the light. 'There's a man's head on this one,' I said. 'And lettering . . . PHILIPPUS II D G HISP.REX.'

Theo looked up. 'Has he got a very long jaw?'

'Yes.'

He nodded. 'Philip II of Spain. It's an Armada coin, struck in England. Many of *them* about.'

I picked up another coin. It had the same crossed branches as the gold one I'd looked at in the crypt, but the date was 1598. The lettering was clearer on this one: PHS D G HISP Z REX DUX BRA. I read it out to Theo.

'Dux Bra,' he repeated thoughtfully. 'Duke of Brabant. The Spanish king asserting his rule over the Netherlands, and adding a dukedom or two to his titles.' He rummaged through the coins scattered on his desk. 'There are several of these Duke of Brabant ones.' He looked up at me. 'Maybe your headless man is a Spaniard.'

'He was tall and had very light eyes,' I said. If I'd had to place a bet, I'd have said the man was more likely to be a Dutchman than a Spaniard, but I decided to keep that thought to myself for now.

Theo began to put the coins back into the pouch, and I handed him the ones I'd been looking at. He was frowning in thought, and presently he said, 'You'd have had coinage from many lands when you were at sea?'

'Yes,' I agreed. 'I still have a large collection of foreign money, in all shapes and sizes, and—' Then I saw why he was asking. 'You think the dead man was a sailor?'

'It's a possibility,' he said. 'A traveller, anyway, and—'

There was a tap on the door, and Jarman Hodge came into the office. 'Am I disturbing you, Master Davey?' he asked. 'Morning, Doctor T.'

'No, come in,' Theo replied.

I sensed a tension between them. Theo hadn't quite forgiven his most efficient and valued agent, then, for coming to me about Artemis before reporting to him.

Jarman glanced at the pouch. 'That the headless man's?' he asked. 'I've been told about him,' he added. 'Met Tomas and Matthew outside.'

'Yes, it's his,' I said. 'Heavy with coins, most of them not English.'

Jarman nodded quickly. 'Aaah,' he murmured.

Theo waited, and when he didn't go on, said testily, '*Aaah*?

Are you about to tell me something, Jarman, or are you going to stand there and wait for me to guess?'

'No, sorry, chief, course not,' Jarman said hastily. 'It's about the man found in the gutter behind the tavern. He's not local, that's for sure, everyone seems to be agreed on that, and—'

'Everyone?' Theo interrupted. 'What do you mean by that? Hardly anyone saw him, just Gabe and me and the lads who came for the corpse. Oh, and the lad who found it and came to report it.'

Jarman waited patiently till he'd finished. 'I went round the taverns and the lodging houses,' he said, 'describing him and asking people if they'd seen him. Seems he'd been about for a couple of days or so, putting up in one of the cheapest of the lodging houses, and he'd apparently drunk his way right down the row of taverns.'

Theo turned to me. 'Didn't you smell alcohol on him?' he demanded.

'Theo, he was found in a channel leading into a cesspit,' I said crossly. 'You know quite well what he stank of, since you were there. If he also smelt of ale, or whatever he'd been drinking, then no, I didn't smell it.'

Theo grunted something, but I didn't think it was an apology.

'So this man wasn't a local,' I said to Jarman. 'Any clue where he *was* from?'

'Well, he tried to pay for his drinks in one place with a foreign coin, and when the dullard who'd been serving the brandy refused to accept it, the man got very angry and said words to the effect that it was that or nothing, it was all he had, and someone else in the tavern pointed out to the tapster that it was a gold coin, and was he too stupid to see, which set off a bit of a rumpus, seemingly. Which is probably why quite a lot of people recalled the dead man when I asked,' he added.

Theo nodded slowly. Then he said, 'What led them to conclude he wasn't local? Was it simply that nobody knew him and he had foreign coins?'

'Ah, no, I should have said,' Jarman replied. 'He spoke with a heavy accent, and several men said they thought he was just slurring his words because he was so drunk, only a woman he'd been with said he'd talked like that even before he'd had a drink.'

'I don't suppose anyone recalled his name?' Theo asked.

'No. Sorry, chief,' Jarman said.

'We'll go on asking,' I said. 'There may be others who had contact with him.'

Jarman turned to me. 'There's something more, Doctor T.' His mouth was turned down in a grimace. 'Don't reckon you'll like it, though.'

I sighed. 'You'd better tell me anyway.'

'Seems he had a hidden pocket deep in his tunic. Someone said they'd seen him reach inside his clothes and when his hand emerged it was holding this small leather purse, or maybe a wallet. There was a drawing in it, tight-folded, or a little painting, rather, because this man who saw it said it had colours on it, blue and green and bits of brown.' He'd been looking at me sympathetically, and now Theo was doing the same.

I didn't have to ask why.

When I'd finished inspecting the dead man's clothes, I'd wrapped the sweaty shirt up in the rest of the stinking garments and thrown the lot out of the crypt, an action which straight away made the stench in the crypt considerably less pungent. The garments had been sluiced with cold water, but this had done little, if anything, to launder them.

Now I was going to have to return to that noxious bundle, extract the tunic and this time go through every inch of it until I found the secret pocket and whatever it was hidden away inside.

'I'd better go and look for it, then,' I said tersely.

I flung myself out of Theo's office and stomped off up the road.

The bundle of garments was in the small, enclosed courtyard behind the house. Nobody lived there: it was the subject of some complicated and confused inheritance arrangement. Clearly, no one was desperate to take possession, and as a result the old place was slowly but steadily crumbling to ruin. The crypt, however, was sound, and whoever was responsible for the house was happy to receive Theo's rent in exchange for its use as a mortuary.

The door at the front had been closed, locked and barred for so long that it probably would have taken a battering ram to force it open. The modest little door that gave admittance to the cellar steps was in the rear courtyard, which was closed off from the road by a sturdy wooden gate. The keys to both were usually in Theo's keeping.

I unlocked the yard gate and, closing it behind me, stood looking around. I spotted the bundle immediately, lying to the right of the doorstep. It had been sheltered by the house from the worst of the snow, and I only had to brush off a light layer. I was glad of my heavy gloves, nonetheless, for the pale sun was doing little to raise the temperature.

I unrolled the thick cloak and spread out the other garments on top of it, the sweat-encrusted shirt still tightly rolled inside the other items. Then I began my examination of the stiff, padded tunic.

It was a garment purchased for show and not for long, hard wear. There was some braid edging decorated with gold thread, but the thread was of poor quality and already unravelling. The wool batting was coarse and had gone into lumps. The lining was full of small tears where the cheap fabric was pulling apart, and the outer layer had been inexpertly darned and was encrusted with old food.

I examined every part of it and I found nothing. Then I took off my gloves and tried again. At the second attempt I discovered the secret pocket: a seam had been unpicked right at the base of the left armhole, and the opening had been re-closed by a tiny pin. I only found it this time because I pricked my finger on the pin.

I removed it and felt inside the pocket. It was about the size of my palm, extending either side of the considerably narrower opening. It was empty.

I threw down the tunic and swore.

When I'd finished I tied up the bundle again and put it back against the wall. Whatever had been in that secret pocket was gone, as was whatever else the dead man had carried hidden in his clothes. I was feeling guilty because I should have searched through his garments properly once I'd finished with the corpse, but now somebody else had done so, and it was too late.

Someone had killed him, disposed of the body and then, presumably, discovered where the corpse had been taken and come under cover of darkness to go through the dead man's clothes. Perhaps this person had known the secret pocket was there and gone straight for it. Perhaps, working in the bitter chill of night, his hands had become even colder than mine, and he—

No. That wasn't how it happened.

It was at least possible that the man had been killed because of what he was carrying. Unless they were desperate, surely no assailant would choose to go through the victim's clothing *after* he'd been dragged out of the foul ditch. The search would come first – and probably a good distance away from the cesspit – and the body disposed of so ignominiously *after* the killer had found what he wanted.

If my reasoning was sound – and I was increasingly sure it was – then I had been reprimanding myself for nothing. Whatever the man had carried that someone else wanted badly enough to kill him for it had been taken immediately after death. Even if I had searched right through his garments and managed to discover the pocket under the arm, there would have been nothing in it.

Feeling as if I'd been granted a reprieve, I put my gloves back on, strode out of the yard and, locking the heavy door, hurried off to report to Theo.

SEVEN

One of the men in Theo's outer office informed me I'd just missed him, and that he'd gone haring off somewhere with Jarman Hodge and hadn't said where he was going or when he'd be back. 'Shall I tell him you called by, Doctor T?' he asked.

'Er–yes, very well.' I thanked him and then went out to the yard to fetch my horse.

My head was full of alarming thoughts concerning the two dead men. Bearing in mind last night's attack – not to mention its proximity to my house, and the increasing likelihood that the deaths were somehow connected to the presence of my uninvited guest – it was all the more imperative to talk it all over with Theo, and with Jarman too. With that denied me for an unspecified time, I came up with an alternative. I wanted to see for myself the area of concentrated taverns and lodging houses where the first victim had met his demise, and speak to some of the many people who reckoned they'd seen him in the days he spent there. Accordingly I set off down to Plymouth.

On the way I called in to see one of my patients. He was a very old man named Enos. He'd been at sea all his working life, and since retiring had used his time constructively by working on the garden of his pretty cottage on the northern fringe of the town. His wife had died many years ago – before I returned to the area – and now, in increasingly frail old age and with his gardening days, like his days at sea, behind him, he was cared for by his daughter Beth.

Beth had a husband and two sons, and I'm sure she loved and tended them just as diligently as she did her father. But she and Enos were devoted to each other; their minds were in sympathy, and they took delight simply in being together. Both knew that their days together were limited, but as Enos had once wisely said, it was the same way for everyone lucky enough to have someone in their life who they truly loved.

Today they were sitting together in the small room with the window from which you could see the distant sea. It was where Enos spent his days and his nights, the steep stairs being beyond him, and it was comfortably crammed with a variety of objects that eloquently spoke of him, from his worn old leather chair to the row of books, the clay pipe and the beautiful tobacco jar on the shelf over the fire.

Beth went away to prepare refreshments and I pulled up a stool and sat down next to Enos. We dealt swiftly with the matter of his health – the linctus I'd brought him last week had helped with the cough, he reported, and, indeed, his colour was better than when last I'd seen him – and then he rubbed his hands and said, 'So, Doctor Taverner, what is new in your world?'

I waited while Beth set out mugs of cordial and a platter of small, sweet biscuits, then told them about the two dead men. I did not pass on all the details – no need for them to share the horror of cesspits and beheadings – and, although both of them were more than intelligent enough to detect that they weren't hearing the full tale, neither mentioned it.

'One of the men carried foreign coins, you said,' Beth remarked after a moment's thought, 'and the other spoke with an accent. Do you conclude that both are foreign, and of the same nationality?'

I shrugged. 'I don't know. There are always a lot of foreigners in Plymouth, so it's not necessarily relevant to these men's deaths.'

'Except that the deaths occurred within a very short time,' Enos observed. 'Which suggests they may be linked.' I glanced at him, and his eyes were bright with interest.

'Indeed,' I agreed. 'It's been pointed out to me that the second man might have been a sailor, and had picked up the coins in the various ports he visited.'

'He could equally well have been a merchant,' Beth said.

'His hands did not show signs of hard manual work, which might support that,' I said to her, 'but, on the other hand, not every man who goes to sea spends his life manipulating heavy objects.'

'I have been thinking about this matter of the accent,' Enos said. 'We tend to assume that by an accent we always mean a foreign accent, but that is not in fact so. I once had a ship-mate who came from the northeast,' he went on with a reminiscent smile, 'and we had a devil of a job working out what he was talking about.'

Beth turned to me. 'You have examined both men, Doctor, and are well placed to make comparisons. I would not suggest that a man's nationality is apparent in his appearance, but what of the two men's features and apparel? Were there any obvious similarities, or, indeed, differences?'

I remembered the decapitated man's shirt.

'Perhaps there were,' I answered.

Sensing that I did not want to say any more, she turned the conversation to the weather, and all three of us expressed the sincere but faint hope that there would not be any more snow.

Then – Enos was starting to look tired – I took my leave.

I left Hal with the ostler and went on foot down to the least respectable parts of the town. I shouldered a way through the crowds on the quay and managed to find the stinking little alley that led to the cesspit and the narrow channel feeding into it. There was no need to revisit the place where the body had been found, however, and I turned away and started walking along the row of taverns and rundown lodging houses at the far end of the quay.

Jarman had said the dead man had visited all of them, so it didn't much matter where I began. However, it was now two days since his body had been found, more than enough time for the story to have been heard, gasped about and endlessly discussed by pretty much everybody. Even those who hadn't actually seen the man knew enough to speak authoritatively about him, and by the time I reached the fourth inn I had realized I was wasting my time.

I'd already found the place where the man had attempted to pay with a gold coin – that was the second place I tried – and my questions having almost started another fight, I'd quickly left.

The fourth inn was called The Crown and Sceptre, a some-what grandiose name for such a small and simple place, but it was cleaner than its neighbours, the ale looked and smelt inviting, so I ordered a pint, sat down on a bench set in a corner behind the door and discovered happily that the ale lived up to its promise.

I had just decided I'd pursue my enquiries at another two or three taverns and then give up and go home when someone said very quietly from right beside me, 'You the feller asking about him in the cesspit?'

I turned, startled, and saw a woman of twenty-five or so, half hidden by the door. She was dressed in dark garments, a thick shawl over her head and drawn forward to conceal her face. Her light-coloured eyes were sharp with intelligence, her expression wary. She was pale and drawn, and the hand clutching the edges of the shawl together was very thin, the bones showing sharply.

'I am,' I said, keeping my voice down.

She nodded. 'They told me, back up the quay. I was with him, see.' She hesitated, and her eyes narrowed. 'Paying for information, are you?'

Several answers ran through my head, but I just said, 'Yes.'

She edged round the door and sat down on the bench. 'He buys me a drink and we set a price. Only when it comes to it, he can't. That riles him, but I was expecting it and he missed, pretty much.' She drew back the shawl and the reddish-brown hair beneath it, and I saw a faint bruise on the side of her jaw.

'He punched you,' I said.

She shrugged. 'Like I said, he didn't quite miss. I've had much worse,' she added.

I looked at her. I was tempted to remind her of the dangers of her way of life, to advise her to do all in her power to change it, but I have learned over the years to keep my mouth shut. I do not believe that many women, if any, choose to do what she did, and to assume they can simply and easily find an alternative way to make enough money to scratch a living is insulting.

'What can you tell me about him?' I asked. I reached in

my pouch for some coins, opening my hand to show them to
her and then closing it again.

She nodded, understanding. 'He were a cocky little sod.
Dressed up in fancy clothes, but they'd been too hard worn
and weren't made to last. Money in his purse – you'll have
heard about the gold coin?' I nodded. 'There was more where
that came from, and he bragged about it so much that soon
everyone on the quay knew.' She shot me a shrewd glance.
'That why he were killed, eh?'

'Perhaps.'

She was still giving me that look, and now she said, 'I don't
reckon it were, and neither do you, I'll wager. You attack a
man to rob him, you make off soon as you've got what
you're after, stands to reason. You don't drag his corpse down
a tiny alley and shove him in a cesspit. That's like a comment,
and not a kindly one.' She nodded again. 'That's *personal*,
that is.'

She had come up with something I hadn't given much
thought to. And she was right.

'He was foreign, or so I've heard,' I said.

'Not him!' she said scornfully. 'He were deep in his cups,
like what I said, and stumbling and slurring, repeating himself
over and over. He weren't from here,' she went on, leaning
closer and poking my arm for emphasis, 'and he used words
I didn't know and said them funny, but English were his mother
tongue, just like it is yours and mine.'

'You seem very sure of that,' I remarked.

She rolled her eyes. 'This place is full of foreigners,' she
said scathingly. 'Sailors from all over. Some can manage a
word or two of English, some more, some none at all. You
think I can't recognise a native-born Englishman when I hear
one?'

I wasn't entirely convinced, but what she said did make
sense. Beginning to unfold my hand, I said, 'I don't suppose
you found out his name?'

Now, for the first time, she smiled. She had lost a couple
of teeth, but the remainder were large and white. 'Stick another
coin or two in with that lot,' she said, 'and I'll tell you.'

I should have clarified whether she meant she'd tell me if

she'd discovered his name or not, or if she had and was going to reveal it. Still, either way I could spare her another couple of coins.

I reached into my pouch again.

Neatly gathering all the coins in one quick grasp, she said, 'He had this little ditty he sang, something about Malin Piltbone and his canny ways, and how you had to get up early to catch him out, and he were that smug and pleased with himself, him with all that money in his purse, but he were wrong, weren't he? Someone did catch him out, and he ended up deep in the shit.' She laughed, tucking the coins away somewhere within her enfolding cloak.

'That was his name? Malin Piltbone?'

She was getting up. 'That's what he said it were,' she confirmed.

'And you, who are you, and where do you live, if I need to talk to you again?'

But she was already through the door, banging it closed behind her. I leapt up, but by the time I'd wrested it open again and hurried out on to the street, she had gone. I looked each way, but she must have headed straight up one of the many passages and alleys leading into the maze of buildings behind the quay.

I went back inside to finish my ale, then headed off to fetch my horse and ride home.

I spotted Jonathan's gelding in the stables when I reached Rosewyke, and Samuel informed me that he had arrived a short time ago.

I went inside, and into the kitchen. Sallie was laying out bread, ham and pickles on the table, where she had already placed a big platter of cheese, two mugs and a jug of ale. She must have heard the door, because she went over to the dresser and returned with another mug, platter and knife. 'Just in time, Doctor,' she said. 'No doubt you're hungry.'

'Always, Sallie,' I replied.

Jonathan had stood up from his chair at the table, and I waved to him to sit down again. 'Let's eat together,' I said, and he smiled.

Celia was standing by the hearth, and, turning to greet her, I saw that she was rolling up Jonathan's cassock. 'He came for this,' she said. I thought she sounded slightly flustered.

'Yes, I did,' Jonathan agreed. 'I really wasn't expecting it to have been washed and dried so efficiently, however – thank you again, Sallie, I am very grateful.'

'But—'

I got no further. Celia, still by the hearth and out of Jonathan's line of sight, shot me a very expressive look, eyes wide open, mouth in a grimace, head jerking in Jonathan's direction, and Sallie, who was standing beside me, nudged me very hard in the ribs.

I had obviously missed something. But I was too hungry to waste time puzzling over exactly why it must be kept from Jonathan that it was Celia and not Sallie who had washed the blood out from his cassock and put it by the fire to dry.

I pulled out a chair, sat down and reached for the bread.

'I wondered if Mistress Brownyng might like to speak to me again,' Jonathan said as he, Celia and I began to eat. 'But I understand she's sleeping.'

I chewed, swallowed and said, 'I haven't seen her since early this morning. I will rectify that once we've eaten.'

'The fever is fading, and her long hours of slumber can be doing nothing but good,' Celia said. 'Don't worry, Gabe, she hasn't been neglected. Sallie and I have kept an eye on her, and Sallie is confident she can persuade her to eat something solid tomorrow.'

'She managed some sips of my nourishing beef broth this morning,' Sallie said, putting the replenished ale jug back on the table. 'Well I say broth, it's more like a thin gravy, not a lot of substance to it, but it's a start, isn't it, Doctor?'

I agreed that it was, thinking yet again what a good woman she was. She had her hands full running my household without having to tend to the needs of a frightened and not very gracious stranger, and yet her happiness that her patient had managed even a little sip of broth was illuminating her face.

Jonathan took his leave once we had eaten. The daylight was fading now, and, as he said, he needed to be back in Tavy

St Luke's. I saw him off, the laundered cassock tied in a roll behind the saddle, then went back in the house.

Sallie was clearing the table. 'What was all that about pretending it was you who washed the vicar's cassock?' I asked her.

She gave me the sort of look women always give men when some small subtlety of female behaviour has entirely passed them by. 'Oh, dear me, Doctor,' she replied, shaking her head and smiling.

But she didn't offer an explanation.

I crossed the hall and went into the little parlour. Artemis Brownyng was lying with her head and shoulders propped up on pillows, anxiously looking towards the door. When she saw it was me, her tense expression relaxed.

'Doctor Taverner,' she said. 'I was going to come and find you.'

Swiftly I went to sit beside the bed. 'I don't think you should be thinking of getting up yet,' I said. 'Even though you are obviously feeling better – and I am very glad of it – you have had two days of high fever, eaten virtually nothing, and you will be very weak for some time.'

'*Weak*,' she repeated bitterly. 'Always, *always*, the woman is the weaker vessel.' Her dark eyes narrowed in anger, and again I noticed the thick black eyelashes. With the heavy, dark brown hair, the elements of Artemis's beauty had an exotic quality.

I stopped studying her appearance and thought about her remark.

'Not necessarily,' I said. 'Nature has in general given women smaller bodies, less muscle and lighter bones, but in my experience the female sex makes up for this by an ability to think quickly, to see deeply, to understand others. To give birth,' I went on, warming to my theme, 'and to fight like wild animals to protect their young.'

She was watching me uneasily, and straight away I understood why.

'I know you are carrying a child,' I said gently, 'and of course you are aware that I know.' For all that you try to cover it up, I thought, for even now she was clutching the bundled blankets to her belly.

She was silent for some moments, then let out a long, weary sigh.

'I think perhaps that by hiding the evidence from my own eyes I seek to conceal it from others,' she said. Then with a violent gesture she flung the bedding away.

She was lying on her back; a position that displayed the rounded bump of her belly most clearly. 'Look,' she said bitterly. 'See the result of my shame.'

After a moment or two I drew the blankets up again, tucking them round her. 'You are recovering from a high fever,' I said calmly. 'Not a time to risk becoming chilled. Now,' I continued, 'tell me if you have other symptoms; a headache, perhaps, or—'

'You are not horrified? Disgusted? Planning to hurl me out in the snow because of my sinful, immoral behaviour?'

I met her eyes. Until our exchange progressed, I had no way of knowing if she was referring to her pregnancy or the fact that she had been pulled out of the river with stones tied round her waist. It seemed best, I decided, to answer as if it was both.

'First, I shall not hurl you out into the snow,' I said firmly. 'I am a doctor and you are my patient, and I have taken an oath to do no harm. I shall care for you until you are well again, and on that you have my solemn word.'

I thought she relaxed, just a little.

'Second, you are, as we have agreed, pregnant, and about six months along.'

'Yes,' she said dully. 'That woman who came to see me said the same, and that's about right because he's—' She stopped, closing her mouth abruptly.

'The woman is a midwife, and our friend, and her name is Judyth Penwarden,' I said.

'Judyth. Yes, she said that was what I should call her.' She frowned. 'Was that yesterday?'

'The day before.'

The frown deepened. 'How long have I been here?' she demanded.

'We brought you here three days ago.' She was watching me intently, and I thought now was the moment for the whole tale to come out. 'A man called Jarman Hodge saw you in the river and he pulled you out. He believed you were dead. He discovered the stones tied round your waist, and he removed them and threw them away. He works for the coroner, Master Davey, and—'

'The coroner! Oh, no, no! Oh, *God!*' She was throwing the blankets back again, putting out a foot, but I eased her back.

'Wait! Let me finish,' I said.

She stared up at me.

'Jarman knows what becomes of suicides. He does not believe it is right, and so he covered up the evidence. Then he came to find me – this house is close to the river – and we planned to say that he had found you in the water but that we would not mention the stones. Then, of course, we discovered to our joy that you were alive. And you have been here ever since,' I finished.

This time she was silent for even longer.

'You have tended me, you and your womenfolk, with care and tenderness.' She could not meet my eyes. 'You summoned a midwife and a priest, each of whom was compassionate and kind.' She paused, and at last raised her eyes. 'I wished to end my life, and with good reason. But it seems it was not to be.' She gave another deep sigh. 'I know I should be thanking you profoundly for all you have done, but—'

I waited, but she did not continue.

'But you have woken to a life which still threatens the same problems you sought to escape through death,' I said softly. 'You are pregnant, you are unwed. Your parents are dead and if I judge aright, you are friendless and alone. Those are indeed grave burdens, but you are strong – that is evident by the swiftness of your recovery.' Her eyebrows went up a little, and briefly she looked pleased. 'Could you not gather your courage and find the right path to take? You have just said that you have met with compassion and kindness here, and although the world is harsh, these qualities exist elsewhere too.'

'I do not doubt my own strength and courage,' she whispered. 'Or I didn't, until recently.'

A long, deep shudder went through her, and her face twisted into an expression of profound fear.

'What has happened?' I asked. 'What has terrified you so?'

She shook her head. 'Oh, Doctor, you can have no idea,' she muttered. 'They are ruthless, they are hard on the trail, they sense what they have sought so long and so far is within reach, and they will do anything to recover it.'

I thought of the man in the drainage ditch and the headless man at my own gates. Of the pale, black-bearded face at the window. Of a man with foreign coins in his purse, and another with a carefully hidden wallet that someone had stolen from his corpse.

'Will you not tell me?' I asked.

And, very slowly and determinedly, she shook her head.

Wait, I told myself. Be patient. She will have to reveal the truth of the matter, in time.

I got up. 'Your water jug is empty,' I said. 'I will go and fill it. You must keep drinking, after the fever.'

I was in the doorway when she called me back.

'Doctor?'

I returned to the bedside. 'Yes?'

She was reaching under the covers, and now she drew out the canvas pack with the single leather strap. 'Whoever found me found this too, it seems.'

'We made sure it was safe,' I replied.

She unfastened the remaining strap and turned back the flap. I wondered what she was about to show me. Was this to be the start of her revelations? But she had just indicated she wasn't going to tell me anything.

I waited.

She felt around inside the pack, touching the contents, frowning. 'It's not—' she began anxiously. Then her expression cleared and she smiled. 'No. Here it is.'

She pulled out a small bag made of what looked like soft, fine suede. It was about the size of my palm, and its sides bulged with whatever was inside. She unpicked the knotted leather strings that held it closed, then simply stared at the contents.

'These I was given as a token of what is to come, and they

have a certain value,' she said eventually, 'which I am told is by no means insignificant.' She paused, clearly nervous, or perhaps embarrassed. 'I have no money with which to pay you for your care and your kindness, Doctor, but—'

'I have not asked for payment, nor shall I,' I interrupted.

She nodded. 'That is what I thought you would say. Nevertheless, I do not like to be under an obligation, even if it is only I who believe it exists.' Now she was clutching the little suede bag in one hand, and very carefully she tipped out one of the objects inside, holding it in her closed fist so that I could not see what it was. 'I was given these as token of very much more to follow,' she said, her voice trembling with emotion. 'Now I believe that what was so fervently promised will never come to pass, and that all hope is gone.' She forced a smile. 'Take these and offer them for sale, Doctor Taverner. What you are paid for them will, I am quite sure, more than repay what I owe you.'

'But I've just told you, you don't owe me anything!' I said, disturbed by her insistence. 'Keep them, whatever they are, and when you are well again, sell them yourself, for you will have far greater need of the money than I, and . . .'

I stopped.

For she had leaned towards me and very firmly placed the little object in my hand.

It was round, and small, and fragrant.

It was a nutmeg.

I almost blurted out that this was not the only nutmeg I had seen recently, but managed to hold back. Artemis was already frightened and very anxious, and to be told that I'd discovered ten or a dozen of the big seeds shoved in the mouth and throat of a dead man was hardly going to lessen her distress.

'What am I to do with it?' I asked instead.

She held out the suede bag. 'Not just the one, but these too. I *said*,' she added impatiently. She pushed the bag against my hand and I took it.

'These really are valuable?'

She nodded.

'Then I shall indeed sell them, but whatever money they bring will be yours.'

Her dark eyes were fixed on mine, and she smiled very faintly. 'We shall argue about that once the coins are in your purse, Doctor.'

'I will remove one, as you just did,' I went on, 'and take it down to the Plymouth quayside, where I'll ask—'

'*No!*' she hissed. 'Not Plymouth, Doctor, for God's sake, not if you value your skin, for it is where they began and *far* too close by, and you risk—' Abruptly she stopped.

'But you just told me to offer them for sale!'

'Yes, yes, but not in Plymouth!' she said in a harsh whisper. 'You must be very careful, for it is not at all safe, and if it were to become known that you had them for sale, and word spread to–er–to someone who might be interested, then they might follow you back here to your house.'

'But this house is strong,' I pointed out.

And stopped, for she had gone very white and I realized that her terror was not for my safety but her own. I was momentarily irritated, but then, remembering that she was alone, pregnant, with no money and no home, and that there had been a pale oval of a face at the window only two nights back, I decided she had every reason for her fear.

'I will take the sample further afield, then,' I said.

'Somewhere they don't know you,' she insisted.

I reflected briefly that somewhere affording total anonymity was not practical, because apart from anything else, I was not at liberty to go off on a day or more's journey, which was what I'd probably have to do to make absolutely certain I wasn't going to be recognized. The winter season was no time for a physician to absent himself, and besides, the roads were clogged with snow, and travel would be difficult and very uncomfortable. Her dark eyes were narrowed as she stared at me, waiting for my answer, so I merely nodded and said, 'Very well.'

EIGHT

I set off early the next morning. The sky was clear, and there was no wind to speak of, but the temperature had dropped overnight and the thin rays of the sun had done little to raise it. Accordingly I was very warmly clad, and I carried a supply of food in a bag tied to the saddle.

Sallie had been very reluctant to let me go, and looked up at me worriedly as she handed over the bag.

'Not that it's for me to say,' she added, clearly embarrassed at her own insistence. 'But it's so cold, Doctor, and the roads may well be blocked, and surely there is enough to occupy you here?'

I took her hands, one still clutching the strings of the bag. 'You are right, dear Sallie, on all three counts, but I hope to be home by tonight, or tomorrow morning at the latest.'

It was probably wildly optimistic even to say I might be home tonight, for my mission involved a journey of not far short of forty miles, and I'd be going over the moor where the snow would lie thickest. But I didn't think I'd share that with Sallie.

She was still frowning. 'What'll I tell Miss Celia?'

I was sure that the fact I was leaving so early largely to make sure I avoided my sister's inquisition had not passed her by.

'That I have someone I must see, and I may have to stay overnight. Now the sooner I leave the sooner I shall be back,' I added firmly. 'Thank you for the provisions, Sallie. They will be a great comfort.'

She pushed a thick blanket into my arms and finally let me go.

As I rode up on to the moor, I discovered I had underestimated the strength of the wind. Hal didn't like it any more than I did, and, unlike me, it wasn't as if he had a reason to be out in the cold and far from the comforts of home.

The wind had one advantage, however, in that for quite a lot of the road over the high ground it had blown the snow into drifts, leaving the way fairly clear. I was heartened to see that the surface had been trodden down by other travellers; if other men and women were going about their business undeterred by the conditions, then it made me less of an irresponsible idiot for doing the same.

As we began the descent it seemed to me that the temperature rose a little, aided, probably, by the fact that we were now protected by the bulk of the moor behind us. The snow was melting here and there, and I found little streams running down off the hills. We stopped, Hal had a drink, we both had some much-needed food, and then we went on.

We rode down into Dartmouth soon after noon, and as we travelled the road along the west side of the river, deep in the valley, we were not only in full sunshine but sheltered from the wind, and it became almost balmy. Almost.

I always like visiting Dartmouth, having got to know it well in my years at sea. I made friends in the town with whom I keep in touch, quite often riding down to pay a visit although more typically in summertime.

I did not believe that, by sharing the secret of Artemis's little bag with the man I had in mind to call on, I would be taking much of a risk. He was someone I had known for years, he was wise and well informed, and I had always detected an innate kindness and a sense of chivalry in his nature. These qualities would, I was quite sure, make him as unlikely to use what I was about to share with him to bring harm to Artemis Brownyng as I was.

His tiny house was a couple of streets behind the busy waterfront, which was visible through a broad gap between the buildings in front. It was a location that afforded wonderful views out over the river, the harbour and the sea beyond. I had wondered, when he first invited me to his home, whether the constant presence of water was not a pain to him; like me, he had been forced to give up his life as a sailor, but, far less fortunate than I, the reason for this had made him unsuited to other work. He had lost his right leg, and the injuries to his left leg had left it twisted and unable to bear his weight for long.

He had been on one of the ships I'd served on, and it had been I who amputated his leg. I had felt guilty for a long time that I could not have done a better job on the remaining one, until eventually he had lost patience and told me he was still alive, so matters could be worse.

His name was Henry Sparre, he was a Devonian like me, he was perhaps ten years my senior and since he had lost his leg, he had occupied himself teaching local lads whose parents' ambitions for their offspring rated education as the most likely step to fortune and fame. Henry taught anybody's sons, provided the father could pay, from boys whose regular schooling had lit the fire of intellectual curiosity in them and were consequently apt and willing pupils, to the sort of resentful lads who reckoned the hours spent in school were more than enough, and utterly failed to appreciate someone trying to force yet more learning into their thick skulls.

Henry had told me once that while the latter category might have formed the majority, the hours spent struggling with them were more than compensated for by the boys who appreciated what he offered them and whose minds consequently bloomed under his tutelage.

Teaching biddable and not so biddable boys was not, however, Henry's sole source of income. An intelligent and astute man residing in a busy port did not have to look far for an enterprise in which to invest the modest wealth he brought ashore with him when he had been forced to abandon the sea: for more than a decade now, Henry Sparre had been quietly and unobtrusively making himself rich by investing in trade.

I left Hal with an ostler at the inn on the north end of the quay, giving the man a handful of coins and telling him my horse needed a few treats to make up for the ride, then I strode along the quay, passing the Cherub, and turned to the right into the narrow, intersecting network of narrow streets that clustered behind it. In a few moments I was standing in front of Henry's door.

In the brief time it took for someone to come and open it,

I looked up at the house. It was two storeys high, although Henry's condition had led him to arrange his living arrangements on the ground floor. The white paint looked quite fresh, and the brass knocker on the door gleamed in the sun. As the door opened, revealing a stocky, heavily-muscled man with gingery hair and a truculent expression, I said cheerfully, 'Good day, MacNab! I see you're looking after the property!'

And the dour face of Henry's manservant, nurse, companion, and whatever else he might be, broke into a welcoming smile.

'What are you doing in Dartmouth, Doctor?' he asked. 'Not come specially to see the master, I'll warrant, else you'd have sent word?' There was a faint note of interrogation in his voice, as if to make sure I was aware of my minor breach of social good manners in turning up unannounced.

It probably wasn't his place to question a visitor, and perhaps I should have ignored the remark and pushed him aside, demanding to be announced instantly, but MacNab was devoted to Henry, and he cared for him with efficiency, diligence, tact and kindness, even if he did act like a guard dog. You didn't tangle with MacNab unless there was no alternative, so I smiled and said, 'I have come to ask Henry's help, MacNab, on a matter of some urgency that has only just arisen.'

MacNab nodded, then strode along the passage and opened a door. 'A visitor, Master Henry,' he said. And stood aside to let me go in.

Henry was sitting at a wide desk placed in the window, which looked out on to the narrow street. He had books and papers spread out, a quill in his hand and an irritated expression.

'What–Gabe! Good God! How grand to see you! Come in, draw up a chair! MacNab, fetch us something tasty, would you? And a bottle and two mugs, if you please!'

I sat down, craning my neck to see what Henry was working on. He appeared to be drawing a map, and there was a series of arrows leading from specific places to little boxes crammed with his small, neat writing.

'I'm disturbing you,' I said.

He grinned. 'You are, but nevertheless I'm delighted to see you. How are you?'

As I made some vague answer, I was thinking to myself that it would be far more pertinent to ask him how he was. He was pale, but then it was February, and like anyone else who finds it hard to get about out of doors, he'd probably been stuck inside for weeks. His face was thin, the cheekbones and brow ridges prominent, and his clothing looked loose on him. His remaining leg was concealed by the warm wool blanket spread over his lap. As always, the flat space where the lost one should be was a slight shock. Henry's wound had been very high in the thigh, so there wasn't even a stump. My main battle the day I worked on him had been to stop the frightening flow of blood from the femoral artery.

My inspection of him hadn't been as unobtrusive as I'd hoped. 'I do quite well, Gabe,' he said gently. 'Although I shall never cease to be grateful to you for saving my life, you are no longer my physician.' *And I don't want to hear your observations*, he might have added. There was no need, however, for I read it in his face.

He would suffer pain on a pretty permanent basis, I thought. I hoped he had ways of dealing with it; that MacNab knew what to slip into Henry's hot drink when it got too bad. I wanted very much to offer some suggestions – I had picked up much from both Black Carlotta and Judyth on the subject of the control of pain – but in light of what Henry had just said, I held my peace.

In any case, distraction was a way of coping; which, I realized, was probably why Henry chose to spend his time tutoring.

We were interrupted by MacNab with our refreshments – small, hot savoury pies containing cheese and onion, a jug of ale – and when he had gone again, Henry said, 'Now, what can I do for you?' He smiled. 'What is so important that it has brought you over the moor and down into Dartmouth on a bitter February day?'

I told him.

He had the intellectual's ability to sit silently and not interrupt with distracting questions, and he listened intently as I described the eruption of Artemis Brownyng into our lives and what we knew of her story, adding every detail I could think of concerning the death of the man in the gully and the decapitated corpse left at my gates.

Some moments after I'd finished he seemed to bestir himself from his utter stillness, and he turned to look at me. He raised his eyebrows slightly. 'And?' he asked.

'Hmm?'

'What else?' He made an impatient sound. 'Why, specifically, have you come to me? What do you believe that I know, that you can't find out in Plymouth?'

With a reluctance I didn't really understand, I reached inside my tunic and, feeling inside the suede bag, took out a nutmeg. I laid it on Henry's desk.

His eyes widened as he stared at it. 'Good grief,' he muttered. 'You must have been to London recently, Gabe. Meeting your colleagues in that Symposium of yours, I suppose?'

I shook my head. 'No. It is the currency with which Mistress Brownyng offers to pay me, this and its fellows, for all that I have told her there is no need of payment.' I paused. 'She tells me to be very careful. She tells me it is not at all safe. When I proposed to take her offering to Plymouth to find a buyer, she responded in horror and commanded me to go considerably further afield. She feared, I believe, that others would have been very interested in what I was up to and pursued me home to Rosewyke, where Mistress Brownyng is still in my care as she regains her strength.'

'With good reason,' Henry muttered. He had picked up the nutmeg and was turning it between his fingers and thumb

'You recognize it?' I indicated the nutmeg. 'You know why it should arouse such interest?'

'Yes, and yes,' Henry replied, 'but that wasn't what I meant; I was observing that she has good reason to fear what men might do to get hold of this little nut and its fellows, as you quaintly refer to the rest of them, because two men have already been murdered.'

'And you think their presence in the area and their brutal deaths are connected?'

Henry sighed resignedly. 'Of *course*, Gabe.'

I took a deep swallow of ale. It was very good. Then I said,

'Go on, then. Tell me all about this nutmeg. Why, for a start, did you assume I'd acquired it in London?'

But he didn't answer; he was reaching behind him to a tightly-packed bookcase, from which he extracted a carefully-drawn sketch map. He spread it out on his desk, covering the books and documents. He gave me a moment or two to study it, and after some time I finally recognized what it depicted.

'Francis Drake's circumnavigation,' I said softly. 'You drew this?'

He nodded. 'Some of my more lively-minded lads are avid for travellers' tales, and I like to think that a boy who learns about this great world of ours from me may one day find his way around it as a consequence. See,' he hurried on, his face alight and his body tensed in his eagerness, 'Drake rounds Cape Horn and sails into the Pacific Ocean, all the way up the west coast of that great land mass, and then he leaves land far behind him and sails west—' he traced the route with his finger '—until west becomes east, and he finds himself in the East Indies, where among other places he lands at a port called Ternate—' he pointed '—and proceeds through the Banda Sea to Java, then to the south of India to the Arabian Sea, down the east coast of Africa, around the Cape of Good Hope, up the west coast and, eventually, home to where he started.' He paused, eyes distant. 'What a voyage,' he murmured. 'What courage the sailors had, those puny men in their little ships.'

I waited for him to return from wherever he had been in his thoughts. Then I said, 'Your pupils are lucky to have you, Henry. But what has Drake's voyage to do with Artemis Brownyng's nutmegs?'

He nodded, frowned, then said, 'They say Drake was never slow to spot an opportunity, and out there in those hot and steamy islands with their incredible fertility, he observed a busy trade in what they produce in such lavish abundance.' He looked at me enquiringly.

'Nutmegs?' I offered.

'Nutmegs grow profusely only in one place, which is the Banda Islands, specifically Neira. Or so I understand.' He looked at me intently. 'But you are close, Gabe. It was another spice, cloves, that caught Drake's attention, and they say the profit on the clove cargo that he purchased in Ternate was so enormous that covetous eyes were lighting up all over London.'

'But Artemis hasn't got cloves, she's got nutmegs,' I said.

'Where the desire exists for one spice, hunger for others will follow,' Henry replied. 'And since the days of the Romans there has been a busy and highly profitable trade in pretty much anything and everything that adds savour to a dull, bland diet, not to mention the spices' much-vaunted medicinal qualities. And what a convenient cargo! Little could be less arduous to transport over very long distances than clove buds, pepper berries, cinnamon bark, mace and nutmeg, and—'

'Mace?'

'The nutmeg is the fruit's kernel, mace is the protective matter that surrounds it.'

I was still thinking about what he'd just said concerning profit.

'And there's really as much money to be made in this trade as they say?' I asked. 'They're worth more than gold?' That was what my friend Jasper had said, although I still found it hard to believe.

Henry was silent for so long that I thought I'd have to prompt him, but then he turned to me with a grin and said, 'Sorry. I was just trying to think of a word other than money, since the word does not do justice to the potential profits.' He paused, and I guessed he was working something out. 'They say the percentages can run into the thousands, if not the tens of thousands.' While I was trying to absorb that astounding fact, he added, 'And that if as little as one-sixth of a cargo manages to avoid all dangers and obstacles and end up back in London, the man who purchased it will still make a decent profit.'

Slowly I shook my head. 'I'm amazed the whole world isn't making its way east to carve out their share,' I remarked.

Taking my flippant remark seriously, Henry said, 'For one thing, few men have the means, and the ones who are busily engaged in funding voyages usually do it as a consortium, sharing both the costs and the profits.' He shot me a swift glance, quickly looking away. 'But there is another factor that undoubtedly deters all but the brave and, perhaps, the unimaginative.'

'Which is? I asked softly, for once again he seemed to be far away inside his own thoughts.

'Have you sailed east, Gabe?' he asked.

'To the Arabian Sea and as far as India, but no further,' I replied.

He nodded. 'It was the same for me. But I speak with many men who have gone beyond. Some have room in their heads only for cargoes and profits, and their talk concerns little but how they struck this deal in one place, that better deal elsewhere, how much they expect to make and what they propose to do with it. Other men, however, see below the hard-nosed, covetous surface to the darkness and the mystery beneath.'

'Mystery? What do you mean?'

'Those eastern islands that are enclosed by the Spanish islands of the Philippines to the north, Celebes to the west and New Guinea to the east—' in a swift, darting movement he hastened to show me on his map '—are in an area of the world that is frighteningly alien,' he said. 'They are ringed by a circle of volcanoes, many of which are as violent as they are unpredictable, and men sail close to them at their peril. And such places are always hidden behind clouds of superstition, myth and legend. Have you heard tell of the Devil's Triangle, Gabe?'

'No. Where is it?'

'Somewhat to the north and west of the islands we are speaking of, between the Philippines and the hidden land they call Japan. But it is an area that inspires dread, so that men are reluctant to sail there, whispering its name – the Sea of the Devil, sometimes the Dragon's Triangle – and skirting it when they can. They say Kublai Khan lost an entire fleet there, his ships consumed by the dragon that rose up from the depths.'

'I do not believe in mythical fleet-eating dragons,' I said crushingly, 'and I'm quite sure you don't, either.'

He smiled. 'Perhaps not, but even the least superstitious cannot deny the alarming conditions in the region, for thunderstorms, typhoons, tidal waves and underwater eruptions are all commonplace. Or so they say.' He leaned towards me, dropping his voice to a whisper. 'Imagine the sea cresting in a great hump beside your frail ship, Gabe. Imagine something huge rising from incalculable depths. Imagine your terror as you wait for it to break the surface. What will you see? A new land? A monster? A portal to somewhere unknown and unimagined?'

The echoes of his words sounded once or twice in the room. As they faded I said, determined to break the spell he had just woven, 'It could just be a very large wave, Henry.'

He looked at me for a moment, eyes narrowed in consideration.

Then he laughed.

I went back over what we had just been saying and realized something. 'You still haven't explained why you assumed I'd acquired the nutmeg in London,' I reminded him.

'No, I haven't,' he agreed. 'It's because among the merchants I spoke of – the ones busy forming their consortiums with which to fund more voyages – those far out in the lead are based in London.'

London was where the wealthiest and most ambitious merchants had always tended to congregate, and where in previous centuries the city guilds had been founded. It was no surprise that these hard-headed men with their eyes on the future had been the first to exploit this new treasure from the East.

'They call themselves the Company of Merchants of London trading in the East Indies,' Henry was saying, 'but their renown is already sufficient, in London anyway, that people know who you mean if you just refer to them as the Company.'

'How long have they been operating?' I asked.

'After several months of typical indecision—' Henry smiled reminiscently '—the late Queen finally signed the precious document recognizing their existence on 31st December 1600.'

I had not realized it was quite so recent. 'Why was she indecisive?' I demanded.

'Oh . . .' Henry paused, probably working out how to explain something rather complex in a few words that I would understand. 'At the time she was walking the usual knife edge with Spain, and for England to push their way into the East Indies trade already established by the Spanish would be regarded as provocative, to say the least. King Philip had good reason for being wary about us,' he added wryly.

He was right. The Armada had destroyed Spanish faith in her fighting ships roughly as much as it had increased our confidence in our own. In addition, our ships had taken far too many heavily-laden Spanish galleons lumbering their way back from the New World for Spain to have any faith that we would play this fledgling new game by their rules.

The Spanish believed we would meekly accept their carving-up of every newly-discovered area of land and sea on the globe between them and their near neighbours, the Portuguese, the dividing line running north to south straight down the Atlantic. Broadly speaking, Spain had originally claimed the Caribbean and the New World, Portugal the East Indies. But then, of course, a couple of decades ago Philip became king of Portugal as well, and the Spanish appeared to think this gave them rights to the whole world.

It wasn't really any wonder that the English didn't like them.

'What changed the Queen's mind?' I asked.

'For one thing, even back then it was increasingly apparent that war with Spain wouldn't go on for ever. Our present King, of course, established peace, which meant our privateers no longer had any reason to attack enemy shipping,' he added. 'Besides—' he made the age-old gesture of rubbing his thumb against his fingertips '—there's a very large pie out in the Eastern Islands, Gabe, and the Queen wanted to make sure we had our slice. And why buy from the merchants of other nations? If they could find their way out there and back again with their priceless cargoes, why couldn't we?'

'And now we're doing it? This company of London merchants are financing voyages that come back groaning under the weight of their cargoes?'

He grinned. 'Well, not exactly, but in a minor fashion, yes. They have a fine captain called Lancaster who's made the trip a couple of times, although strictly speaking the first voyage was before the Company was founded. He set out again in 1601, and although the voyage could hardly be said to be a total success, at least Lancaster established that it could be done, and we can do it.'

I thought he had finished. I hoped he had, for I was busy trying to absorb all that he had told me already. We sat in a reflective silence for a few moments, and then he said, 'You mentioned foreign coins.'

'I did.' I'd told him about what I'd found on the headless corpse by my gates, and described the coins. 'My friend the coroner believes they may be Dutch, minted by the country's Spanish rulers.'

'From what you say, they are.' Henry was frowning, his expression concerned.

'And?' I prompted. 'Why does that fact cause you to look so worried?'

He sighed. 'Because the London Company isn't the only concern so enthusiastically seeking many men's fortunes out in the East Indies. There is also the Vereenigde Oostindische Compagnie, usually referred to for brevity as the VOC and translated as the Dutch East India Company. They got there before we did, they have already established fortified ports and trading bases, they are well-armed and well-equipped.' He paused, a faint, ironic smile on his lips. 'And they're not at all pleased that we've pushed our way in out there to join them.'

NINE

By the time Henry had finished telling me every last fact and piece of gossip he knew about the East Indies and the Company – or so it seemed – the afternoon was almost done, the skies had clouded over and begun to darken, and it was much too late to set out for home.

I said I would put up for the night at the inn where I'd left my horse, not wanting to put Henry – or in fact MacNab – to the trouble of preparing a bed, but they would not hear of it. Henry said it was good to have my company and he'd welcome a little more of it. MacNab said he would enjoy having 'a bit of a chat' with me, and the exaggerated wink with which he accompanied the words suggested he had something to say to me in private.

I walked back to the inn and arranged for the ostler to care for Hal overnight, and on my way back to Henry's house I purchased a bottle of fine brandy. Then the pair of us settled in for the evening, talking about all manner of fascinating subjects, for he was deeply interested in the details of my profession and, for my part, I was eager to absorb just a small part of his extensive knowledge on botany, geology, the history of the countries that made up the world, their legends, tales and religions, and a hundred other sundry topics as well. We ate a very tasty supper in front of a good fire, and I only brought the evening to an end when I saw he was growing drawn with tiredness and was clearly in pain.

I had brought my doctor's bag with me – I always do – and I was about to suggest a remedy to dull the pain and help him sleep, but MacNab picked up my intention and, out of Henry's sight, minutely shook his head. So I bade them both goodnight, and after a brief visit out to the yard, retired to my cosy little room upstairs and what looked like a very comfortable bed.

It was not long before a soft tap on the door announced the expected visitor.

'Come in, MacNab,' I said softly.

He did so, closing the door carefully behind him.

'What can I do for you?' I asked.

'Persuade Master Henry to take his medicine,' he replied promptly. 'And maybe suggest something that might actually work while you're about it.'

I didn't answer straight away. Something of this sort was what I'd been expecting, but it wasn't as straightforward as simply doing what MacNab was asking; what I too very much wanted to do. For it appeared that Henry was already someone else's patient, and physicians don't take kindly to a fellow professional crowding in.

'He has a doctor here in Dartmouth?' I asked.

MacNab grimaced. 'Aye, he does, for all the good it does him. Man's an incompetent, dishes out the same old remedy all the time, says it ought to help when it's obvious to all of us it does no such thing.'

'Which I imagine is why Henry doesn't take it,' I remarked.

MacNab snorted, which I took for agreement.

I was weighing up the options. Yes, it would be unprofessional to prescribe for Henry, even assuming he would accept my offer and his pride would not make him insist he was perfectly all right, thank you. But I was not local, hardly anybody knew I was there, and certainly not Henry's physician. I knew I could help him, and it had been increasingly uncomfortable to watch him trying not to show he was in pain, distracting himself – or so I believed – by that great outflow of riveting talk.

I stood up, picking up my bag. 'Come on, then,' I said to MacNab, who, with a surprised smile and a look of delight, led me down the stairs and into Henry's bedchamber.

It took every one of my most persuasive arguments to overcome Henry's resistance, and in the end I think he only gave in because he realized I wasn't going to. He called me an interfering bully and a know-all, but that was when I'd just folded back the bedclothes to look at his stump and his twisted left leg, and I agreed with him that was exactly what I was.

It was clear from my examination that MacNab cared for

him efficiently as well as devotedly, for the stump was clean and tidy, and the skin covering the amputation was soft with fragrant oils.

But even my lightest touch caused Henry a lot of pain.

I covered him up and sat down beside him. Then, with MacNab lurking in the doorway, I told him about Judyth, and Black Carlotta, and how I'd put my male professional pride deep in my pocket and listened to what those two compassionate, knowledgeable and experienced women had to say on the subject of pain. How I'd been forced to acknowledge that they knew as much if not more than I did, and the fact that I'd attended the King's College of Physicians in London and been taught by stern old men with rigid views weighed little against the depths of wisdom they had inherited from the generations of women who had preceded them.

I took a certain preparation out of my bag and mixed a very small amount in a glass of hot water. Henry, bless him, didn't ask what was in it, and I was humbled by his trust, even as I accepted and pitied the depths of desperation from which it came. He made a face – the potion is very bitter – and I apologized, saying it tasted much better when sweetened with honey.

The preparation I had used contained both an analgesic and a soporific. The concentration was weak – Henry was new to this – and at first I wondered if I'd erred too far on the safe side, for he began talking again – that distracting chatter – and he was still twisting around in pain.

But then, as suddenly as the light vanishes when a candle flame is blown out, he changed.

The marks of long agony left his face. A small amount of colour rose into his cheeks. His eyes wide with astonishment, he began to say, 'Good grief, Gabe, it's–it's lessening! I don't—'

MacNab had come right into the chamber, face full of alarm, and I thought I saw him surreptitiously cross himself.

Then all at once it was as if the strings and sinews of pain that held Henry in his tight knot had been undone. His body relaxed, then slumped, and as MacNab hurried forward to ease him down in the bed and plump up the pillows supporting his head, he turned on his side, gave a deep sigh and went to sleep.

For a few moments neither MacNab or I spoke. Then he said in a barely audible whisper, 'How did you *do* that?'

'Several different substances made into a very old remedy, known since ancient times,' I whispered back.

He looked at me dubiously. 'Why doesn't everyone use it?' he hissed.

The long answer was that pain and suffering were deemed by the church to be a part of man's lot, or, more specifically, woman's lot. *In sorrow shalt thou bring forth children*, as the Book of Genesis commands, and the male sex were similarly doomed to bodily suffering in this life. The short answer – and the one I provided for MacNab – was that physicians could not prescribe what they had not been taught to use.

Some time later, MacNab and I watched as Henry fell into a deep sleep. The harsh lines of pain had been smoothed out of his gaunt face, and the tension had left his body. MacNab whispered, 'Thank you, Doctor,' and he spoke as fervently as if it had been his own pain that I had just relieved.

'I'll stay with him awhile,' I said quietly.

'I can do that, I usually—' MacNab began.

'Take a night off,' I said with a grin.

And, responding with a nod and a smile, he slipped away and I sat down on the comfortable chair beside the bed.

I sat with Henry until he started snoring. Then I crept away to my own room.

I had asked MacNab to call me early in the morning, and he did, tapping on the door and delivering a large jug of hot water. A short time later I went down and joined Henry at the table, where MacNab was setting out platters of bacon, egg and fried bread. The amount on my platter was roughly twice the size of Henry's portion, and, catching my eye, MacNab murmured, 'You've a long ride ahead of you, Doctor. Best to set out with a full belly.'

When he had returned to the scullery, Henry slid a folded piece of paper across the table to me. 'What's this?' I asked.

He leaned towards me. 'You didn't need to come all the way to Dartmouth to find out about that particular cargo you spoke of,' he said.

I unfolded the paper. Henry had written a name – Jacobus Schuer – and an address in Plymouth.

'Who's this?'

'Someone you can trust,' Henry replied.

'Judging by his name, he's not English,' I observed.

Henry grinned. 'And anybody who doesn't share your nationality is untrustworthy? Don't tell me that's your view, Gabe. I won't believe you.'

'Of course I don't think that,' I said shortly. 'It's merely that if this man is Dutch—'

'He is.'

'—if he's Dutch, then, as we established last night, some of his fellow countrymen are deeply involved in this business.'

'*Some* of them,' Henry said, emphasising the first word. He sighed. 'I am trying to help you, Gabe. Jacobus is a good man, I've known him a long time, he is a successful merchant, like many men in Plymouth, and he is extremely knowledgeable about trade with the East.' When I did not reply, he gave a tut of irritation and said, 'Please yourself, but you're not going to learn more about this cargo and why men are dying all by yourself.'

He was absolutely right.

I refolded the piece of paper and tucked it inside my tunic. 'Thank you, Henry. I will seek out this Jacobus Schuer and ask for his help.'

'Tell him I gave you his name,' Henry suggested. He smiled again. 'He's suspicious of strangers asking questions, and he'll shut the door in your face unless somehow you manage to convince him not to.'

I reflected that since two men apparently involved in this dangerous cargo were already dead, Jacobus Schuer had good reason for his caution.

Before I left I summoned MacNab, and explained carefully to him and Henry how to mix the potion I'd administered for

Henry last night, how to make absolutely sure not to use too much, and that the amount in the little bottle should be sufficient for several months.

'And then I shall return,' I promised. 'In the meantime, you know where to find me.'

I took my leave. If I'd felt any twinge of conscience over treating another physician's patient, it was annihilated by the pleasure of seeing Henry's smile.

Celia woke early. She knew without checking that Gabe hadn't returned. When called out in the night to a patient he tried very hard to move quietly, soft-footed on the stairs and avoiding the creaky ones, but he never quite succeeded. He was too large and heavy not to make some small sound, and normally Celia would stir, register that her brother was going out or coming in, and go straight back to sleep.

But this time she didn't know where he had gone and when he would be back. She had gone downstairs yesterday morning to find no Gabe and a worried Sallie, the latter distressed because it was very cold and no day for a long ride. And she could give Celia no clue as to where Gabe had gone.

'It'll be to do with *her*,' Sallie had said in a sharp whisper, jerking her head in the direction of the small parlour. 'Mark my words, he'll be off on some errand to help her, as if having her in this house and all of us running round after her like she was royalty wasn't already enough!'

'I know, Sallie, and it's easy to forget that most of the extra work falls upon you, and you have quite enough to do already,' Celia had replied.

But Sallie had a kind heart, and having vented at least some of her anger, she said more softly, 'Well, someone has to help her, the poor soul,' and left Celia to her breakfast.

Now, this morning, it was a full day and night since Gabe left. He had warned her he might not be back, but nevertheless Celia was uneasy. She got out of bed, dressed and went downstairs. She could hear Sallie busy in the kitchen. *Good*, she thought. *I can speak to Artemis privately.*

She went along the short passage and into the morning

parlour. Artemis was sitting up in bed, brushing out her long dark hair in smooth strokes with an old and worn ivory-backed brush.

Celia closed the door and went to stand beside her.

'My brother the doctor has not yet returned,' she said. 'It is very cold outside, and journeys taken in this weather always contain an element of danger. I believe his mission concerns you.'

Artemis's dark eyes narrowed. 'What if it does?' Before Celia could reply she went on, 'It's private. Between him and me. *Secret.*'

'That may be,' Celia said, holding on with difficulty to her impatience. 'I do not care about your secret, Artemis. I care about my brother, and his well-being. If you tell me where he has gone, I will set about organising my friends and setting out to meet him.'

'Well, you can't because I don't know where he's bound,' Artemis said tersely. She flung the brush down on the bed.

'But you must have . . .'

But then Celia stopped. Because it was all at once clear that Artemis wasn't protecting this secret, whatever it was, to be difficult; she really didn't know where Gabe had gone and when – if – he would return,

Artemis was also becoming worried.

Compassion overcame anger, and Celia crouched down beside the bed and took Artemis's hands. 'He knows the region very well,' she said, 'he has friends and patients all over the place, and there are many doors he'll have been able to knock on if the weather conditions became too severe for safety.' She knew she was reassuring herself as much as Artemis. 'Now,' she went on briskly, standing up, 'I shall fetch you some good, nourishing food and a hot drink, and we shall look after you while we wait for Gabe's return.'

By the middle of the morning, Celia could restrain her impatience no longer. With no clue as to Gabe's destination there was no point whatsoever in going out to look for him. She considered riding down to Withybere to see if Theo – or more likely Jarman Hodge – knew where Gabe had gone, but there was someone else in whom she would much rather confide her anxious fear.

She went into the kitchen and said to Sallie, 'I'm going to ride into Tavy St Luke's, because I need to talk to his reverence about . . .' She stopped.

But Sallie knew full well why Celia wanted to go to Jonathan.

'Good idea, Miss Celia,' she said. 'If the doctor comes home I'll tell him where you are. Might drop a strong hint about unreasonable people riding off in terrible weather without a word as to where they're bound,' she added in a cross mutter, 'and worrying those that care about them half to death.'

Celia smiled. 'Yes, and add an even stronger hint from me too,' she said.

Sallie detained her only long enough to fetch a jar of last autumn's quince jelly '—For his reverence, because he likes it—' then let her go.

'—and I know it's foolish to worry, but it's so cold outside, and he's gone haring off on some business concerning our patient, and there's a dark side to all this and two men are already dead,' Celia blurted out, 'and so I–I—' She stopped.

They were sitting by the fire in Jonathan's small room, and now that she was here, and trying to put her fears into calm, sensible words, it was at the same time a huge relief just to *talk* to him and very embarrassing because quite obviously there was little or nothing he could actually *do* and so he'd realize it was just for the comfort of being with him that she'd come and he'd think–

His quiet voice interrupted her tumbling thoughts. 'And so you came to share your worries with a friend,' he finished for her.

She looked up, meeting his eyes. 'I'm sorry, I'm disturbing you, you must have so many calls upon your time.'

He considered her words. 'Not particularly busy just now. I do of course have calls on my time, but for the moment I've answered most of them and I've put the remainder into God's capable hands.' He paused, then added softly, 'You are not disturbing me, Celia. It is as always a joy to see you.'

She was both delighted and surprised at his last comment and, watching as he lowered his eyes, she reckoned she wasn't alone in the feeling of surprise.

'What should we do, Jonathan?' she asked after a moment. 'Of course I'm sure Gabe really is all right, it's just that–'

'Just that he is away on an unexplained absence in very poor conditions,' he said. 'Naturally it is worrying. One thing we might do,' he went on quickly, 'is to reflect on the wider picture.'

'What's that?' she asked, already interested.

'Your unexpected guest is pining for her absent lover, the father of her child, whose name is Edwyn and who has sailed off on a voyage to make his fortune. It is six months since he left, and she has had no word. Coinciding with her appearance in the area, a man has been found dead with nutmegs pushed into his mouth, robbed of the contents of a secret pocket, which a witness reported to have been a document. A second man was left without his head at the end of the track to Rosewyke, and in his purse were coins produced by the Spanish rulers of the Netherlands. Neither of them was the man who attempted to break into Rosewyke, the first because he was already dead when the would-be intruder appeared, and the second because the face at the window was dark and bearded and the decapitated man was clean-shaven, light eyed and fair. If we assume that the bearded man was looking for Artemis Brownyng, then we have a link between the lady, the nutmegs and the man with the Dutch coins, who let us say for the sake of argument was a Dutchman.'

He was looking brightly at Celia, as if expecting her to make an intelligent comment. 'Er–' she began. 'It's to do with trade? With some very precious cargo that this Edwyn was seeking and that the others both want?' Then, for he was nodding as if to say go on, she added, 'But what about the nutmegs?'

'Let us assume that they comprise the very precious cargo,' he replied. 'Demand far outpaces supply, especially as the more unscrupulous merchants market them now as a cure for plague, which without doubt they are not. But it's where they come from, Celia!' he exclaimed, leaning forward towards her, his eyes bright.

'Yes?' she said encouragingly.

'They grow far away in the east, on islands in a sea half a world away, and our London merchants are busily seeking a source and a means of bringing the cargo safely home. However, others reached and secured this source before them, and these others are Dutchmen.'

'So–' She struggled to comprehend a voyage to somewhere half a world away. 'So you're saying this Edwyn has gone all the way to these islands in the East? For *nutmegs*?' Before Jonathan could reply, she added, 'And how on earth do you *know* all this, stuck out here so far from London and merchants and trade?'

He sat back, smiling. 'It's at least possible that this explains the long absence of Artemis's lover, yes. As to how I know, we may live in the quiet of the countryside but nevertheless we are close to a very busy port. People from all over the country call in at Plymouth, as do ships outward and inward bound to and from ports as far away as men's perpetually questing natures have taken them. It is more than likely that Edwyn's ship sailed from Plymouth, especially in view of the fact that it is where Artemis came in her despair. And once I—' He hesitated, and she had the distinct impression he was weighing up whether or not to say what was in his mind. After a short pause he said, 'And travellers love to talk.'

She was all but certain it wasn't the remark he'd almost uttered. But she was too intrigued by what else he'd just told her to push him, so she tucked her feet up under her, snuggled into her chair and said, 'Tell me what these travellers have to say about the islands in a sea on the other side of the world.'

As I came down off the moors and into the Tavy valley, I wanted more than anything to go home, eat, see my patient and talk to my sister. But I made myself ride on; I had the name of a fresh contact tucked inside my tunic, and before I sought him out, I knew I must call on Theo.

He was in his office, and Jarman was with him.

I sent up a brief but fervent prayer of thanks.

'Where have you been, Gabe?' Theo demanded even before

I'd pulled up a chair. 'Two days since you reported on that second corpse, and you failed to return and tell me what you found out about the first body and Jarman's rumour of a document in a secret pocket.'

'No. I'm sorry, Theo. The secret pocket was empty,' I hurried on before he could ask me again to explain my absence, 'but his name was Malin Piltbone, and although he spoke with a heavy accent that wasn't local, he was English.'

'Could have told you that,' Jarman Hodge said laconically.

Yes. I recalled him saying that he too had asked around in the quayside taverns.

'I've been to see a contact in Dartmouth,' I went on. 'And before you make some comment about it being no time to look up old friends, Theo, it was because this man is making a tidy sum through trade, and he told me more than I could take in on the subject of nutmegs.'

'And nutmegs are what we found in this Malin Piltbone's throat,' Theo said. 'What of it?'

I reached inside my tunic and drew out Artemis's little suede bag. 'My patient wishes to pay me for her care,' I said, 'with these.' I opened the drawstrings and the nutmegs rolled out on to Theo's desk. 'She warned me against trying to sell them in Plymouth, but my Dartmouth friend has provided the name of a man he trusts. I am on my way to visit him.'

'Take Jarman with you,' Theo said, and it wasn't a suggestion but an order. 'There's danger here, Gabe. Sinister foreigners and Dutchmen loose in the town, two men dead already and I don't want a third, especially if it's you.'

I wanted to protest but Theo had clearly made up his mind. I stood up, and Jarman followed me out of the office.

'What's this fellow's name?' Jarman asked as we rode off into Plymouth.

'Jacobus Schuer.' Jarman chuckled. 'What's funny?' I demanded.

'A Dutchman, from the sound of it,' he observed, still grinning. 'Sinister foreigners and Dutchmen,' he added. 'Just as well you didn't tell Master Davey *that*.'

*　　*　　*

Jarman knew the location of the address Henry had provided. It was an elegant, three-storey house with smart whitewash on the plaster and well-maintained woodwork, and it was set in a row of similarly grand houses up above the stink and the crowds on and around the quays. It fronted the street, and walls on either side extended to the rear and appeared to enclose a narrow space, presumably a yard or garden. Whatever Jacobus Schuer did to earn his money, he was clearly very successful.

Jarman and I tethered our horses to a ring set into the wall and Jarman went up the short flight of steps to bang on the knocker. It was brightly-polished brass, and in the shape of a full-sailed ship. The door was opened not much more than a crack by a tall, well-built man dressed in plain dark wool whose heavily hooded dark eyes studied Jarman suspiciously and then turned to me. The thin lips of his trap of a mouth parted only for the one curt word: 'Yes?'

'This is Jarman Hodge, coroner's agent, and I am Gabriel Taverner,' I replied. 'I'm a physician. We wish to speak to Jacobus Schuer, please. His name was given to me by Henry Sparre of Dartmouth.'

The man stood exactly where he was, not increasing the gap in the opening by as much as an inch. 'Wait.' The door slammed. Presently it reopened, the man stood back and said, 'Come in.'

He led us down a dark, narrow panelled hall and opened a door at the far end. The room was filled with light, and a man sat in an elegant and costly chair behind the desk set in the window. There was a leather folder bulging with documents on the desk, and a large wooden box with a clasp and padlock.

'I am Jacobus Schuer,' he said, the accent of his natal land evident. 'How do you know Master Sparre? Why did he send you here, and what do you want of me?' There was a detectable tremor in his voice.

The dark-clad man had softly closed the door and was standing against it, his eyes watchful. I noticed belatedly that he had a dagger in a sheath on his belt, and that his right hand was hovering uncomfortably close to the hilt.

I sensed his suspicious antipathy. It would have been cause

for apprehension, if not actual fear, but I was not afraid and I didn't think Jarman was either.

There *was* fear present in the elegant, well-furnished room, however: the dark manservant was anxiously watching his master, and the face of Jacobus Schuer was pale with dread.

TEN

'To answer your first question,' I said pleasantly, for the uncomfortable silence had gone on quite long enough, 'I sailed with Master Sparre many years ago, and as ship's surgeon attended him when he was so badly wounded and lost his right leg.' Jacobus Schuer's pale eyes were watching me closely. I thought I saw his tense expression relax slightly, and wondered if the fact that I was aware of the nature of Henry's devastating injury was a reassurance that I did really know him. 'It was I, in fact, who operated on him,' I added quietly.

Jacobus considered that for a few moments. 'You went to Dartmouth to treat him?'

It was undoubtedly a trick question, for Jacobus presumably knew Henry had his own physician in Dartmouth. 'No, I went to ask him about a matter on which he has a great deal more knowledge than I have.'

'And what was that?' Jacobus asked.

Once again I withdrew the suede bag and placed a nutmeg on the desk.

If Jacobus's fear had begun to lessen slightly, the sight of the small brown nut lying in a shaft of sunlight instantly increased it again, and to some way beyond the previous level. His face paled, he put a hand over his mouth and from behind it whispered, 'Why do you bring this to me? What do you know? *Who told you*?'

The last three words were an agonized hiss. The manservant made a soft noise of protest, stepping forward to stand closer to his master.

I put my hands up, palms out. 'I mean no harm, and I am sorry to cause such dismay. I went to see Henry to ask about the trade in this very costly spice because I have a small amount to sell.' I paused, wondering how much I should reveal. Deciding that unless I was frank with Jacobus he'd

probably have his manservant show Jarman and me out, I
said, 'I've been warned that for some reason the mention of
a cargo of nutmeg here in Plymouth is likely to arouse intense
and probably unhealthy interest, and that is why I rode to
Dartmouth to consult Henry. Although he provided much
valuable general information, he knew nothing of any
clandestine cargo.'

For this mysterious cargo, it struck me suddenly, was of
course what this matter was all about. Artemis's lover Edwyn
was missing, she had a sample of nutmegs hidden away, two
men had died and here was Jacobus Schuer out of his wits
with fear.

His face had now lost what small amount of colour remained,
and he looked as if he was about to faint. The dark servant
clearly thought so too, for swiftly he went over to a little side
table and poured a measure of what looked and smelt like
brandy.

'And why,' he said when a couple of gulps had restored
him a little, 'should you imagine that I do?'

I shrugged. 'Henry Sparre said you could help me,' I
said. I made as if to turn away. 'But if you can't, then please
accept my apologies for having disturbed you, and we shall
wish you good day.'

I waited, but he kept silent.

The manservant opened the door. I bowed and went out
through it, Jarman behind me. The servant edged past us in
the corridor and opened the street door, and then Jarman and
I were outside and the door firmly closed on us.

'Now why did you do that?' he demanded. 'He was terrified, and I'd put money on him having a great deal he could
have told us!'

'Wait,' I said. 'He's terrified, I agree, and I'm hoping that
means he'll—'

The door opened again and the manservant beckoned us
back inside.

'You are right,' Jacobus Schuer said. 'There is indeed a valuable cargo that has disappeared, and more than one interested
party is looking for it.'

Jarman and I were seated opposite Jacobus, and now all three of us had a glass of brandy before us.

'And you have an interest in this cargo?' I asked.

He smiled grimly. 'No, Doctor Taverner, I do *not*,' he replied. 'However, I do have interests in many other cargoes – I am after all a merchant – and unfortunately and for some reason I cannot fathom, the belief has spread along the Plymouth quayside that this missing shipment is among them.'

I thought I could see a reason for his fear. Not pausing to check the impulse, I said, 'And these interested parties have come knocking on your door to persuade you to reveal what you know?'

'But I know *nothing!*' he said angrily.

I strongly suspected he was lying.

'Henry told me you are extremely knowledgeable on the subject of trade with the East Indies,' I observed. 'It is, of course, why he sent me to you.'

'He shouldn't have done,' Jacobus muttered. He took another large mouthful of brandy. He had, I observed, been drinking the generous measure very quickly, and his cheeks had flushed. 'The last thing I want is men like you turning up with your questions and your demands to be *told*, and assuming I'll somehow know where that blasted island is and—' His hand flew to cover his mouth, and above it his eyes looked at me in horror.

'Island?' I echoed.

'Master Schuer,' the manservant said warningly.

Jacobus shot him a quick glance.

The man was shaking his head, frowning. He was standing out of the light, and I couldn't tell if his expression was alarmed or threatening.

Jacobus had clearly read it. He nodded, and began to mutter something about misleading talk and damaging rumours, but then all at once he sat up straight in his chair, banged his fists on his table and shouted, 'Damn and blast it, Gulworthy, I'll speak freely in my own house if I've a mind to, and this man is surely to be trusted because Henry sent him!'

The manservant's hooded eyes stared unblinkingly at him for a moment. Then he gave a visible shrug and leaned back against the door.

Jacobus was fumbling with the padlock on the large wooden box. He dropped the little key a couple of times, swearing to himself under his breath. Jarman leaned forward to help, but Jacobus waved him angrily away.

Jarman and I exchanged a glance. Then we waited.

Finally the box was open, its lid thrown back to bang heavily on the desk. Jacobus delved down into the tightly-packed documents, some with red wax seals attached, some yellowed with age and the old parchment thick with ancient dusty odours.

Jacobus straightened up. He was holding a black leather wallet about the size of a hand. He laid it on the desk, opened it and withdrew a piece of thick paper, folded so as to fit neatly inside the wallet. He spread it out, smoothing it so that it lay flat. Its surface was painted in shades of blue, green and brown. It appeared to be a landscape.

Jarman didn't make a sound, although he must surely recognize it from his own description. And so did I: the wallet and its contents had been in the secret pocket inside Malin Piltbone's tunic the night before he was murdered, and missing when, acting on Jarman's information, I'd gone to check through his noisome bundle of clothing a couple of days later.

Someone had removed it before shoving Piltbone's corpse into the drainage ditch. And now it was in the possession of Jacobus Schuer.

I bent over the painting, studying it very closely. Jarman did the same.

It was a map. It depicted the shoreline of an unnamed land, the blue sea at the top of the page. It seemed likely this was the north, although not every mapmaker conformed to the convention. There was a narrow inlet winding its way southwards inland from the coast, to the east of a small promontory, in a shallow bay bordered on the other side by a larger headland bisected by a second inlet. There was an arrow pointing to the first inlet, from which after a short initial channel a second branched off to the west and a longer one to the east, the main channel continuing to end in a fork some short way further inland. Going on to the west, the coastline was only faintly indicated, with another inlet some distance away and, further west and opposite the coastline, a long, thin spit of land reaching out to meet it.

There were only five words written on the map. Two said *The Island*. The third and fourth were very faint and I did not recognize what they said. It looked like *Nieuwe stad*, but that made no sense. The last appeared to say *chaw*.

Jarman was breathing over my shoulder. I sensed he was longing to speak, but he kept silent.

I straightened up. 'Where is this?' I asked, hoping the display of only mild interest was convincing.

Jacobus grunted. 'I was hoping you would tell me,' he replied. He had, I noticed, refilled his glass, although no more brandy had been offered to Jarman or me.

'Hmmm,' I murmured. '*Nieuwe stad*? Is that Dutch?'

'It is,' he replied. 'Not much help, however. It just means new settlement, and it appears quite often when a new territory is first mapped.'

'How did you come by it?' I refolded it and slid it back across the desk to Jacobus, maintaining the air of indifference.

But he pushed it back inside the leather wallet and immediately shoved it back. 'Take it, for God's sake, take it,' he said urgently. 'I don't want it in my house, I haven't slept since it's been here, it's—' Firmly he shut his mouth on whatever he had been about to say next.

'Very well.' I picked up the wallet. 'But you haven't answered my question.'

His face was very red now, his eyes bloodshot and his mouth loose and wet. The glass was once again empty. 'What question?' he said dully.

'Where did the wallet and the map come from?'

He waved an expansive hand. 'Oh . . . I'm known to be an antiquarian—' he had trouble with the five syllables '—and people bring me such items, thinking they may spark my interest and I'll pay accordingly for them.' His expression darkened. 'But I don't want that thing. Won't have it in my house. Too—'

Whatever his final word might have been, it was drowned out by the manservant's sudden loud clearing of his throat.

* * *

'D'you reckon he'll regret his generosity once he sobers up?' Jarman asked as we mounted our horses and set off.

'He may, but I reckon the regret will be less than the relief,' I replied. 'He was very frightened.'

'He was,' Jarman agreed. 'Has to be it, surely?'

'If by *it* you mean whatever your witness saw Malin Piltbone tucking away in his pocket that wasn't there when I checked, then yes.'

'A map of an unknown, unnamed island,' Jarman mused. 'You'll have your work cut out for you trying to find where *that* is, Doctor T.'

We rode on until our ways parted, Jarman's down to Withybere, mine on to Rosewyke. I started to make some mild remark wishing him a quiet night when he put his hand up to stop me. 'Sorry, Doctor, but there's someone following us,' he murmured very softly. Then, in his normal voice, he said, 'I'll wish you the same, Doctor T, with no midnight calls from the sick and the wounded to drag you out of your warm bed.'

As he spoke I saw him staring intently over my shoulder. I kept up the chatter until he said, 'It's all right. He's gone.'

'What did you see?' I demanded.

'Man on a chestnut horse. Long legs, looked tall, although it's hard to tell when someone's mounted. Fair-faced, light eyes that I could make out even under the brim of his hat.' He paused.

'And he was watching us? He'd followed us, perhaps, from Jacobus Schuer's house?'

Jarman shrugged. 'Couldn't say. Probably.'

There was something more: I waited, and then Jarman said in a rush, 'Maybe I shouldn't say this – it's disrespectful, somehow, when you recall how he died.'

'Disrespectful?' I echoed. 'And how *who* died?'

He muttered something I didn't hear, then said, 'Straight away he put me in mind of the man found dead by your gates. Except,' he added, 'this one still has a head.'

The light was fading when I got back to Rosewyke. Samuel came out to take Hal, and I could hear Tock in the stable, muttering to a restless horse.

'We have guests,' I observed to Samuel. I couldn't see the horse to identify the rider.

'His reverence and Mistress Penwarden,' Samuel replied.

He led Hal into the stable and, carrying my bag, I headed for the house. While I was happy to hear that Jonathan and Judyth were within, nevertheless it posed the question as to why they had come . . .

Sallie was clearing away the remains of a meal. 'They've just finished, Doctor,' she said, greeting my return after a two-day absence in the midst of a very cold February as if I'd simply been out for a breath of air. But then she paused in her task and looked at me, her face creasing into a smile. 'It's good to have you back,' she said softly. Then, turning back to the table, she added, 'Go and join them in the library, I'll bring a tray.'

Celia and Judyth sat in the chairs either side of the fire – which was radiating a wonderfully welcome heat – and Jonathan had pulled out a chair from the table. All three looked at me as I went in, and I read the same relief in them I'd just observed in Sallie.

When we'd greeted each other, and hoping I was right in deducing from their demeanour that nothing life-threatening had been happening, I said, 'Sallie's bringing me food. While I wait I'll explain what I've been doing, then all of you can tell me what's gone on here.' Not giving any of them the chance to protest – Celia looked as if she'd very much like to – I drew out a chair next to Jonathan and hurried on, 'I've been to Dartmouth to see my old friend Henry Sparre because he trades in spices. I needed information about Artemis's bag of nutmegs and she warned me it would be dangerous to consult anyone closer to home, which I decided meant dangerous for *her*, in case it invited another dark-bearded face peering through our widow. Henry referred me to someone he trusts here in Plymouth, however – a very wealthy merchant called Jacobus Schuer – but before I could ask him anything he gave me this.' I took out the wallet and spread the map on the table. 'Jarman and I – Jarman was with me – decided it must be the object that Malin Piltbone had hidden away inside his tunic and that was stolen before he was–before the body was disposed of. Before you ask, it seems to depict an island but there's no clue to its location.'

'We think Artemis's Edwyn sailed to the islands in the Eastern Seas,' Celia said, 'and that he—'

'That he's gone missing along with his cargo?' I interrupted.

'Yes. His extremely valuable cargo, and he, as we have been told, is a man hungry to make his fortune before he weds his bride.'

Sallie came in and set before me a huge slice of hot pie and gravy and a tankard of ale the size of a small bucket. I thanked her and began to eat.

'I know you're hungry, Gabe,' Celia said somewhat tartly, 'which I will take as your excuse for not asking why our guests are here.'

I waved my knife in the air. 'Sorry,' I said.

Jonathan smiled at Judyth. 'You first.'

Judyth's silvery eyes regarded me steadily. 'Artemis has become very distressed,' she said. 'In your absence Celia sent for me, thinking quite rightly that extreme agitation is not beneficial for someone still weak from fever. Artemis is calm now, largely because I mixed a mild sleeping draught for her, and the fever has not returned.'

I had momentarily forgotten about Artemis. I didn't think it was a good idea to admit it, but, closely watching Judyth's expression, I saw that I didn't need to.

'And what of you, Jonathan?' I asked, turning to him.

'Celia sought me out,' he replied. With a glance at Celia, who nodded, he went on, 'She was concerned at your continued absence in such bad weather. To distract ourselves, we set to discussing this whole mystery of Artemis, her missing lover and the cargo of nutmegs. We felt the need of an aid in our attempts to picture the world, and Celia mentioned the globe in your study. We returned to Rosewyke, hoping to find you returned. Instead we found Artemis fretful, fearful and threatening to leave and seek sanctuary somewhere safer – that was what she said – and Celia sent Samuel to ask Judyth to call, hoping she could persuade Artemis to stay.'

Questions were filling my head. I asked the most important first. 'Why on earth did she want to leave?'

Celia suppressed a sigh. 'Why do you think, Gabe? She's frightened. And she's right to be, for it seems highly likely that dark-bearded face at the window four nights ago was looking for her. Or perhaps for something she has, or knows, that will lead whoever it is to this extremely valuable cargo you just mentioned.'

'That's madness!' I protested. 'Why should she imagine she'd be safer out in the wilds on her own than under my roof with the protection of all of us?'

Celia tutted with impatience, Judyth sent me a pitying look, and Jonathan said quietly, 'Because if she left she could find another refuge that is not known to those who pursue her.'

I could only excuse my slow-wittedness by reminding myself I was very tired.

There were other things I wanted to ask them, but I did not think I was in a state to take in the responses. So I settled on something simple: 'What did you learn from consulting the globe?' I asked, looking from Celia to Jonathan. 'I have many maps, too, we could go through them.'

But Jonathan and Celia had exchanged a wry smile, and Celia said, 'We haven't looked at the globe yet.'

'Why ever not? It's there in its usual place, on the high shelf in my study!'

Celia had blushed slightly. 'Because you told me I must never ever even *think* of touching it unless you're there, and even then you must be the one to bring it down off the shelf!' she said in a angry rush.

I started to smile. 'Celia, when I said that I'd only just acquired the globe, I was totally fascinated by it, it was my treasured possession and you were eleven years old.' I almost added that she'd been a rather clumsy and very headstrong eleven-year-old, but it didn't seem wise to add fuel to that particular fire.

'Well, you were *very* insistent,' she muttered. She still looked cross.

I got up and went to fetch it.

We sat round the table, Celia, Jonathan, Judyth and I, and slowly I turned the big globe on its spindle.

It is a beautiful thing.

I purchased it in 1592, soon after I first sailed with Captain Ezekiel Colt on the *Falco* as his ship's surgeon. The *Falco* was nimble and fast, and her captain could have held his head up in the company of the Queen's most audacious sea dogs. Captain Zeke and his crew had money in their pockets – a great deal of money – and I spent a huge portion of my winnings on my globe. We were on a shore run in Greenwich, the Queen had paid a visit and met a notorious pirate (notorious largely because she was a woman) and it's quite possible I would not have parted with such a vast sum if I hadn't been drinking all day.

Not that I have ever regretted my purchase. The merchant who sold it to me said the globe was French, probably made around 1560, and the gores which depicted the land masses, the islands and the oceans of the earth were engraved on very thick paper. The script was a work of art, as were the sea dragons rearing their heads out of the waves and the wonderfully characterful image of Triton. The globe sat snugly in the cup of its wooden frame, firmly supported by six carved legs around the frame's circumference and one in the middle, under the earth's southern pole.

I put my spread fingers on the Atlantic Ocean and gently spun the world round. For a moment I was back in my past: the Caribbean, the Mediterranean, the Arabian Sea, those vast expanses that other men now explored with such enthusiastic relish while I lived my quiet country life in Devon . . .

Jonathan cleared his throat quietly, and I came back to the present.

'Here we are,' I began, stilling the gentle revolutions and putting a finger on England. 'Here the Channel emerges into the Atlantic Ocean, here the trade route runs down the west coast of Africa and on south to the Cape of Good Hope.' I followed the words with my finger. 'This is the Indian Ocean, and to the north is the Arabian Sea. Here is India, and beyond is Cathay, and further still the many islands that comprise the East Indies. On we go, following in reverse the great voyages of the circumnavigators – Magellan, Francis Drake – and here is the great continent that the Spanish claim as their own. Here

is Cape Horn, here the Caribbean Sea, where other nations
challenge that claim. Here is the Atlantic once more—' I
moved on swiftly now '—and here we are in Plymouth and
back where we began.'

'If we are right and Artemis's lover and his priceless cargo
are both missing,' Celia said, breaking the silence, 'then where
could he be? More importantly,' she went on before any of
us could reply, 'how are we – how is *anyone* to find him,
friend or foe, in half a world of sea, land and thousands upon
thousands of islands?'

'We have the map,' Judyth said. It was still spread out on
the table, and she touched it lightly. 'An island with a new
settlement, so called in Dutch, yet the title – The Island – is
written in English.'

It seemed none of us had any comment to make on that
little peculiarity. But then Jonathan spoke.

'The Spanish and the Portuguese were, of course, the first
to trade in the riches of the newly-discovered lands,' he said.
He had been staring at the globe but now he glanced up
apologetically, as if aware he was telling at least some of us
what we already knew. 'For some time they were unchallenged
in their ruthless division between them of the globe and its
treasures, although for as long as our country was at war with
Spain, our ships had the excuse they needed to plunder whatever cargo the Spanish brought back with them. But the King
made peace, after which our merchants accepted that they
would have to seek their treasures for themselves rather
than—' Diplomatically, he stopped.

'Rather than stealing them from the Spanish,' I finished for
him. 'Yes, Jonathan, I know. I would point out, however, that in
the case of those weighty cargoes of silver and gold from the
New World, the Spanish plundered the treasure in the first place
and had no more right to them than the men who took them.'

Jonathan gave me a wry smile. Diplomatically, he made no
comment. 'Both the English and the Dutch are now actively
and openly pursuing trade routes and contacts in the East
Indies,' he said instead, 'forming companies to—'

'The London Company and the VOC,' I interrupted. 'Henry
Sparre told me about them.'

Jonathan nodded. 'And so we find ourselves in competition with a new contender, as hungry as we are for dominance in the region,' he went on. 'Which brings us back to Edwyn Warham, the cargo, a missing ship that may either be called the *Leopard* or the *Luipaard*, and the curious matter of both English and Dutch writing on Gabe's map.'

It was a measure of how tired I was that it took a moment for the import of what he'd just said to penetrate.

'What's this about a ship called the *Leopard*?' I demanded. 'How did you find *that* out, and why haven't you told me before?'

Jonathan held up his hands. 'It's only an idea, Gabe,' he said. He glanced at Celia.

Celia nodded. 'I remembered that when Artemis was delirious, she muttered Edwyn's name,' she said. 'Well, she called him Ned. But she was also raving about a leopard, and I thought she was having the sort of tangled and frightening nightmare you have when you're feverish, because she said the word strangely and it sounded like *luipaard*. I was telling Jonathan and Judyth earlier, and Jonathan said could it perhaps have been the name of a ship.'

'A Dutch or an English ship,' Jonathan added, 'because—'

'*Luipaard* is Dutch for leopard,' I finished for him.

Judyth was staring into the fire, but both Jonathan and Celia were watching me eagerly, clearly expecting an enthusiastic response.

I didn't feel as excited as they were, but, again, it might have been fatigue.

'It could indeed,' I said, 'and we should bear the possibility in mind. Alternatively, it could just have been an imaginary leopard in a nightmare.'

There was a short and not very comfortable silence.

With an impatient sigh, Judyth pushed back her chair and stood up. 'I must go,' she said. 'I have a labouring woman to see before I make my way home, and I am of no use here since I have nothing to offer that might help us determine wherever it is that the map depicts.' She picked up her heavy cloak, swirling it around her shoulders.

I rose too. 'I'll see you on your way,' I said.

But she held up a hand. 'No need, Gabe, thank you. I shall look in on Artemis before I leave, and that is best done alone. Good evening, Celia, Jonathan.' She nodded to them, gave me a swift smile and was gone.

I did not like to think of her setting out alone in the cold and the fast-growing darkness. But there was no point in telling her: she would reply that it was her job, that she was almost more often out in the dark during the night than at home in her bed, and that it was none of my business anyway.

A part of me felt very sad.

I turned the globe again and, addressing Celia and Jonathan, said, 'Right, now let us examine the route from the East Indies back to England.'

If either of them noticed I'd spoken more sharply than the remark demanded, they were kind enough not to mention it.

Some time later, Celia rose, stretched and said 'I've had enough for tonight. I shall bid you both goodnight—' she gave Jonathan a very sweet smile'—and wish you good luck in your deliberations.' She briefly rested her hand on my shoulder. 'Don't stay up too late, Gabe, tomorrow will bring its own duties and responsibilities.'

By which she meant, I was quite sure, *don't keep Jonathan up too late.*

We heard her quick steps crossing the hall, and on the first few stairs. Then the house fell silent.

'We can do no more for now, Jonathan,' I said presently. 'Celia is right, you must go home and we should both get to bed.' He didn't reply. When I looked up at him, I saw that his expression was dark, his eyes unfocused. 'What is it?' I asked.

He stirred. 'Oh . . . I was quietly but fervently hoping and praying that whatever transpires in the East Indies as we and the Dutch stamp our mark does not lead to the brutality of what happened in the lands of the New World.' He sighed. 'But I fully expect it will.'

I waited, sensing there was more he wanted to say.

'You are aware of what I was doing in the final decade of the last century,' he said presently.

I did, but I let him remind me.

'I was recruited into Francis Walsingham's spy network,' he went on, 'where my job was to determine between what was true intelligence from what was blurted out by the desperate trying to stop the pain, or by the devious-minded trying to even an old score by falsely accusing another. But I was aware – far too aware – of what others around me were doing, and among other things I would far rather I did not know, I learned of the utter ruthlessness of men who not only saw it as their right to plunder the wealth of another race, but decided that, as men, women and children of a different faith, that other race must be wiped out.' He glanced up at me. 'What vicious horror we do in the name of God, Gabe. And what, I wonder, would be the reaction of the God who came to us as a man, and who told us that his greatest commandment was that we love one another?'

His voice had risen and, as belatedly he realized, he looked towards the door, frowning.

'Celia will not have heard,' I said gently. 'Her rooms are at the far end of the upstairs corridor.'

He nodded, not speaking.

After a moment I said, 'Jonathan, why do these things you just spoke of have to be private between us? I am honoured that you confide in me, but Celia is intelligent and no sheltered little miss. She would understand, I believe, that sometimes we are driven to do things we later regret.'

He didn't answer for some time. Then, rising to his feet, he said, 'I can't tell her of my past.' Gathering up his cloak, he added simply, 'I'm ashamed.'

ELEVEN

That night I dreamt I was back at sea. I was on a ship very like the *Falco*, and we were running fast under full sail. Now and again stretches of rocky shore appeared to starboard, materialising out of the mist and then melting back into invisibility; my dream self did not question why the strong wind did not blow away the mist. I was in my surgeon's cabin, trying to sew a pair of breeches together because one leg had become detached, and Theo was yelling at me to hurry up because the Queen was waiting at Greenwich and wanted to give me a ruby. Then, in the way of dreams, instantly I was up on deck, the wild sea roiling and foaming as the *Falco*'s prow carved through the huge waves, the ship responding in that devilish dance of hers that threw her crew and everything else not fastened down against bulkheads, down companionways and sometimes even over the side. I had my hands on the rail and I knew I was secure, my body instinctively moving with the *Falco* and not against her. I yelled aloud with the joy of it, and Captain Zeke gave me a mug of brandy and shouted right in my ear, 'Greenwich! Look!' and then I saw he was pointing not at the south shore of the Thames but at an enormous wave that was rising up straight ahead and, even as I stared at it in horror, manifesting itself into a vast sea dragon.

I woke up.

Moonlight penetrated my chamber, and it was very cold. I was still half in my dream, and the sea dragon was as vivid in that moment as the quiet domestic details of the room.

Three things occurred to me.

The first was that I hadn't been terrified by the storm or the sea dragon; on the contrary, I'd revelled in the danger and the sheer strangeness.

The second was that I understood just how much I grieved for the life at sea that I had lost.

The third was that I'd stood there on that violently bucking deck, the *Falco* beneath me unable to decide whether to pitch or to toss and maliciously deciding to do both, the horizon all but invisible through the sea spray, the rain and the mist, and I had felt wonderful. Not nauseous, not vertiginous; in fact, not the slightest suggestion of sickness.

It was only a dream, I told myself.

I had dreamed what I wanted to be the truth: that I could go to sea again and not suffer the terrible effects brought about by that head injury; that damaging, devastating blow that came about when a careless sailor let a rope slip so that a heavy wooden crate crashed into my head, just behind my right ear. My last experience of a sea voyage had been the nightmare of the homeward journey across the Atlantic, throwing up constantly and violently, my guts heaving out from my empty belly trickles of yellow bile that burned as it came up.

Reason would suggest, I thought, watching the very first of the daylight creeping into the room, that when I dreamed of being at sea, some sense of self-preservation would make it a very bad experience, just in case I was tempted to try again,

But it had been a glorious experience.

And I discovered how very much I wanted to try again.

I was up and about very early; I knew I wouldn't sleep again. The house was quiet, and when I went soft-footed down to the kitchen to poke up the fire and prepare a hot drink, Sallie had not yet risen.

I took my drink up to my study and spread out my nautical charts and land maps. I tracked the route a ship would take from the islands of the East Indies to England. I studied the island groups and the individual islands along the way. Celia was right: there were thousands of them. The idea of comparing the outline of the map Jacobus had given me with every single one of them was extremely daunting, and pointless, surely, in any case, since the map looked very much like the sort of sketch that someone draws for the benefit of another person who already knows where it is.

Nieuwe stad. A new settlement, the writing not to call it by its name but to indicate its location, at the mouth of that river, or stream, that went southwards inland and branched into several different channels.

It must be somewhere, I reasoned, known to both the Dutch and the English, and it was the Dutch who had established a settlement there. Since their merchants were as active in the islands of the East as we were, and their sailors just as busily sailing the length and breadth of the oceans between northwest Europe and the East Indies, that small fact was very little help whatsoever.

I needed to consult someone whose knowledge of that long journey was a great deal better than mine. My mind went straight to Jacobus Schuer, who undoubtedly knew more about this mystery island and the missing cargo than he'd been prepared to admit. I thought briefly of returning to his elegant house, forcing my way in past the dark-clad manservant with the watchful eyes and insisting that the old man revealed the extent of his involvement. But then I remembered how terrified he'd been; also that ominous manservant, still and silent as he stood before the door, his attention intently focused on his master as if alert for the first sign of distress.

Another more worrying possibility occurred to me.

I recalled the moment Jacobus had mentioned the island. And the manservant's instant hiss of *Master Schuer.* As if to silence him before he could utter some indiscreet remark?

I sat back in my chair. I could hear the sounds of the house beginning to stir: Celia's door opening, her sweet voice singing an old country song, Sallie, moving about in the kitchen.

Realizing that I was too impatient to go down and share a pleasant, sociable breakfast with my dear sister – that in fact I didn't want to talk to either her or Sallie just now – I hurried down the stairs, gathered up my bag, grabbed my heavy cloak from where I'd thrown it across the old sea chest and headed for the door. 'Going out, Sallie,' I called in the direction of the kitchen. Before she could respond – she'd only got as far as 'Good morning, Doctor' – I was out in the yard and Samuel had hastened into the stable to prepare my horse.

I went to see Theo.

Jarman would have reported back to him when we'd parted after our visit to Jacobus Schuer. He'd have described the map – which I had returned to its leather wallet and tucked inside my tunic – and he'd have told Theo what we'd found out. Theo might not be a merchant or a seaman, but he was a Devonian, a Plymouth man born and bred, and he was the coroner: not much that happened within his area of responsibility passed him by.

I realized as soon as I went into his office that he'd been expecting me.

'Jarman says you've got a map,' he said, not wasting time on a greeting. He raised his eyebrows in expectation.

I took it out and spread it on his desk.

'This man Jacobus Schuer was pale and shaking with fear,' he remarked, staring down at the sketch of the island.

'He was.'

'He didn't reveal how he'd come by this—' he waved a hand at the map '—except to say he was known to be a dealer in such curiosities?'

'Yes.'

'Yet you and Jarman reckon it was stolen from the body dumped in the cesspit channel?'

'Malin Piltbone. Yes. We know from Jarman's witness that he had such an item, in a wallet.' I put the wallet on his desk beside the map. 'It wasn't on the corpse, and we surmised that whoever killed him took it before they put the body in the ditch.'

'If that means he was killed for it, then why did his killer take it to Jacobus Schuer?'

'Er . . .'

He grinned. 'No, Jarman and I couldn't come up with an answer to that either.'

I was about to summarise everything that I had discussed with Jonathan, Celia and Judyth the previous evening but Theo got in before me.

'Jarman and I talked at length when he reported back here,' he began. 'Jarman's been quietly asking a few questions down on the quays, and he reckons there's something going on. People are more wary than usual, and it's not just that body in the cesspit that's got them wondering and muttering.'

'He didn't mention this to me yesterday,' I observed.

'Well, you know Jarman. He looks, he listens, he works out a possible sequence of events in the privacy of his own head, he tests it to see if it's viable, and if it is, sometimes he comes and tells me about it.'

He sounded rueful, if not annoyed, but I knew he valued his agent, even if he did follow his own path more than his superior would like. 'You're lucky to have him,' I muttered.

'I *know*,' Theo muttered back.

'So what did he find out?'

'Hasn't told me yet. He was here earlier, said he had something to check. Wait with me, if you have the time, and you can hear what he has to say.'

So I pulled up a chair and did as he suggested.

We were finishing off a platter of hot ham rolls when we heard the outer door open. Theo had observed that I appeared to be hungry – my stomach had been rumbling – and sent for refreshments. Not liking to embarrass me by having me eat alone, he joined in.

There was a tap on his office door and Jarman Hodge came in.

'Morning, Doctor T,' he said. 'Thought you'd be here.'

'What have you to tell us?' Theo demanded.

'There *is* something. People are talking, being watchful. I sought out that doxy you talked to, Doctor. The one that said she knew Malin Piltbone.'

'I remember,' I said. I remembered as well that I'd thought she was intelligent, and probably beautiful too, if you could ignore the tangled hair, the dirt and the missing teeth.

'Goes by the name of Kataryn, or more usually Kat,' Jarman went on. 'She's a sight too good for the life she leads, but she had a child her husband wouldn't accept was his, he slung her out, the child died and Kat ends up scraping a living on the quay.'

There was a short silence. I wanted to ask if there was not something better for the woman, but I held back. If there was, she'd no doubt be doing it.

'She's one of your sources, Jarman?' Theo asked. 'I seem to recall you've spoken of her before.'

'She is and I have,' Jarman replied. 'She's good. Doesn't miss much, and she's got a sharp mind. She says there was nothing about her–er–her encounter with Malin Piltbone that she didn't share with you, Doctor, but your interest in the man sparked hers, seemingly, and she's done some asking round.'

'I hope she hasn't aroused dangerous suspicion,' I said.

Jarman gave me a look. 'She can take care of herself, I reckon. None of them would last long if they couldn't.'

'Maybe I could—' I began.

But Theo said quite sharply, 'Go on, Jarman.'

'You're not the only man who's been trying to find out about this Piltbone,' Jarman said after a moment. 'There's a big man with a black beard and a mean look about him for one, and he's been trying to frighten folk into revealing what they know, which isn't making him any too popular.'

'Know about what?' Theo demanded.

'Malin Piltbone,' Jarman replied. 'He's aware the man's dead, and he wants to know where the body is and what happened to the clothes and the effects.'

'He's after the map,' Theo and I said together.

Jarman grinned. 'Seems he's not too familiar with the ways of coroners, and hasn't any experience of a body being tucked away in some crypt or cellar till the cause of death's been determined, and the corpse's identity as well, if that proves possible.'

'Where does this large bearded man think Piltbone's body is?' Theo asked.

Jarman shrugged dismissively. 'He's been making a nuisance of himself round the local churches, I'm told. There's probably one or two clergymen mounting a watch in case he comes by in the night and starts digging up recent burials.'

I was barely listening. I was thinking about the big man

with the black beard. Who quite clearly had not just been doing the round of the churches, and who obviously was not as dumb as Jarman believed . . .

Somehow he knew about Artemis Brownyng. Knew she had been in Plymouth, knew – or so it must surely be – that she had been in the river, pulled out again and taken away somewhere to be tended and nursed back to health.

My house.

'He's my intruder,' I said, interrupting Jarman. 'The face at the window, five nights back. I *told* you, Theo!' I added angrily when he made no comment.

'You saw a pale face with a dark, heavy beard,' he said. 'Yes, I grant you it could have been the man after Piltbone's wallet and map, but there are any number of other men with black beards.'

After a tense and irritable pause, diplomatically Jarman resumed his account. 'He's not the only interested party. Now Kat didn't see this herself, mind, she heard it from one of her–from a man she knows. There's two foreigners been spotted doing the round of the quayside taverns, and the word is they're Hollanders. Somewhat alike to look at, both of them being tall, long-limbed, fair-skinned, light eyes, sombrely clad in good quality garments. Well, I say two, but seemingly that's now become one.' In case Theo or I had missed the point, he added, 'So, it appears that to start with, we had two pairs of colleagues, partners, what have you, the two Hollanders and this Piltbone and the bearded man. They're in the same town, haunting the quays, and one pair possess something the other pair want very badly. One man gets murdered, his corpse is robbed, and then the very next day—'

'One of the other pair is beheaded!' I exclaimed. 'It *must* be so! The man was just as you described, Jarman, and . . .'

The black-bearded man hard on Malin Piltbone's trail had peered in through my window. The body of the decapitated Dutchman had been found at my gates.

The surviving man of each of these pairs of conspirators knew about Artemis Brownyng and had found their way to my house.

And it seemed highly probable that both of them would kill to get what they wanted; they had already done so.

I wanted to leap up and race home to defend my household. I wanted to turn Rosewyke into a fortress and keep my sister, my servants and my uninvited guest safe from ruthless strangers. I resisted the urge, although it wasn't easy. I argued with myself, reasoning that it was daylight, the house had strong doors and windows, that Samuel and Tock were keeping the gates barred and were already on the alert for strangers.

My time was better spent working out where the threat came from. Why it was that helping a secretive stranger by taking her into my house had brought an unsuspected danger to us all.

Theo and Jarman were muttering about something, but I ignored them. I had come to Theo's office this morning for a specific purpose, and, recalling belatedly what it was, I said, 'There's a missing ship loaded with a very valuable cargo at the bottom of it all, and I don't believe we are going to make any significant progress in this dark business until we find out where the ship has gone, what she's carrying, who the cargo belongs to and who is trying to appropriate it.'

They were both looking at me. Theo was scowling, Jarman was trying not to smile.

'I have no idea where you've been these past few minutes, Gabe,' Theo said – and now he too was grinning – 'but that's exactly what we've just been saying.'

The realization that I had just missed the entire exchange was more than a little embarrassing. Thinking swiftly, I said, 'Yes, my mind was indeed absent. I was recalling that my purpose this morning was to seek out someone familiar with the new trade route to the eastern islands. Someone other than Jacobus Schuer, who is too terrified to be of any use as regards reliable information.'

Theo and Jarman were watching me, clearly waiting for me to go on.

'And I–er–I haven't come up with anyone,' I finished lamely.

Jarman frowned. 'But you know Gilbert Baynton, surely?'

'Gilbert Baynton?' Theo echoed.

'Rich merchant, very fine house in one of the streets up behind the quay where those with enough money live above the stink and the bustle.' Jarman shot a glance at me. 'Your sister knows his daughter.'

Yes. Celia had renewed her friendship with Sidony Baynton – or Scrope, for that was her married name, although she was now a widow – back in the autumn[4], although it had been largely because Celia wanted a favour from her.

'I know Gilbert Baynton, of course,' I said. 'But I thought he dealt in Spanish wines?'

'He does,' Jarman agreed. 'He is not a man to miss a new opportunity, though, and like as not he spotted the possibilities of trade with the islands of the Eastern Seas quick as anyone. He's already brought in a cargo of pepper on a ship belonging to someone else, and the word is he has a ship making the journey right now. This time,' he added, lowering his voice, 'it's one of his own vessels, and when she returns she'll be filled with goods that are Master Baynton's alone.' He paused, his expression thoughtful. 'He'll make a fortune,' he said softly. He grinned. 'Another fortune.'

Theo leaned back in his chair, regarding his agent and shaking his head. 'How in heaven's name do you do it, Hodge?' he demanded. 'How do you find out all these things? Are you able to make yourself invisible, so that you creep into libraries and hidden rooms and dark corners in taprooms, listening to men who believe they are speaking their secrets in private?'

'I keep my eyes and ears open,' Jarman said modestly. 'And people talk to me.'

I met Theo's bright eyes, and said softly. 'I believe, Master Coroner, that is the best answer we shall get.'

But I was thinking about Theo's suggestion that Jarman made himself invisible, because, in a way, that was precisely what he did. He was slim, of medium height, with mid-brown hair, unremarkable hazel eyes, clean-shaven, plainly dressed, modest and quiet in his manner. To those who did not know

<hr>

[4] see Magic in the Weave

him, he was unassuming and self-effacing. Only those who did were aware of the razor-sharp brain perpetually fed by very sharp ears and ever-observant eyes.

'. . . you'll be away to visit Master Baynton, Gabe?'

Theo had been addressing me, and once again I'd been too deep in my own thoughts to hear.

I shot to my feet. 'Yes, right away,' I said briskly.

And before I had caught up with myself, I was out of Theo's office and on my way down to Plymouth.

I was admitted to Gilbert Baynton's house by his tall and taciturn manservant Phillips. Recognizing me, he greeted me courteously and led me through to a room at the rear of the large central hall. To judge by its furniture and fittings, this was the master's preserve: generous-sized dark oak table, leather-seated chair with beautifully-carved arms that looked old enough, costly enough and vast enough to have welcomed the buttocks of Henry VIII, shelves of fine books, a globe twice the size and probably four or five times the value of mine. A window gave on to the rear of the house, affording a fine view over rooftops and chimneys to the bustling quayside and the sea below.

Gilbert Baynton was swift to arrive, and he closed the heavy door firmly behind him, shutting out the rapidly-increasing sound of a small child having a major tantrum, at least two women trying to reason with him and a third screaming almost as loudly as the child.

He leaned against the door, breathed out audibly and said, 'Good morning, Doctor Taverner.'

I returned the greeting, then, nodding towards the source of the noise, said, 'Oh, dear.'

He moved round to sit behind his desk, pulling up a chair for me. 'Please, sit down,' he muttered. 'Yes. My grandson objects to having his boots put on, which means he will not imminently be taken out for his walk, which means my household must endure that hellish noise a little longer.'

'I can barely hear it with the door closed,' I said diplomatic-ally. 'Is Sidony well?'

'She is, thank you, although I wish she would—'

But, either out of loyalty or love, he did not allow himself to continue.

His daughter Sidony had married young and been widowed only two or three years later, leaving her with her little boy, Myles. According to Celia, Sidony had never felt deeply for her late husband and had married him in a fit of pique at her father's mild suggestion that perhaps it would be wise to wait a year or two before taking on the responsibilities of marriage and her own household. Moreover, bringing up a child as a sole parent did not present the extreme difficulties it would for a woman of a different station for, as soon as the poor young husband was dead, Sidony had moved back into her father's home and demanded a nurse for her child and a personal maid for herself, enabling her to revert wholeheartedly to the giddy and facile pursuits she had enjoyed as a young single woman.

I felt sorry for Master Baynton, his peaceful existence and the calm of his elegant house invaded by a self-centred daughter and an over-indulged little boy who seemed to have a *very* loud voice.

Gilbert Baynton picked up a small brass bell and rang it, and when Phillips reappeared, requested refreshments. When the door had closed again, he turned to me and said, 'What can I do for you, Doctor?'

So I told him. About the missing ship, her cargo, the indications that she had been on a voyage to the East Indies, and about the interest that several mysterious men appeared to be taking in the matter.

I did not mention Artemis Brownyng, her presence in my house or her absent lover. Neither did I tell him about the two dead men.

He did not speak for some moments after I had finished. Phillips came in with a tray, a glass decanter, two glasses and a platter of small savoury biscuits, and when he had gone Baynton said, 'You have come to consult me, I imagine, because you are aware of my interests in the islands of the Eastern Sea.'

It wasn't a question, so I merely nodded my agreement.

'And what is the reason for your interest?'

I had thought him a sophisticated, mannerly man, courteous,

considerate, self-effacing. Now, looking at the set of his jaw and the hardness in his light eyes, I recognized the calibre of the man behind that polite and kindly mask. And I understood how he had made so much money.

'Two men have been killed,' I said bluntly. I had hoped it wouldn't be necessary, but I had reckoned without Master Baynton's true nature. 'Enquiries I have made lead me to believe the missing ship is on her way home from the East.'

'She set out from Plymouth?' he asked sharply.

I shrugged. 'It appears so. And in addition there is this.' I took out the wallet, removed the map and handed it to him.

He unfolded it, smoothed it and studied it.

Presently he looked up and said, 'Do you expect me to tell you where this is?'

'There is very little to distinguish it,' I replied. 'Does it yield any clue, to a man such as you who is, I am sure, becoming familiar with the route to the East?'

He smiled, clearly recognizing the flattery but opting not to comment on it. 'Words in both English and Dutch,' he mused. 'A new settlement, on an inlet between two headlands, one to the northeast and one to the southwest. And the single word, *chaw*.' He pushed the map back towards me.

'You have no idea where it might be?'

He thought for a while. Then he said, 'As I am sure I need not tell a former ship's surgeon such as yourself, Doctor Taverner, as soon as ships discover a new route to somewhere deemed advantageous for trade—' he smiled faintly '—their masters look out for likely ports along the way where they may re-provision, take on water and effect repairs.' He got up, walked to the side board on which his globe stood and beckoned me over.

'Here are the islands of the Eastern Seas: the Molucca Islands, the Philippines, Neira and the other islands of the Banda Sea.' He pointed. 'Here is Ternate, where Francis Drake procured a cargo of cloves, and here is Java, where he also called. Portuguese possessions, in Drake's time.' He glanced at me. 'But now matters are less . . . certain.'

'Both ourselves and the Dutch seek a share in this trade,' I said.

'We seek it, and we are finding it,' he replied curtly. 'The Company of Merchants of London have already dispatched two voyages to the islands, although they met with limited success.'

'And the Dutch fare better?' I asked.

'They believe they are the natural successors to the Portuguese,' he replied. 'Time, however, will tell.'

I wanted to pursue the point, but before I could he said, 'Now, let us say that this little island of yours is visited by both English and Dutch ships. It could be here, here, here, or here—' in rapid succession he pointed to Ceylon, two ports on the east coast of Africa, the Cape of Good Hope '—but the settlements in these places are well-established, and a map depicting them would surely be more detailed . . .'

He paused, a hand to his face, frowning.

Then he pointed to a tiny speck of land barely visible off the southwest coast of Africa, perhaps a quarter of the way across the Atlantic Sea.

'That,' he said softly, 'is a possible location. It was discovered in the early 1500s, by the Portuguese, of course—' he smiled briefly '—and they recognized straight away how useful it would be for ships returning from the East. They tried to keep it to themselves, but it was an impossible secret to guard, given that soon both we and the Dutch were also using the sea route. They carried out some planting – fruit trees and the like – and deposited sheep and goats, but there was no real attempt at settlement, and they constructed no defences. The Dutch knew of it, an Englishman named Cavendish came across it in the late 1580s, and Drake himself visited on his way home.' He paused, shooting a quick glance at me. 'And a ship called the *Ascension*, which was part of the Company of Merchants's first fleet, called there a couple of years ago, allowing the Company to mark its claim. In their own minds, anyway,' he added in a murmur.

I stared at the spot he had indicated. I had sailed those southern Atlantic waters; for a few moments I was back in my own past, heading south, on the deck of a ship whose full sails buffeted above me, whose timbers creaked as she rode the huge waves. There off to port was the reddish-brown smudge that marked the distant coat of Africa . . .

The sudden stab of longing for the life I had once led struck like a blade.

With some effort, I brought myself back to the present.

I turned to Master Baynton. 'Does this island have a name?'

And he said, 'They call it St Helena.'

TWELVE

I left Gilbert Baynton's house with my head aflame with facts, thoughts and possibilities that totally failed to coalesce into a picture that made any sense.

Master Baynton had suggested a location for the mystery island on Malin Piltbone's map. I wondered fleetingly why he had been so helpful – although there was no reason why he shouldn't have been – and also how much faith to put in what he'd told me. I reminded myself that he was a merchant; one who had just begun trading with the islands of the far Eastern Seas. He ought, then, to be a reliable source of information . . . Jarman had mentioned a cargo of pepper – my thoughts rambled on – and revealed that Master Baynton had his own ship out on the high seas, and when she returned laden with spices – *if* she did, for there was no guarantee – then no doubt the profits would be vast.

I wondered if Jarman's information went as far as knowing the name of Gilbert Baynton's ship. No, I thought, for if Jarman knew it he'd have told us.

Assuming, however, that this vessel had sailed from Plymouth, then her name was perhaps something I could find out for myself. So I turned Hal's head down one of the narrow streets leading towards the sea, and presently was leaving him in the care of the ostler who'd seen to him before.

Ships lined the quay, many of them ocean-going, all of them thrumming with activity. Some of them were familiar, and I was on the point of approaching one – a tub of a boat which traded up and down the coast, as far as Bristol to the north and Portsmouth along the south coast – when, further along and at the end of the line, I spotted a vessel I knew a great deal better.

She was a familiar sight in Plymouth, calling in as she did at frequent if irregular intervals over the years. She had been built in the mid 1570s, one of the new type of sleek ships which were smaller and faster than the huge, lumbering warships of Henry VIII's day. She was one of a class known as race-built galleons whose distinguishing feature was their greatly reduced upperworks, which gave them an unusually low profile shaped like the crescent moon. But smaller did not mean less formidable: of her 700-ton displacement, more than thirty tons was taken up by her weapons. Another design innovation was the heavy artillery mounted in her bows, so that, unlike her predecessors, she could fire straight ahead.

She was a weapon; built to be dangerous and fast, every other consideration sacrificed to increase her deadly potential. The convenience of her crew was of no account at all, which was no more than an ordinary seaman in the Queen's navy expected. When it came to those of the ship's company whose primary role was other than sailing her or firing her guns, the facilities provided by this particular race-built galleon left almost everything to be desired.

Her name was the *Nightbird*, and she was the first ship I sailed on when I signed up in 1584. To begin with I served in the ranks of the ordinary seamen, and as one of the younger ones it was tough. But a practical fighting force is ever on the lookout for particular talents and skills, for it is far from efficient to waste a man skilled at navigation to swab the decks, or set one who can sew a torn sail with his eyes shut in a heavy sea to scraping vegetables. I had long been fascinated by blades; as a boy I had spent hours with my blacksmith grandfather Ralfe, watching him while he transmuted metal with fire and ground blades to a lethal sharpness on his granite. Grandfather Ralfe was renowned for his skill, and all the barber surgeons and the sawbones of the area came to him; as he worked he taught, and I learned how to take a blunted and horribly stained knife, axe or saw and restore it to clean, precise, ruthless efficiency. Not long after I joined the *Nightbird*'s company, my ability was spotted, the ship's captain Gidley Furneaux decided he'd make use of it, and I was put to working with the ship's surgeon.

Mark Snell was a tough man; a hard taskmaster who never, ever accepted second best. He saw more in me than I was aware I had, and he made up his mind to turn me from the underling who looked after his medical instruments into his apprentice. Whether I liked it or not.

At first I loathed the whole process. The nearest I came to performing an amputation was holding down the victim while Mark Snell worked, and that was more than close enough. When the time came for me to wield the blade, I was so frightened, so nauseous, that I didn't think I could stand up. Snell told me brusquely that I had no choice, it was an order. Then, as I stood with the knife in my shaky hand, he said quietly right in my ear, 'Don't keep the poor bugger waiting. You and I both know you can do it. Get to it.'

It's amazing what a determined man can do on a wooden leg; my first amputation survived to spend a further decade in the Queen's service, and whenever our paths crossed he always stood me a drink and thanked me.

My thoughts so deep in the past, I had wandered the length of the quay and now I stood looking up at the *Nightbird*. A man was standing at the rail looking down at me, and I called out a greeting. He responded courteously but guardedly, so I said, 'Is Captain Furneaux on board?'

'Who wants to know?'

'Gabriel Taverner. I was once of the ship's company.'

I hadn't expected an open-armed greeting, for the *Nightbird* was a warship and you can't just stroll up and board her when the mood takes you. The man stared at me for a while longer – he was a decade or so younger than me, and I didn't recognize him – then said curtly, 'Wait there.'

I did not wait long. It was not he, however, who presently came thundering down the plank to vigorously shake my hand and slap me on the back in delight but another, older man, his skin tanned, stretched and deeply lined, his eyes the bluer for the contrast, his hair still thick and unruly but now pure white.

'Good old Gabriel Taverner!' he yelled cheerfully, landing another hard slap. 'Come up, we'll share a tot or two.'

Accepting that the tot or two would be very generous and probably extend to several more, I quietly abandoned my plans for the rest of the day and accompanied Gidley Furneaux to his cabin.

*   *   *

Although I had often seen the *Nightbird* in Plymouth and more than once had a drink with her officers, this was the first time Captain Furneaux and I had sat down together. He gave me a sketchy outline of what the *Nightbird* had been doing, saying merely that she'd been on the eastern run and describing the delights of some of the more notorious ports, and I knew better than to press for details. Then he asked me what I'd been up to.

I told him about serving on the old *Mandragora* with the legendary Captain Pemberthy, under whose command I'd first killed a man and had the heavy gold coin I'd been awarded as my prize made into the earring I still wear; about the *Pandion*, where I'd first been ship's surgeon in my own right; about voyages to the Caribbean, the Mediterranean, the Indian Ocean, the south Atlantic and on into the bitter cold of the far, icy regions. About Captain Ezekiel Cole and the *Falco;* and, finally, about the accident that had turned me from a sailor to a land-bound country physician.

When I finished, Captain Furneaux silently poured me another tot.

Presently he said with what I thought sounded like false brightness, 'So, a good life, is it, that of a country doctor?'

'It is.'

I should have said more. Should have enthused about the house that I have grown to love, my loyal household, my good friends the coroner and the vicar; my beloved sister; Judyth; and I was angry with myself that I didn't. But just at that moment, sitting with Gidley Furneaux in his cabin, hearing the sounds of shipboard life all around me, smelling the familiar smells, intensely aware of the lively sea slapping against the *Nightbird*'s hull and the gentle rocking as she responded to the ceaseless motion, I couldn't.

I thought Captain Furneaux probably understood.

He did not speak for a while, then said, 'What brings you to seek me out, Gabriel?'

It took me some moments to recall.

I had gone to the quay with the intention of finding out the name of Gilbert Baynton's ship. Now – admittedly after quite a lot of brandy – I couldn't really recall why it had seemed so important. I sat there in Gidley Furneaux's cabin, twisting my glass to and fro, and I remembered something that Celia had told me last night.

Without pausing to think, I heard myself say, 'Do you know of a ship called the *Leopard*?'

He repeated the name under his breath, then shook his head. 'One of ours?'

'No, a cargo ship. If, that is, such a ship exists. Possibly English, possibly Dutch.'

'Then she'd be the *Luipaard*,' the captain said pedantically.

'It's probable that she sailed from here, and she may have been on the route from the Eastern Seas—' I ignored the interruption '—and have put in at St Helena.'

He shook his head again. 'I've been that way recently, like I said. I don't know of this *Leopard*, though. It's likely she'll have reprovisioned at St Helena if she was on the way home from the East. I'm told many of them do, and we encounter merchantmen who speak favourably of the place. What's your interest?'

But instead of answering, I asked another question. 'I've been speaking to a merchant here in Plymouth by the name of Gilbert Baynton. Seems he too has a cargo of goods on its way home from the East. D'you know of the ship?'

It was unlikely that he would, and yet again he shook his head. 'Go and ask Ashley Bryme,' he said. 'It's his job to know the ships that put in to his harbour.'

Which, of course, I already knew; Ashley Bryme is the harbourmaster.

I could sense that the captain was curious as to why I had asked about the two ships. I did not want to deflect his questions or lie to him, so I got up to go and he accompanied me back to where the gangplank led down to the quay.

As we shook hands I heard myself, 'Is it far, to St Helena?'

He grinned. 'Six weeks, a couple of months, maybe more, maybe less. Why? Want to pay a call?'

I very nearly said yes.

I made my way to the succession of taverns that run in an almost unbroken line behind the quay to order some food. I had taken too much drink on an almost-empty stomach, and I needed to think. I was heading for one I have frequented before when I spotted Ashley Bryme barging his way into one a little further along. It was not one I knew, largely because it was usually crowded and eating there would take too long for a doctor in a hurry. As I pushed in among the throng in the harbourmaster's wake, the smell of the food on offer was already making my mouth water; this tavern was busy for a very good reason.

I eased my way in beside Bryme as he waited to shout his order. I introduced myself, then added, 'I would like to ask you some questions, Master Bryme. If I pay for your meal and we eat together, will you indulge me?'

He was watching me with round brown eyes, a slight smile on his fleshy face. He was a short man, and the size of his belly suggested a fortuitous fondness for food that had made my offer one he was more likely to accept than refuse.

'By all means, Doctor Taverner,' he replied. And he rubbed his hands together in anticipation.

We found a place to sit at one end of a long table, facing each other across it. I ate my food quickly; it was good, but I didn't give it the appreciation it deserved. I quickly discovered two things: that it wasn't a question of persuading the harbourmaster to talk but rather of getting him to stop so that I could ask my questions, and that he talked with his mouth full.

He was deep into an account of the intricacies of his job, just embarking on a rant at how people took his diligence for granted and how would they like it if they had to manage without him, *that'd* soon stop men asking what he did all day, when he paused to take a gulp of ale. I seized my chance and said, 'I'm trying to discover the movements of two ships, the first a trading vessel belonging to Master Baynton and the second a ship that I believe was either called the *Leopard* or the *Luipaard*. Have you come across them?'

He actually stopped eating. He sat quite still, mouth open, knife spiking a large piece of turnip dripping gravy on to his platter, and I thought I saw several expressions flit across his face. Then, recovering, he shoved the turnip into his mouth and began rapidly chewing it. 'I *do* know the name of Gilbert Baynton's ship,' he mumbled through the food, 'although you'll need to convince me why I should share it with you.' He gave me a knowing grin. 'Master Baynton's bringing in an entire cargo of spices this time,' he went on, 'or that's what the word is, and likely as not he'll make the same success with pepper and that as he's always done with his Spanish wines. Now don't go expecting me to tell you any more, because for one I've no more to tell and for two, Master Baynton likes his private affairs to *stay* private and not be gossiped about by the likes of us.' He gave me a smug look.

'And the *Leopard*?' I persisted.

He bent over his platter, slicing into a piece of meat and dunking it in a pool of gravy. 'Never heard of her,' he muttered.

And as I watched, his florid face paled and I had the impression he was very scared.

He'd probably told the approximate truth in everything else he'd told me, but as I watched him, taking in the sudden and very evident lessening in his enthusiasm for his meal and the fact that all at once he was evading my eyes, I knew the last statement was a lie.

I was thinking hard as I fetched Hal and set off for Rosewyke. I was slightly surprised that the daylight was already beginning to fade; I'd clearly spent considerably longer with Gidley Furneaux and Ashley Bryme than I realized.

As we rode out of the town and on to the quiet paths along the Tamar and then the Tavy, the sharp, cold air quickly cleared my head and something occurred to me that I ought to have thought of before.

Someone had killed Malin Piltbone and taken the wallet containing the map out of his secret pocket. If, as seemed likely, the man had been murdered purely so that his killer could acquire the map, why then had he taken it to Jacobus Schuer? For money? But how much money would that rough and not very informative sketch have been worth? Jacobus Schuer was, on his own admission, an antiquary, but the little map wasn't old, nor did it give much away.

I realized belatedly that I ought to have asked Schuer how much he paid for it. It was too late to turn back and bang on his door now, and anyway I was tired.

Why else might the killer have left the map with Jacobus Schuer?

To hide it, perhaps? Could the killer have come up with Jacobus's house as a safe place to conceal it from other interested parties? And then Jacobus, greatly alarmed at the escalating violence – I saw again that decapitated body – had decided he'd much rather the map did not remain in his possession and passed it on like a hot stone to me.

I rode on, so deep in my own thoughts as the gloom of approaching evening settled around me that it wasn't until I was almost home that I realized someone was on the road behind me.

The tall man had been following the doctor and his long-maned black horse for much of the day. To the small village to the northwest of Plymouth, then on into the port, almost losing him when he slipped into a tavern yard to leave his horse in the stable lad's care, but managing to pick up the trail again and track him to the elegant house in the quiet street above the quay. A long wait, then the big man had been on the move once more, all the way to the far end of the quay, where he went on board a ship of the navy and did not emerge for some time, to make his way to a tavern and eat a substantial platter of food.

But he hadn't been alone: he'd sat at a table in the far corner with the fat harbourmaster, their heads close together as they bent to their food. The tavern had been thronged with people, and it hadn't been hard to weasel his way through the crowd and stand close enough to pick up a word or two of that muttered conversation.

He had little interest in this Master Baynton that the big man asked about, merely noting that whatever he was about, he was one more of the growing band of wealthy merchants investing increasingly large sums in the new trade with the islands of the East.

But then the big man had mentioned the *Leopard*.

The word had hit like a fist.

When, at last, the big man had left the tavern, fetched his horse and set off on the road for home, there had been no option but to follow him. And now here he was, tired, hungry, very cold, and increasingly tempted to put heels to his chestnut mare, close the gap between them and catch up to his quarry, then demand to know what he was up to, at knife point if necessary.

He fought the urge and held back.

He knew where they were bound. He had been to the house called Rosewyke before. He had observed from the shadows; this silent, still watching was a skill perfected over the years, and he thought his presence had not been noticed sufficiently to make anybody wonder who he was and what he was up to. There had been a moment yesterday when the nondescript fellow riding back with the big man had turned and looked straight at the spot where the tall man stood under the trees, but nothing came of it.

The weary ride went on. The tall man tried to keep himself alert by reviewing what he had found out. The big man was a doctor, he was called Gabriel Taverner, and somehow – the tall man did not yet know how – it had happened that this Taverner had Artemis Brownyng in his house, where it seemed she was being so carefully protected that she might as well be in a castle.

He made a soft sound of frustration, and the chestnut mare cocked an ear. He muttered some soothing words.

The problem was – he resumed his line of thought – this doctor was all of a sudden ever-present. The tall man had managed to tell himself that the secret was so well-buried that there was no danger of anyone uncovering it, even an over-inquisitive doctor. But then the damned man had mentioned the *Leopard*.

Admittedly the fat harbourmaster had said he'd never heard of her. But the tall man could clearly see that he was both lying and extremely frightened, and he was quite sure this observant Taverner had seen it too.

'The *Luipaard* is safe,' the tall man whispered aloud. Dear God, she *must* be safe; he said a swift prayer. Ned was clever.

He was also slippery, and so greedy for the vast sums they stood to gain if all went according to plan that he surely wasn't going to take any risks; he'd even promised, on a solemn oath, not to reveal anything to Artemis . . .

But supposing he had done? Supposing, in the face of her distress as he set off all those months ago, he had tried to comfort her by telling her more than he should have done?

And God alone knew what would happen if he really had, and if that stern and forceful man in his island fastness who had set up, masterminded and financed this whole scheme found out . . .

Abruptly the tall man arrested that thought. There was no way he could know for sure, and the more he dwelt on it, the more he began to believe Edwyn had broken his oath.

Very deliberately, he turned his mind to the facts he did know.

The map was gone.

Ned said that had to happen, *must* happen; it was a vital part of the plan. It had been safely placed in Malin Piltbone's keeping. Not that Piltbone had known it was a deliberate move, a plant; or at least, the tall man hoped not. Then the two Dutchmen had followed him, attacked him, Pieter Rutger had hit him too hard on the temple and Piltbone had died. Rutger and his companion had extracted the map in its wallet from Piltbone's inner pocket, then they had shoved nutmegs down his throat and rolled him into the stinking filth of the gutter that led to the cesspit at the far end of the row of taverns.

The tall man wondered, to begin with, why they had done all that. Why they had not left him in the entrance to the dark little tunnel where he had breathed his last. His death would have looked like the conclusion of one more tavern brawl, surely?

Then it had occurred to him that they did what they did to confuse whoever turned up to investigate. To make it look not like a fight – a struggle over something Piltbone had that someone else wanted – but a killing that somehow made a point; that said, *This man did a great wrong and thus he is repaid.*

It was that morning when the investigators turned up that the tall man had first seen the doctor, and the large man in the black formal robe who he later understood to be the coroner.

But then – the tall man's racing thoughts flew on – Piltbone had not been alone; the Company would not have risked sending just the one agent to do the job. Piltbone had been accompanied by a brutal, ruthless bastard called Rogeus Kytson. The nature of the man showed in the cold, dead eyes. The heavy black beard that hid the lower half of his pale oval of a face concealed the harsh twist of his thin mouth, but those who knew him were in no doubt at all what he was capable of. And, possibly in revenge for the death of Malin Piltbone, Kytson had slaughtered Pieter Rutger.

Cut his head off.

And the tall man, watching, had not expected the sudden swift, terrible violence. Despite his best efforts – he had never run so hard – he had been too far away to intervene. He had watched Kytson ride away and then gone to kneel over the decapitated body.

Poor Pieter. They'd been kinsmen, although not close kin, and also friends.

He had said a prayer, in their own tongue.

He hoped Pieter's soul had lingered long enough to know.

And he'd been back in his place of concealment when the priest on the bay cob rode up.

He had been deep in his own thoughts, and, jerking back into the present, he realized that the doctor had almost reached the track that branched off the road and was about to enter his own property. Just for a moment he stopped.

He's sensed my presence, the tall man thought.

By good fortune he was in a patch of deep shadow, and gently he drew the chestnut mare to a halt. Movement caught the eye, he was well aware, and if he and the horse stayed absolutely still, they probably would not be seen.

They waited.

Then the big man turned back towards his house and kicked his horse into a trot and then a canter for the final leg of the journey.

The man on the chestnut murmured some quiet words, and

his horse's ears twitched in response. Taverner looked tired, he thought. It must be good, he reflected bitterly, to anticipate the comforts of home: the groom and the simple-minded man coming to greet him and take away the black horse, the house-keeper with her platter of food and her jug of warmed, spiced ale ready waiting, the bright-eyed, pretty sister.

And the woman hidden away in some inner room behind the heavy shutters and the curtains.

THIRTEEN

I stopped just before the entrance to the Rosewyke track.
There had definitely been someone there, following me
on the road. I'd been deep in my thoughts, and the presence
of a pursuer had barely registered. While there was nothing
suspicious about a fellow traveller on the more well-frequented
stretches, however, having someone close behind me as I
reached the very gates of my home was more disturbing.

I turned. Gazed back down the road. The light was fading,
and although most of the track was still perfectly visible, there
was a stand of fir trees beside the place where it bent in a
gentle curve, and they cast a deep shadow.

I waited. Nothing moved. Nobody called out.

Losing patience, I kicked Hal into motion and cantered up
the track to the house.

Once again, both Jonathan's and Judyth's horses were in my
stables.

'They might just as well move in,' I muttered irritably, but
very quickly I regretted the moment of bad temper. Judyth
was there to tend her patient; Jonathan, no doubt, had found
time in his busy schedule to return to the mystery that was
preoccupying my household and me. I should be grateful to
them. I *was* grateful to them. It wasn't their fault that I was
tired, hungry, perpetually anxious about the accumulating
number of dangers, real and imaginary, that threatened my
household, and increasingly frustrated at my inability to make
progress . . .

Sallie gave me a quick, sympathetic glance as I stomped
into the kitchen. 'Oh, dear,' she murmured. 'Bad day, Doctor?'

'Not great, Sallie,' I replied, trying to summon a smile.

'You're earlier this evening,' she went on, busy at the hearth,
'and in time to eat with the others. It's not ready yet, mind,'
she added.

'Thank you, Sallie.' I went across to her and gave her a hug, which made her blush and mutter 'Get away with you, you'll have the pan over!'

Crossing the hall, I heard Judyth's voice, speaking softly. I went along the short passage to the little parlour, pausing at the half-open door. Artemis was out of bed, sitting on the edge of it and fully dressed in clean clothes. Judyth crouched in front of her, holding both her hands, and I thought from her anxious and slightly stern look that she was trying to impart something of weight.

Artemis looked up and spotted me, and some change in her expression alerted Judyth. Turning, she saw me in the doorway, frowned slightly and shook her head. Then she returned her full attention to her patient.

As she should, I told myself as I walked away. But all the same, it felt uncomfortably like a dismissal.

I went towards the library, but Sallie must have heard my footsteps because she emerged from the kitchen and said, 'They're not there, Doctor, they're up in your study.'

Fighting the childish protest that they were all making themselves so thoroughly at home in my house and managing so well without me that I might as well not be there, I climbed heavily up the stairs.

Celia and Jonathan sat side by side at my desk, heads together, so intent on what they were doing, so absolutely focused on each other, that when I coughed quietly to alert them to my presence, Jonathan jumped and Celia flushed.

'They were all on your desk, quite a lot of them still lying open!' Celia said. 'We're being very careful, and . . .' She stopped, eyeing me nervously.

Jonathan had stood up, and in doing so had managed to move half a pace away from my sister. 'I apologize for our presence in your study, Gabe,' he said quietly. 'We did not think you would mind.'

'Oh, sit down, Jonathan!' I said. 'Of course I don't mind. What is it you're being so careful with, Celia? Oh, I see.'

My charts and maps still lay on the desk from where I'd been looking at them this morning.

I sensed there might soon be a further round of apologies,

so I pulled up a stool, sat down next to Celia and said in what I hoped sounded a genuinely encouraging tone, 'What are you doing, and have you found out anything?'

Celia had a piece of paper in front of her, a quill in her hand, but she covered up whatever she'd been writing too quickly for me to see what it was.

'We've been following the route home from the Eastern Sea and looking for an island that resembles the one depicted in the dead man's map,' Jonathan said. 'You do not have marine charts for the farther end of the journey – from its starting point – although we found a map that depicts the islands in some detail.' He drew it out from beneath several others. 'The Banda Sea, Ternate, Java—' he pointed to the places as he spoke '—Sulawesi, the Moluccas. And here to the north—' he was pointing to my globe now '—is China, and beyond to the northeast, Japan.' He paused for a moment, as if the very names of these distant places were drawing him far away from my study in the quiet Devon countryside. I knew exactly how he felt. 'Then, following the homeward journey, India, Africa, round the Cape and into the Atlantic Ocean and finally to England.'

Celia and I waited for him to go on, but he was still gazing at the globe.

With a quick glance at him, Celia turned to me and said, 'It's a hopeless task to try to identify one island among the hundreds, perhaps thousands, of others out in the Eastern Sea, especially when all we have to aid us is a very simple sketch map with few details and no scale, and depicting only a short stretch of the island in question. It gives little indication of how long the stretch of coastline is, even less of how large an island it is a part of. And in any case,' she went on before I could comment, 'we decided it's not likely that it's out there, because if the crew of this missing ship and whatever she's carrying were trying to escape attention and hide, they'd hardly have done so in the very area of the world where the journey began and where, presumably, people would be looking for them.'

It was a simplistic view of cargo ships and the merchants who controlled their movements, but in essence she was right.

'It is perhaps more likely,' Jonathan added, 'that they would use up all of the supplies they took on board at the start of the voyage in order to travel as far as they could before re-provisioning.' He seemed to have emerged from his reverie, and it was good to have his intelligent mind fully back with us. 'We studied the east and west coasts of India, in particular those areas where the Dutch have established settlements, and we looked for some time at the dotted islands between India and Ceylon, but we found nothing that was very like the dead man's sketch. We went on to Africa, but—'

Suddenly losing patience with this long and detailed account, Celia said, 'You asked when you came in if we'd found anything, Gabe, and we did.' She turned to Jonathan, a hand on his arm, and said quietly, 'I'm sorry to interrupt, but Gabe's tired and hungry and I believe he would quite like to proceed straight to the discovery.'

Perceptive Celia, I thought. She was absolutely right.

Even as she spoke, Jonathan had been spreading out a large chart. It depicted the southern Atlantic; specifically, the sea off southwest Africa, between the Cape of Good Hope to the south and, to the north, the great bulge of land that stretches out to the west.

'Here is the small group of islands that the Portuguese discovered,' Jonathan began, 'and that they named after their admiral, Tristão da Cunha. Here to the north is Ascension Island, another Portuguese discovery, although it is believed they have little use for it other than as a source of fresh water and food, in the form of sea birds and turtles. And here, between the two, is St Helena.'

He pointed to the island, and as he did so, Celia uncovered the piece of paper she had been concealing. It wasn't writing; it was a drawing. Leaning over it, I could see the familiar stretch of coastline: the two headlands, the bay, the inlet that divided and re-divided as it continued inland. But Celia's drawing went much further, for it included the entire island on which the detailed section on the dead man's map was located.

I looked from her sketch to the chart. Then I stepped over to my bookshelves and drew out a large leather-bound volume that, presumably, Celia hadn't known about. It consisted of a series of maps, and one of them depicted the islands off the southwest coast of Africa.

I found the right one and laid the book on my desk. The outline of the island was identical to the one on the chart, although it was significantly larger, and showed the rivers and the topography; the mountains, coloured brown, that soared so steeply as the land rose away from the coast.

I reached inside my tunic and took out the leather wallet, then spread Malin Piltbone's map between the land map and the chart.

It wasn't precise – not as good as my artistic sister's version – but it was close enough.

'St Helena,' I said, echoing Jonathan's last words.

Celia looked at me sharply. 'You don't appear to be surprised.'

What she probably meant was *you don't appear to be impressed.* I thought I'd better explain.

'I am amazed at how hard you've worked, and how you arrived at your conclusion. No, I'm not surprised, because this is a conclusion that I too have reached, but then I had the help of two men, both of them experts in their fields, who told me much that I did not know.'

'Tell us,' Celia said, and I didn't blame her for the peremptory note in her voice.

'To recapitulate, and at the risk of repeating what you already know, I visited Henry Sparre in Dartmouth, he sent me to Jacobus Schuer in Plymouth,' I said quickly, 'and at Jarman Hodge's suggestion I consulted your friend Sidony's father, Celia, and asked about trade routes to the East, since Jarman informed me that Master Baynton has now extended his interests considerably further afield than Spain.'

'I knew that already,' Celia remarked. 'Sidony's told me a dozen times how much she's looking forward to spending the profits from her father's new venture.'

'It was Gilbert Baynton who first mentioned St Helena as a place where ships coming home call in,' I continued, ignoring the interruption. 'Then I went down to the quay and I spotted one of the ships I sailed on alongside; it was my first ship, in fact. I went aboard and spoke to her captain, who confirmed

that our missing *Leopard* might well have called in at St
Helena.'

'And could they be hiding there?' Celia demanded. 'Could
her company do that, and find the means to support themselves? Would there be fresh water? Could they find food?
Fish, game, plants?'

'I believe so,' Jonathan said softly. He paused, then went
on. 'The Portuguese explored the possibilities of St Helena at
the same time as they were investigating the neighbouring
islands, and discovered it to be uninhabited. However, trees
grew abundantly, the land appeared to be fertile, and they
planted vegetables and fruits, later releasing livestock – goats
in the main – which apparently have flourished.'

I imagined he was probably remembering what he had
learned when in the employ of the Queen's spymasters,
and the guarded, slightly furtive expression on his face
suggested I'd guessed right.

I thought about that. Good God, but they'd had a long
reach, Walsingham and his successors. Elizabeth's loyal and
fanatical servants had been presented with the prospect of the
world rapidly opening out before them as her sailors,
merchants and adventurers sailed bravely further and further
around and across it. They hadn't hesitated to take their place
among every other nation of Europe that had the ships and
the men to forge a route. They even had the excuse, had
anyone possessed the temerity to demand one: Walsingham
had been haunted all his long life by the fear that a Catholic
conspiracy would slither its way into England and murder his
beloved Queen, and he had imbued those who worked alongside him and who came after him with his ruthless philosophy:
Catholics spelt danger, and must be stopped wherever in the
globe they were encountered.

I'm sure it was a great deal more complicated than that,
and also that Jonathan could have explained the true picture
at great and detailed length. But it was not the moment to ask
him to do so: for now, it sufficed to recognize that the most
powerful urge among those men of the organisation which had
once employed him was the need to *know,* and it had driven
them to find out about pretty much everything, including a

very small island some five thousand miles away. Jonathan's retentive memory had done the rest.

Celia was studying Piltbone's map. She put her finger on the dot that was marked *Nieuwe Stad*. 'Those words are not Portuguese,' she said. 'They're Dutch.' She looked at Jonathan. 'Have they an interest in St Helena too?'

Jonathan smiled. 'Every nation wanting to establish a trade route to the Eastern Islands has an interest,' he said. 'The Portuguese, the Dutch, and, of course, the English.'

She frowned. 'If ships of all these nations are calling in,' she said, 'then surely it isn't much of a hiding place for the *Leopard*.'

'I don't think calling in is quite the right expression,' I offered. 'We're not speaking of a port like Plymouth, and passing ships will still be rare, I imagine.' But something that Jonathan had just said was nagging at me: 'The English have an interest?' I asked him.

Again, he paused before speaking. I remembered what he'd said to me only last night: he couldn't reveal to Celia what he had done in the past because he was ashamed. Now I was asking him to speak to me of something he can only have learned about in precisely that phase of his life that he was trying so hard to put behind him.

I felt for him. But I still needed to know.

And then I heard Gilbert Baynton's voice in my head, uttering his grudging discourse on the nature of the route from the East home to England, and I realized Jonathan did not have to tell me after all.

'There's a new trading organisation recently formed in England,' I said. 'It's called the Company of Merchants of London trading in the East Indies, and they have a ship called the *Ascension* which called at St Helena two years ago, and the Company have marked their claim to it.'

Jonathan stared at me. 'Indeed they have,' he agreed. 'But let us not forget their rivals, the Dutch, who have their own East Indies trading company. They too know about St Helena, and I do not imagine they will yield an island so conveniently located on their new sea route to the East purely because the English ask them to.'

*   *   *

We went down for our supper.

Judyth came to join us when we were halfway through. She had taken a bowl of the thick broth and a little basket of bread in to Artemis, and told us to begin without her. When she took her place at the table, she was frowning, and I thought she looked tired.

'You were speaking very seriously to your patient earlier,' I said. I wondered why all at once it was difficult to know how to start a conversation with her, when once it had been so easy.

She glanced up at me, quickly returning to her food. 'Yes.'

'Is she not improving? I thought the fever had gone down and not returned?'

Judyth sighed. 'Physically, she is improving. The fever has indeed gone, and the congestion in her chest that was threatening to overcome her has cleared. She is a strong woman, and now that she is rebuilding that strength by eating properly, it becomes clear that she is usually healthy.'

I waited. 'But still you are concerned?

I sensed Celia and Jonathan watching. I had the feeling that both of them were aware of something I didn't know; that Celia – who I thought was trying to signal something to me with her eyes – was in some way trying to warn me; to whisper *be careful what you say next!*

Judyth put down her spoon. 'I have already told you what ails Artemis Brownyng,' she said coolly. Glancing briefly at Celia, she added, 'So has Celia.'

I tried to think back to the conversations we'd had about Artemis. I had been closely involved with her at the start, when first I'd thought she was dead, then that she might well die even after we'd got her back to the house; but then Judyth had arrived to care for her, and, respecting that Artemis probably needed a midwife more than a physician, I'd stepped back.

Now it appeared I'd somehow offended Judyth by what I'd done.

And in my head a more honest part of me was saying *something much more interesting and a great deal more challenging came up, and the problems of a pregnant and deeply distressed woman did not compete.*

I was about to say something in my own defence when abruptly Celia spoke. Her expression was anguished, as if the subtle undercurrents in the room distressed her. 'I told you she doesn't want the baby, Gabe. Remember?'

'Of course I remember!' I said impatiently. 'But—'

'But what?' Judyth said sharply. 'But let her wait until she has her child in her arms, then she'll think differently? Then everything will suddenly and miraculously be all right?' I was framing a reply – not easy, when the onslaught of her angry words had taken me completely by surprise – when she added, 'Everything will *not* be all right, because Artemis will still be alone, homeless and with no money, and—'

'She has a bag of nutmegs,' I said. I'd thought I was being helpful, but the look that Judyth shot me suggested otherwise.

'And what do you propose she should do with them?' she demanded. 'If we are right in thinking that it is nutmegs which constitute this very valuable cargo that Edwyn Warham has run away with, then how is a woman entirely alone in the world with a newborn baby meant to gain any advantage from a small bag of them? Take them to a merchant, such as your Gilbert Baynton, perhaps? And what is the first question he'll ask when she turns up with a sample of the very commodity that half the merchants in the country, as well as this new London company, not to mention the Dutch, are hunting for? He'll say *Where's the rest of them?*'

There were so many responses I could have given. But all I could think of was that I'd been wrong in assuming that while Judyth had been caring for Artemis she had been deaf to what else had been going on in the house. On the contrary, she seemed to have picked up pretty nearly everything, and she had not only summarised the situation in a few brief words but in addition – as a true healer always did – she was considering them purely as they affected her patient.

Into the increasingly awkward silence, Jonathan said quietly, 'I believe that what ails Artemis is grief. She loves Edwyn profoundly. She trusted him, and believed his promises of sailing away on this secret mission and returning with the sort of wealth she could barely imagine. She didn't mind about the wealth; she simply wanted to be with him. To marry him.

And now she believes he is dead, for in her mind there is no other reason for his absence and his silence.'

Briefly I closed my eyes. So Jonathan too had gained some deep understanding of the woman Jarman and I had brought back from the dead, and it was only I who had somehow failed. I waited until I was sure the furious little boy who still appeared to live inside me wasn't going to shout his angry protests, then said, 'I am sorry that I have been absent from home so much since Artemis's arrival. I admit that I have not given as much thought as I should have done to the cause of her profound distress. But I have not been out carousing these past few days.' I felt increasingly sharp words form and fought to hold them back. 'I haven't been making all these enquiries purely to satisfy my own curiosity,' I went on. 'I've been trying to hunt down Edwyn Warham and his blasted ship.' I paused, controlling the rising anger with difficulty. 'If that's not good enough for the three of you, if you believe I should have been here holding Artemis Brownyng's hand and cooing reassuring platitudes, then perhaps you should say so.'

I stopped. The echoes of my loud, accusatory words echoed round the room and slowly faded.

Jonathan stood up. 'You have done what you felt you should, Gabe, and you have hurled yourself at the problem with your usual enthusiasm. Thank you for the food.' He glanced at Celia, his face softening. 'It is late, and I must go. I bid you all good night.' With a bow of the head, he strode out of the room.

Judyth also rose. 'I shall call in to see that Artemis is comfortable, then I too shall leave.'

Celia and I were alone. She looked at me across the table. 'Are you all right?' she asked gently.

'Yes, of course I am.'

She grinned. 'From the way you snapped out that reply, you don't sound all right.'

'I should speak to Judyth before she goes. About Artemis,' I added.

Celia looked away.

I was waiting in the hall when Judyth emerged from the little parlour, quietly closing the door.

'I have left her a very mild draught and she will sleep,' she said in a low voice.

I nodded. Then, before I could change my mind, I said, 'Judyth, what is it? We've–we were—' I wanted to say, *we have grown very fond of each other; we have found time in our busy lives for a small amount of time alone, and the memory of it is very precious.*

I was remembering that supper we had shared in her serene and welcoming little cottage. The things we had said; the confidences we had entrusted to each other. The moment when, as I finally summoned the willpower to stand up and go home, we had at long last done what I'd been wanting to do since we'd met and lost ourselves in that long kiss.

Did she not remember too?

She was watching me, the pupils of her silvery eyes wide in the dim light. She paused, then gave me a brittle little smile and said, 'We are both busy people with many demands upon us. I have work to finish once I reach my home, and so now I must hurry back and see to it.'

I stood there and watched her go.

I went up to my study and poured a measure of brandy from the bottle I keep on my bookshelf. I sat down at my desk, and wondered if I should have another look at the maps and the charts still spread out before me.

'I'm too tired,' I muttered aloud.

And too dispirited, I might have added.

I folded my arms on the desk and rested my head on them. I was aware of Celia downstairs, speaking quietly to Sallie. Presently all was quiet, and I guessed my household had retired for the night.

I stood up. I would turn in too, and perhaps a night of sound sleep might help me to wake in a more positive mood.

But out in the passage Celia was walking to meet me.

'What's the matter?' I asked. 'It's late, we should all be in bed.'

She ignored that.

She put her hand on my arm, then moved to hold my hand.

'It's calling to you, isn't it?' she said softly.

I considered pretending I didn't know what she meant. But this was my sister; she knows me probably better than anyone, she knows when I try to lie to her, and anyway she was absolutely right. I nodded.

'Oh, Gabe,' she whispered.

'I thought I was keeping my feelings to myself,' I said, trying to smile.

'I was watching you, yesterday when you were looking at your globe, then today when we had the charts spread out. And then by sheer bad luck you came across the *Nightbird* at Plymouth quay.'

She'd remembered the name of my first ship.

'Is Captain Furneaux still in command?' she went on.

'Yes.'

There was quite a long pause. 'What are you going to do?' she asked finally.

'What *can* I do?' I replied, my voice rough. 'I can yearn for my old life as much as I like, but it's as distant from me now as it was after that final voyage home across the Atlantic when I not only thought I was going to die but was fervently praying for death as I've never prayed for anything before or since!'

I was shouting now, my angry voice echoing up into the high roof.

'I know, Gabe,' Celia said.

She was already turning away, walking towards her own room. Then she said something else . . . softly, under her breath, perhaps more to herself than to me . . .

It sounded like *but that was then*.

FOURTEEN

I slept deeply, probably because of the second measure of brandy I took to bed with me. I was woken just as the sky was growing pale by a noise that at first I was too sleep-fuddled to identify.

As my head cleared I realized it was a combination of Flynn barking and Celia banging on my door and shouting my name.

I leapt out of bed, stumbled to the door and flung it open. 'What's happened?' I demanded angrily. 'What's Flynn making such a noise about?'

Celia was not yet dressed, wrapped in her warm robe over her nightgown, hair loose and tumbled.

'It was me, I set him off when I started calling you,' she said. 'I'm afraid it's Artemis.' I noticed absently that, despite the fact that she'd just been yelling, already she sounded calm again, controlled. 'She's gone.'

I grabbed my own robe – it was bitterly cold upstairs – and flew down the stairs, Celia right behind me. Flynn was in the hall – thankfully he had stopped barking – and he wagged his tail in greeting. I raced across the hall and along the short passage into the little parlour. The bed we'd made up on the floor was empty, the blankets folded back, the pillows plumped. The little room was orderly; there was no indication of a disturbance.

And the small canvas pack with the missing strap that Artemis had carried was gone.

I went over to the window, which was securely fastened. I spun round, about to go and check on the doors and the rest of the windows, but Celia said, 'I've already checked. Windows all fast shut, front door bolted and barred, but the door to the yard isn't.'

'Was it locked last night?' I demanded. It was usually my last job, but I'd been up in my study drinking brandy and feeling sorry for myself.

'Yes,' Celia said in the same calm tone. 'After Judyth left and you went to bed, Sallie and I cleared up and I checked the windows and doors.'

I almost asked if she was quite sure, and not very long ago I would have done. But there was a new, more thoughtful and serious side to my sister nowadays; a sense of responsibility for other people. The former preoccupation with her own pleasure and gratification had gone. I held back the query.

Flynn had padded silently into the room to stand at my side. I rested my hand on his head, then bent to stroke down his throat and chest. 'Did you not hear her go?' I asked him softly.

'I didn't hear him barking during the night,' Celia said.

'No, nor did I.'

I thought about that for a moment.

Then I hurried through to the kitchen, where Sallie looked up at me worriedly. Before she could ask any questions I couldn't answer, I gave her a nod and went on out through the door and into the yard.

Samuel was standing by the gates, Tock beside him. Tock looked scared.

'What have you found, Samuel?' I asked.

He shook his head. 'Nothing. Gates are as I left them last night, after Mistress Penwarden left, with the bars in their slots just as they should be. I don't reckon anyone's come in this way.'

But what about going out? I wondered. Could Artemis have clambered over them? The gates were high, the top rail reaching my shoulders, and the strengthening struts did not extend far enough to allow much of a toehold. Not for me, anyway, but then I had big feet and wore correspondingly large and sturdy boots . . .

Celia had come out into the yard and stood beside me. 'What did Artemis wear on her feet?' I asked.

'Leather slippers. Flimsy, and badly worn from the miles she'd walked in them.'

I remembered. I'd noticed back there on the riverbank when we thought she was dead that the little shoes were inadequate for the season. For anything, in truth, other than sitting quietly sewing in a room beside the fire.

I glanced down at Celia's feet. She was wearing her indoor slippers. 'Could you climb the gates?'

'You think she went . . .?' Celia began. But then, curtly nodding her understanding, she hurried up to the gates and, after a few brief moments of consideration, put both hands on the upper strut and raised one foot on to the bottom one. In a surprisingly short time, she was sitting perched uncomfortably on the top rail.

Tock was looking at her intently, his face full of anguish. 'No, not good, not safe,' he mumbled, and Samuel said some quiet words in a soothing tone.

'It's all right, Tock,' I said, 'I'm here to catch her if she falls.'

'I'm not going to fall,' Celia said brightly. 'Look, Tock, I'm holding on!'

She was. Her knuckles were white.

I went to take hold of her legs, just in case. 'Could you jump down the other side?'

She turned and looked down. 'It's a long way,' she said. 'I'd never noticed, but the ground slopes away quite sharply, so it's more of a challenge to climb up from outside than from inside. Well, that's what you'd expect,' she added. 'I *could* jump down, yes.' She hesitated. 'Do you want me to?'

I let go of her legs and reached to take her hands. 'No, absolutely not. Come down, before Tock climbs up to rescue you.'

She let her weight fall against me, and when she was safely on the ground, she smiled at Tock and said, 'There, safe and sound now.'

He grunted something, returning her smile. Then he dropped his head and gazed fixedly at his right boot. He was blushing.

Tock has always been devoted to Celia.

Back inside the house, I poked up a blaze in the library hearth and Celia and I sat down beside it. Even the short time we had been out in the yard had been enough to thoroughly chill us; there had been no more snow, but the temperature had dropped sharply

'So you think she went of her own volition?' Celia said.

'It's what appears to have happened,' I replied. 'The bedding has been straightened, her pack's missing, no windows or doors have been forced, and you've just demonstrated that a woman in light shoes can climb the gates on the inside. And, if desperate enough, risk the jump down on the other side.'

'But I'm not six months pregnant,' Celia pointed out.

'No, but then Artemis didn't—' I stopped.

I'd been about to say that Artemis hadn't wanted the child she carried, and that this might have made her less anxious about the damage such an exercise might do to the baby. But my sister had once lost a child, her pregnancy brought to an end in violent circumstances. I didn't want to make her remember that now.

But she knew what I'd held back. 'But she didn't want the baby? Was that what you were going to say?'

I nodded.

Presently Celia said, 'If we accept that's what happened – and I agree there isn't really much of an alternative – we next have to ask why she left.'

I remembered a conversation between Celia, Jonathan and me when I'd asked pretty much the same question.

'Because she's afraid that the man we scared away six nights ago was coming back,' I said softly. 'Because wherever else she went, no matter if it was nowhere near as secure as this house and there was nobody there to look after her, feed her and keep her warm, it would be a place that he, or they, didn't know about and wouldn't go looking for her.'

Celia sighed. 'Yes, it made good sense then and it does now,' she said. 'But, Gabe, it's so cold out there!'

'I know, and nobody in their right mind would flee in such weather,' I agreed, 'but as we were just saying, she's too afraid to be sensible, and—' I heard Celia gasp softly, and stopped. 'What is it?'

'Something has just occurred to me,' she whispered. 'Last night Jonathan said – and none of us disagreed – that Artemis believes Edwyn's absence means he's dead, because it's the only explanation for his failure to come and find her or somehow contact her. But what if it *isn't* what she believes? What if she thinks he's deserted her? That he's achieved what he set out to do and acquired this valuable cargo that's going to make his fortune, but that he's decided he no longer wants to share it with a wife? With *her*?'

'But there's no reason for her to believe that!' I protested. 'He asked her to marry him, he's gone halfway round the world to acquire the means to make their life together very much better! I can't think what on earth would make someone interpret such an absence as desertion.'

Celia sighed. Then, after a short pause, said, 'Yes. It isn't the most logical of conclusions, I grant you, and I understand your objections. But, Gabe, you're not a lonely, frightened and very vulnerable woman who's pregnant with a child whose father she's not not married to, and who – as if that's not bad enough – has gone missing.'

I tried to see it from Artemis's point of view and I didn't really succeed. But I respected that Celia undoubtedly could. 'And this belief that Edwyn has abandoned her would make her run away?' I asked.

Slowly Celia nodded.

'Then we must go after her!' I said. I was picturing Artemis out in the cold, thinking how the icy air was the worse thing for someone recently recovered from a fever, when Celia spoke again.

'I fear,' she whispered, 'that she might try to do what she failed to achieve before.'

And as one we leapt up and raced for the stairs to go and dress.

Outside, we searched all around the immediate surroundings of the house, looking for any sign of Artemis that might provide a clue as to which way she had gone. Samuel and Tock began on a circuit of the house itself; I spotted Tock bending over a patch of hard ground beside the kitchen door, muttering worriedly to himself. Samuel said something to him, and he nodded, straightened up and trotted obediently off beside Samuel.

After searching for quite some time – it was early still, and very cold – we came across hoof prints on the edge of a small copse between the house and the road. There were some horse droppings, still quite moist.

'Someone left a horse here!' Celia exclaimed.

'And recently,' I agreed, studying the fresh droppings.

'Somebody came for her!' Celia's eyes were wide with shock.

I nodded. 'And they rode off together, the two of them on the same horse.' I stared around me, looking for scuffed ground, broken branches. 'But there are still no signs of a struggle.'

'She trusted him, and went willingly,' Celia said after a short silence. 'She *must* have done,' she added more forcefully when I didn't reply. 'Otherwise she'd have found some way of letting us know she was being abducted.'

'Such as what?' I hadn't meant the remark to sound as dismissive as it came out.

'Oh . . .' She didn't have to hesitate for long. 'To have reached this spot where the horse was tethered they had to go right though the house, out into the yard and over the gates. Artemis had only to cry out, or, if he had his hand over her mouth, to kick her heels against the hall floor, or rattle the gates loudly as they climbed over, and even if Sallie, Tock and Samuel were too deeply asleep to hear, Flynn would have picked it up. And we both agreed that he didn't bark till I was yelling your name when I first went downstairs, because neither of us heard it and nor did Sallie, or else she'd have done something about it!'

She spun round to face me, her eyes alight with excitement.

'What if he had a knife to her throat? To her belly?'

But I was objecting for the sake of it; privately I agreed with her. Artemis had been in a state of terror over the possibility that the man who'd appeared at the window would come back and try to reach her, and her fear alone would have made it all but impossible for anyone to take her away without her making even a very small sound. And that was all my bat-eared dog would have required to set up his loud warning barking.

Which led straight to the reassuring conclusion that whoever it was who had come for her, it hadn't been the pale-faced, black-bearded man of six nights ago.

Celia gave me a look. I could see her struggling with her

irritation, but she took a deep breath and said coolly, 'It's possible, of course, but I believe it is far more likely she went with him willingly.'

I was framing a reply when from the direction of the house the air was split with the sound of Flynn barking, and in the very short pauses when he paused for breath we heard Samuel calling 'Doctor! *Doctor!*'

Celia and I turned and ran.

As we emerged from the copse into the open we saw Tock standing by the porch, his face deeply creased with anxiety. Even as we reached him he ran out to meet us, leading us across the front of the house, turning left at the corner to where the little side window of the morning parlour broke the smooth surface of the wall some five feet above us. Flynn was quiet now, sitting beside Samuel with his tongue out.

Samuel said without preamble, 'There's been someone here. Boot prints, some shuffling. Seems like he stood here some time.'

I bent down and looked. He was right.

'Who found them?' I asked.

Samuel put a hand on Tock's shoulder. 'Tock.'

I stood up and said, 'Well done, Tock,' and he beamed with pleasure.

'He calls out, me and Flynn come running to see what he's discovered, Flynn starts sniffing and snuffling, then he began that barking,' Samuel said.

I looked at my dog. 'You're too late, Flynn,' I murmured.

He didn't understand – of course he didn't, he's a dog – but it seemed to me he hung his head.

'What d'you reckon, Doctor T?' Samuel asked.

I didn't reply straight away. I was thinking. Trying to imagine what had happened. Why Artemis had made no noise, why Flynn hadn't barked. I walked back the way Tock had just brought us, round to the front of the house, down the far side to the rear, and the yard gates.

If I hadn't already worked out what must surely have happened, I'd have missed them. But knowing what to look for, I didn't.

I stopped outside the gates. Celia, Samuel and Tock stood

silently watching me, although Celia's expression suggested she wasn't going to restrain her impatience much longer.

'Someone approached the house and left his horse down in the copse,' I said. 'He went across the grass and round to the right of the house, and he stood under the little window of the morning parlour. Somehow he attracted Artemis's attention without alarming her – or, perhaps even more crucially, alerting Flynn – and she opened the window to speak to him. She recognized him, for she knew who he was. Could it have been a pre-arranged plan, so that she was waiting for him?' I paused, thinking. 'He told her to creep softly through the house and leave by the back door, making sure to close and fasten the parlour window. He told her he'd be waiting on the other side of the gates, right here, where we're standing—' I pointed to the cold-hardened ground under our feet '—and he would help her climb down.' Then I led my companions a short way back to what I'd seen as we'd hurried round to the yard gates.

That side of the house faces southwest, and what heat there is in the sun always makes it slightly warmer than the north and eastern sides. As a consequence, the ground in front of the wall was not quite as hard. Halfway along, there were footprints. Only three – right, left, right – and one was no more than the faint impression of a boot heel.

I put my own foot beside the clearest print. It wasn't mine: my feet were much bigger. Celia's were smaller, and in any case the prints had been those of a man's heavy boots. Samuel's didn't match, neither did Tock's. And, in confirmation, none of us ever went creeping along so close under the walls of the house.

'Samuel,' I said, 'please go and prepare my horse.'

He nodded and went into the yard, Tock at his heels.

'You're going after them,' Celia said quietly. 'They've had a good start – will you succeed?'

'I have no idea.'

Whoever Artemis had ridden away with had been careful where he guided his horse, and I found no tracks at all in the fields and patches of winter-bare woodland around Rosewyke. When I rode out on to the surrounding tracks, paths and roads, it was to find them all but empty of people. The few that I came across, invariably in a hurry to complete whatever important mission had dragged them away from their homes on such a bitter morning, listened with poorly-concealed impatience to my query and in most cases were already shaking their heads even before I'd finished. To a man – or in a couple of cases a woman – all of them gave replies that were variations on *No I haven't seen anyone I didn't recognize, and for sure not a man and a woman riding on one horse.*

I rode on to Withybere to see Theo. Not to ask if he'd seen Artemis and her companion, for there was surely small hope of that, but merely to report what had happened.

He heard me out, one hand tapping the desk giving the strong impression that he'd much rather I stopped talking and left him to his work. His expression turned more and more sceptical, and as soon as I'd finished he said, 'For one thing, Gabe, finding a couple of people who don't want to be found and who have a port-full of sea-going craft at their disposal, not to mention a huge area of moorland where few people go and no one's going to spot them, is a pretty hopeless task. For another, why are you bothering?'

'Artemis is my patient,' I said. 'I'm responsible for her well-being, and it may well be that someone has taken her against her will.'

It was a mark of our friendship and our mutual respect that he bothered to answer, and in some detail. 'She *was* your patient,' he began, 'and between you all, you, Jarman, Jonathan Carew, Judyth Penwarden, your delightful sister and your household rescued her, cared devotedly for her and nursed her back to health. The fact that she seems to have shinned up over a gate and ridden away suggests that you succeeded. You say someone might have abducted her, but I've just heard you explain at some length that you and Celia concluded that she went willingly. *And,*' he added before I could reply, leaning forward and poking a finger at me, 'you thought she must have opened the window to speak to this person, since it appears he didn't come into the house, which I think means she was expecting him!'

He sat back with a nod of satisfaction.

'Expecting him,' I echoed. It was pretty much what I'd thought earlier.

And as Theo opened his mouth to elucidate, I said, 'Yes. She was terrified that our would-be intruder with the black beard would return. If she thought it was him outside in the middle of the night, she'd have screamed for help instead of opening the window to speak to him.'

And Theo said, 'Precisely.' Then, frowning, he went on, 'Even if we're right and the woman went willingly and perhaps by prior arrangement, the question remains: where she is now? Where has he taken her?'

I thought for some moments, rapidly running through the points that had led me to my conclusion.

It still sounded astounding, and I was half-inclined to hold back.

But it was all I had, so I spoke.

'I think the *Leopard* is concealed somewhere on St Helena,' I said. Before Theo's doubtful expression could be translated into a scathing comment, I hurried on. 'Artemis's lover, this Edwyn Warham, is there with the ship, because he and whoever is with him must at all costs guard the cargo of nutmegs.' I began to tell him what I'd learned from Gilbert Baynton and Gidley Furneaux about the new importance of such far-flung places to the rapid increase in trading vessels returning from the East, but he quickly held up a hand to stop me.

'Again I ask you, Gabe, why on earth are you bothering?' he demanded. 'I don't know with any accuracy where this island is, but I'm sure it's a very long way from Plymouth.'

'And therefore not your problem?' I said sharply. 'Yet you have the bodies of two dead men on your patch that *are* your problem, and only one of them has a name.'

'Aye, and only your fanciful notion to suggest either of the dead men is in any way connected to this business of the woman in the river!' he yelled.

'But it was *you* who insisted they were!' I protested.

He wasn't listening. 'The trouble with you, Gabe, is that you never know—'

But I was not to find out what I never knew. At that moment the door was flung open and Jarman burst into the room.

He paused only to catch his breath and then panted, 'Another body has been found.' He coughed a couple of times. 'A tall, elegant sort of a man. Long limbs, slim. Clean-shaven, fairish hair.' He stopped to take a breath. 'What you can see of it, anyway, because his head's covered in blood.'

Without a word Theo stood up and reached for the long black robe he wears when about his official business, cramming his cap on his head. With a brusque gesture, he indicated to Jarman to lead the way to the corpse.

I followed on behind.

The dead man had been left at the side of a narrow little lane that was part of a network of paths winding across the countryside to the north of Plymouth. For the most part they led to farms, little hamlets and isolated houses; the area was largely agricultural land, and not heavily populated.

Theo and I stood looking down at the corpse. The lane sloped just there, and a stream of blood had run down the hill. It seemed to be drawing all of our glances. Then Theo nudged me and said quietly, 'Go on, then.'

I knelt on the frost-hard ground and began my examination.

The man had been around thirty, thirty-two. He was clean-shaven. As Jarman had said, he had been tall, long in the arms and legs. His broad-brimmed hat had fallen off and was lying a little apart from the body, and the hair was shoulder-length, light brown and looked clean. Apart, that is, from where it was soaked in blood. Jarman hadn't been exaggerating when he said the victim's head was covered in it, and so thorough was the saturation that the poor man might have been wearing a red cap.

Using my fingertips, I felt beneath the soaked hair to the skull. Right in the crown there was a very deep wound. My probing was very gentle, but suddenly to my horror a large piece of his skull fell away and into my hand.

Jarman made a retching sound, quickly controlled. Theo coughed and cleared his throat. When I glanced up, I saw he'd turned away. He was muttering a prayer.

I went back to the body. Swiftly I felt all over it, searching for the damp stickiness of fresh blood, but found none. It was impossible to say for sure until I examined him naked, but it looked as if the terrible wound on his head was the only one.

Not that there had been any need for more, for whoever had done that to him had attacked him with such savage brutality that he hadn't stood a chance.

Not very long afterwards I was back in the crypt, and yet another man killed by violence lay before me.

I washed the head, but could only bear to look at it briefly, for the injuries were horrific. I could see now why that plate of skull had come away, for he had been struck extremely hard at least three times: a trio of blows with a broad, heavy and very sharp blade, roughly in a triangle, and each so deep that the thick bone of the skull had been breached like an eggshell.

I learned nothing more, and quickly covered the head up with a piece of sheeting. As I lowered it, I noticed that the dead man's eyes were open, and his handsome face wore a slightly surprised expression. I closed the eyes, then tucked the cloth under his chin.

I waited a moment for the shakiness in my hands to subside.

As I stood there I realized that he reminded me of someone: he looked like the decapitated man I'd examined in this very crypt only four days ago.

With a quiet exclamation, I went to look at his clothes and his effects, laid out on the bench under the window. Yes: he'd been dressed in a similar manner to the headless man, and his shirt had been made of that same unknown fabric. As I ran it between my fingers I remembered I'd meant to ask Celia if it was a sort of material she was familiar with, but I'd forgotten.

This man had also carried a pouch of fine leather, and it too contained a lot of money.

'Who are you?' I said softly to the dead man. 'Where did you come from, you and your companion? Are you truly Dutchmen, and are you, as I believe, here because of the *Leopard* – the *Luipaard*, I should say, out of deference to you

– and her cargo?' I paused, staring down at the strong, well-made and otherwise healthy-looking body. 'And whatever is on that ship, whatever its value, was it worth dying for?'

The corpse did not respond.

FIFTEEN

I unfolded a second sheet and covered the body. Then I climbed the stone steps out of the crypt and went along the road to Theo's office, intending to report to him. He wasn't there.

I was at a loss. What should I do next?

I fetched Hal from Theo's yard and rode back to where this latest body had been found. I am not sure what prompted me; perhaps the thought that Theo, Jarman and I had been so utterly transfixed by the violence of the man's murder – particularly by that thin stream of blood – that we had not examined the scene with sufficient care. Reaching the spot, I dismounted a short distance away, tethered Hal and walked slowly to where the man had been felled.

There was nothing on the track. I examined the verge, but there was little growing in this cold winter season and it soon became obvious there was nothing to find. I walked a few paces on down the track, in the direction of the town and the port. I rounded a shallow bend, into a stretch where the track entered a frost pocket, and saw something lying on the hard ground.

It was a short leather strap with a buckle attached.

I pictured the canvas pack that it had once fastened, and the unfaded patch where it had been attached. It had probably come off at a time when the pack's owner had no needle and thread with which to put it on again, and, careful woman that she was – in her desperate poverty, she had no option but to be careful – she had probably tucked it away to reattach when she had the chance.

And now this careful woman – Artemis, of course it was Artemis – had slid a hand inside the pack to the place where she'd put the buckle and strap, and thrown them down on to the track in the desperate hope that someone aware of the significance would spot them.

I stood in the lane, the strap in my hand, working it out.

The man whose brutally cut-down body I had lately examined was the person Artemis had left with. He it was who had left his horse in the copse and crept up to my house, to tap out the prearranged signal on the window and whisper his instructions to Artemis. She had instantly obeyed, creeping out of the sleeping house so softly that she did not even alert Flynn. But my dog would have known who she was, I realized; even if Flynn had seen or heard her, she was a resident of the house, and her presence was no cause for his warning bark. Then she'd have hurried across the yard, clambered up the gate and down the other side into the man's waiting arms, and she'd have been so pleased to see him, and—

'He was Edwyn Warham!' I said aloud.

Surely he was! He had to be.

Didn't he?

But I wasn't certain. I didn't want to accept it, and I understood why: because the man who had ridden away with Artemis was dead.

Even as anguish at how his horrific death right in front of her eyes must have affected her, my mind was already leaping ahead to the next awful realization.

The man who had come to Rosewyke had been killed, and there was no sign of Artemis. Together those two facts strongly suggested that even if she had gone with Edwyn of her own volition, whoever had struck him down and now had her in his control really had abducted her.

If it *was* Edwyn.

But the more I thought about it, the less likely it seemed. Edwyn Warham had gone halfway round the world and back to make his fortune, and wherever the *Leopard* and her cargo were hiding, that's where he would be. If I was right about St Helena, then he was still a very long way from home.

No. It couldn't have been Edwyn who came to Rosewyke last night. Whoever he was, he was now lying dead in the crypt. And now someone else had snatched Artemis . . . Where had he taken her, this man of extreme violence who had just killed again?

Here we were, not a mile from a quayside lined with sea-going – ocean-going – ships. The answer was pretty obvious.

I tucked the strap and buckle inside my tunic, ran back to Hal and rode down into Plymouth.

My thoughts ran round my head in a frustrating loop. I pictured the *Leopard*, concealed somewhere along that winding inlet marked on the map of St Helena. *Nieuwe Stad*. Had whoever had come to the house for Artemis been planning to sail with her down into the South Atlantic so that she and Edwyn could at last be reunited? And was the ruthless killer who had taken her planning the same journey? What a bargaining tool she would be. With her abductor's knife to her throat, would Edwyn Warham yield his treasure or stand there and witness the woman he loved die?

St Helena.

I realized it was becoming an obsession.

As I left Hal in the inn yard and strode on down to the quay, I was peering round every corner in anticipation of that view of the water and the line of ships. Bursting out of the narrow little alley and on to the waterfront, I stopped abruptly, taking it in. Stunned, all over again, by the majesty and beauty of the sea. Moved by the organized, purposeful activities of the sailors and those who attended them.

I knew what they were all doing.

I remembered.

What would it be like, I wondered, to be joining a ship's company again? The *Nightbird*, perhaps; signing on once more with Captain Furneaux, settling into the surgeon's tiny cabin, stowing the tools of my trade tidily in their own spaces, bracing myself for the wide range of injuries and sicknesses likely to present before a doctor on a long voyage? Last time I'd been on this fine ship I'd been a lowly seaman, rising only as far as the role of surgeon's apprentice. This time I'd be king of my own domain. And we'd sail south, down around the great bulge of Africa and on towards the huge, icy blue seas that swirl around the South Pole. Only we wouldn't go that far; we'd head for St Helena, and I would find the missing, mysterious ship that I was looking for . . .

I came out of my reverie, feeling vaguely guilty.

I tried to tell myself that this new, increasingly intense restlessness was for purely altruistic reasons: because I was so concerned about Artemis, now in the company of a man so brutal that he'd all but cut the top of his latest victim's head off, and I was very afraid that even as I stood there in the lane, he might already have bundled her up and be carrying her aboard a ship heading for the South Atlantic as if she was a sack of corn.

I tried to tell myself that it really was not because I was so desperate to go to sea again that I was prepared to ignore the likely consequences.

Then I put my own obsession out of my mind and hurried out on to the quay to start asking anybody and everybody if they had seen a man taking anything remotely suspicious on board a southbound ship.

The tall man who rode the chestnut mare had left her in the care of a stable lad, in an inn on the edge of the town. He had proceeded on foot through the busy town and down to the quayside. He didn't like walking in the town. He was aware he stood out too much: not many local men were as tall as him, and he was aware that his garments and his general bearing marked him out as a foreigner.

He'd once said as much to Ned Warham, when they were in a different port a very long way away and the differences between them and the indigenous population were even more marked. Ned had laughed that full, generous laugh of his and said, 'We're in a port, my friend! Ports are full of foreigners, it's their very nature,' and, still chuckling, slapped him on the back and bought him a tot of the local brew.

The tall man missed Ned.

And he worried about him almost constantly now. Time was passing so fast, so many days had slipped by, and now he might well be—

With some effort he stopped thinking about Ned.

The basic plan was surely sound and still workable – he had told himself that more than once – but it seemed that problem after problem was being hurled at him, and he sensed that his resources were being stretched beyond the limit. His two kinsmen and fellow Dutchmen were dead. He'd not witnessed the death of Goert Shyvers, but he'd been close enough when the big doctor and the coroner bent over his poor bloodied body to make out what they were saying.

One of the Company men was also dead. Unfortunately for the tall man, it was the less dangerous one; the less brutal one; the one who didn't slice one man's head off in a single powerful, skilful blow and land a very heavy and extremely sharp blade down three times on another man's crown so that a triangle of skull came away like a piece of thick pottery.

Once again the tall man was beset with the dangerously undermining fear that he was not equal to the task. That brief, vivid memory of Ned in carefree and happier times had undermined him; now, alone and anxious, he freely admitted to himself that he was less than half the man without Ned beside him.

But there *is* only me, he thought despondently.

And if he failed, not only would Ned suffer – he could not bring himself to use a more powerful word – but the whole point of this long, arduous, risky and almost-completed venture would be lost.

Which, apart from what failure meant for Ned, would also bring down God knew what retribution from that cool-headed, unbending, ruthless man on his island who moved those who served him around the world as if they were actors on the stage.

The tall man shook his head violently, and the image of that lean, tanned face with the intense grey-blue eyes that missed *nothing* slowly faded.

He straightened his shoulders. I will face Walter Haverleigh when I must, he told himself.

Then he emerged on to the quay. He slipped into a doorway. He stood irresolute, staring up and down the long line of vessels. Where to start? What questions to ask?

His gaze snagged once, but his eyes had moved on before the significance of what he'd spotted could register. He looked back again to where whatever it was had caught his attention.

And saw the big man, the doctor – Gabriel Taverner – slowly making his way along the ships lying alongside, stopping here and there to speak to someone on the quay, or on board one of the ships.

Coming straight towards him.

The tall man thought briefly. It seemed a risky idea, and he wasn't at all sure it was sensible. *But what else can I do?* he thought wildly. *I am growing desperate, and I have come to understand that I cannot do this alone.*

Besides, this man is a doctor.

Then he stepped out of the doorway and strode to meet him.

'I believe I address Doctor Taverner?' he said, forcing a friendly smile on to his face. 'Gabriel Taverner, of the house that is called Rosewyke?'

The big man spun round, brows drawn down over the suspicious eyes. One hand was on the knife in its sheath on his belt. 'Who are you?' he said quietly.

The tall man put his right hand against his heart and bowed slightly. 'Hieronymus Petrarcus.'

Taverner's frown deepened. 'A Dutchman.'

'Indeed,' Hieronymus agreed, still smiling.

'What do you want?' Taverner demanded. He still had his hand on his knife.

Hieronymus hesitated. 'I believe – I understand that we have a – a matter in common, concerning which we may perhaps help one another.' *Matter* was not at all the right word, but his command of the English language always suffered when he was under stress.

And so much depended on this opening exchange.

Taverner relaxed slightly; so slightly that had Hieronymus not been on the watch for it in the hope that it would happen, he would have missed it.

'Go on,' Taverner said coldly.

Leaning towards him, Hieronymus lowered his voice and said, 'Not here, in the open. Let us go into the tavern there.' He pointed.

Taverner looked at him, suspicion written all over his

face. Then he nodded curtly and strode ahead into the tavern.

I led the way to a space at the end of a table on the far side of the room, the Dutchman right behind me. I was about to catch the tapster's eye and order two mugs of ale, but the Dutchman forestalled me; 'I will command the ale,' he said, 'for you are here at my invitation.'

I sat down.

Presently he joined me.

'I have been watching you,' Hieronymus Petrarcus said. 'I would not have revealed myself and spoken to you except for the fact that – that a lady has been taken. All else must be set aside to address this, for her abductor will not hesitate to harm her if that is what he decides is necessary to—' He stopped.

'If you've been watching me,' I replied shortly, 'then you will know that dead bodies have been turning up far too frequently.'

He winced. Then he said, 'This I do know, *ja*.'

I raised my eyebrows in silent enquiry. When he didn't reply, I said tersely, 'You said we might be able to help each other. I'm not prepared to help you at all unless you tell me a great deal more of what you know. And we'll begin with the identities of the dead men.'

It was a test: I already knew the identity of the first dead man, and if this Hieronymus Petrarcus, whoever he was, called the man in the drainage gutter by the same name, it might indicate he was being honest with me.

It might.

I watched as he struggled with himself.

The he looked up, stared straight at me and said, 'The first victim was called Malin Piltbone. He is an agent of the Company of Merchants of London trading in the East Indies, to give them their formal title.'

'They are usually referred to simply as the Company,' I murmured.

He shot me a sharp look. 'It was not, I believe, his attacker's intention to kill him. The blow was delivered too hard.'

I nodded. It had been Malin Piltbone's misfortune that this heavy blow had struck him on a part of the skull that is less robust than other areas. 'And who was it who did it?' I demanded, keeping my voice low. 'Who delivered this too-hard blow?'

The Dutchman's face creased worriedly. 'I do not say the right words?' He'd noticed my use of his exact phrase.

'The words are fine,' I said. 'Answer the question.'

He drew a breath, then went on, 'The next victim was called Pieter Rutger. He is an agent for the Vereenigde Oostindische Compagnie, who are—'

'The VOC,' I interrupted. 'I know. Go on.'

'Pieter was accompanied by a second agent of the VOC, a man called Goert Shyvers, and he is the man who was discovered dead this morning and who you and the man who is the coroner discussed as he lay at your feet.'

Not Edwyn Warham. Not Artemis's Ned. I'd been right

I'd sensed emotion behind his words. The two dead men were countrymen of this Hieronymus Petrarcus, and I wondered if they had been acquainted. 'Shyvers was treated decently, as were the other victims,' I said. 'There is a legal process to be followed in the case of sudden death, as I am sure there is in Holland, and within the constraints that it demands, bodies are given the respect that is their right.'

He was waving a long, fine hand. 'I am sure of it, Doctor Taverner,' he said courteously. 'I did not wish to imply otherwise.'

'Go on,' I said. 'You have yet to answer my question.'

He frowned in thought, then said, 'Malin Piltbone was killed by Pieter Rutger. Both Pieter and Goert were slain by Rogeus Kytson, who, like Piltbone, is an agent of the London Company.' He stopped, and I thought he had paled a little.

'You seem very certain,' I observed. 'How do you know this?'

He paused, briefly putting his hands up to rub his face. Then he said very quietly, 'Because of the brutality with which the two were slain. Rogeus Kytson is a killer; that is what he does so well, and that is, I would venture to suggest, why the Company employs him. He kills to order, he kills efficiently, the weapons he uses are of the finest quality and always very well maintained, and his methods are—' Abruptly he stopped.

But I knew this Kytson's methods. He had beheaded one victim as cleanly as if he did it every day, and dispatched the other by hitting him with extreme force with a very sharp and heavy blade.

'He uses a sword and, what, an axe?' I asked.

Hieronymus Petrarcus nodded. 'The sword is Toledo steel, and it is a priceless weapon, very old, handed down from father to son. An inheritance? A– a loom?'

'An heirloom,' I supplied. 'And the axe?'

He looked slightly sick. 'Like a headman's axe. For executions.' He drew a shape in the air.

'What does Rogeus Kytson look like?'

'He is not so tall, but broad, his chest like a barrel, his shoulders wide like this.' He held up his hands some two or more feet apart. 'Strong, so strong, with muscles like a fighter. His eyes are dark, and this darkness is made intense by the pallor of his face. His hair also is dark, and he has a heavy beard that thickly covers his lower face and jaw.'

I'd already guessed who he was, this brutal, professional killer. He had stood right outside my house and, before the fury of my loyal dog had driven him away, I'd stared right into his pale face.

My house, where a lonely, vulnerable and deeply distressed woman had been nursed back to health, only to vanish in the night and fall into the hands of a killer.

'What can you tell me of Artemis Brownyng?' I asked. 'And don't say nothing, because I won't believe you.'

He smiled faintly, and for a brief moment I saw humour in his grave face. 'I will not say I *know* nothing,' he said, 'for it is plain that this is not likely to be the truth, but whether I will *tell* you what I know is another question.'

I glared at him, and he put up his hands as if in surrender.

'Artemis was very much hoping that she would be contacted by a man called Hieronymus Petrarcus. Me, yes, she was expecting me,' he added, nodding repeatedly, as if he imagined I might have forgotten his name. 'But she does not – did not

– know what I look like, only that I am a Dutchman. I had been described to her – my appearance, my nationality, hair colour, eyes, what I wear – and thus she knew what manner of man would come to her window.' He paused, mouthing silently as if planning how to phrase what he had to say next. 'When the man who said he was Hieronymus Petrarcus came and whispered softly at the window, she heard a Dutch accent and assumed this man was me.'

'You are Edwyn Warham's partner,' I said bluntly. 'You must be. Artemis knew this, and so when someone turned up under cover of darkness claiming to be you, she would have leapt at the chance of going with him, especially if he told her he'd take her to Edwyn.'

Hieronymus Petrarcus stared at me, a slight frown on his face. When he spoke, he didn't answer my question. Instead he said, 'The man at the window was not I but Goert Shyvers of the VOC. We are a little similar in our appearance, I believe?'

I stared at him, trying to remember the face of the dead man I had so recently examined.

Slowly I nodded.

Something occurred to me; a stray thought that somehow I believed was important . . . With an effort, I pinned it down.

It had been yesterday. No, the day before.

I'd gone with Jarman Hodge to visit Jacobus Schuer, we were going home and just before our ways parted, Jarman had spotted someone following us. He had been mounted on a chestnut horse, he was tall and fair, and Jarman had said *he put me in mind of the man found dead by your gates.*

Except, he'd added, the man he'd just seen still had a head.

I thought back over our recent exchange, forcing myself to remember. 'Pieter Rutger was the man found at my gates,' I said. 'Goert Shyvers was the man found slain this morning.'

Hieronymus nodded, his expression guarded. '*Ja.*'

'You were seen by a colleague of mine, when you were following us,' I said. 'Only fleetingly, but enough for an impression.' Especially, I thought, when the man who saw you was the ever-observant Jarman Hodge. 'My colleague said you resembled Pieter Rutger. Are – were all of you of a similar appearance, then?'

There was quite a long pause, then Hieronymus shrugged. He drooped his eyes, staring down at the table. 'I have heard it said,' he muttered. Another pause. Then he looked up again, and I saw the pain of loss in his eyes. 'We were related, although not closely.' Shaking his head, he added softly, 'There will be grief for some of my family, when news of these deaths reaches home.'

I waited a few moments before speaking, respecting his sadness. But I was too impatient to wait any longer.

'What does Rogeus Kytson want with Artemis?' I demanded.

He sighed, his expression turning from sorrow to frustration. 'What they all want,' he said bitterly. 'To use her as a bargaining tool.'

'They – these men from the London Company and the VOC – are after the *Leopard* and her cargo,' I said, and I was about to go on, indicating my understanding of how either party having Artemis as their captive would force Edwyn's hand and force him to give up his treasure, but I didn't get the chance.

'*Of course* they are!' he interrupted, his face furious, the words spat out like hard little pebbles. 'They calculate that we – that decent God-fearing men will not stand by and see a woman slain when by yielding the secret of what is hidden, her life will be spared.'

Swiftly I went back in my mind over our conversation. He hadn't admitted he and Edwyn Warham were partners when I'd claimed they were. Unless I was mistaken, he hadn't in fact mentioned him at all.

I wondered why he was being so furtive, when it was quite plain that they must be, for why else would he have been planning to escort Artemis away from Rosewyke other than to take her to her lover and his partner?

Unless I'd misunderstood everything . . .

I looked at him. He was watching me, his light eyes narrowed, and I had the uncanny feeling that he knew exactly what was running through my head.

Before I could speak, he said, 'Last night the surviving men from the two companies were both outside your house, Doctor

Taverner. Both, as you surmise, wished to remove Artemis from your care and use her for their own ends. There is an additional element: Goert Shyvers and Rogeus Kytson believed she could help them in their search for the *Leopard* and her cargo. They were wrong: Artemis was not made privy to the plan.' His eyes slid away, and now he was staring towards the door. 'She will have nothing to reveal when she is asked, even when mere words turn into something very much more severe.' His focus returned to me and he added in a soft voice, 'And it is her grave misfortune that the man who now has her in his power is not the man with whom she left your house. Goert would not have hurt her. It is true that at times he did not know his own strength, but I cannot believe that he would have stooped so deep as to torment or torture a woman. But she is not with Goert but in the hands of Rogeus Kytson, who I fear very much *would*.'

That was a terrible thought. For a moment it filled my mind, then with an effort I shut it off. It was no use sitting here bewailing Artemis's fate; I – we – must find her.

Forcing myself to concentrate, I said, 'Rogeus Kytson must have realized he could not take Artemis by force. He tried that once before, and fled when he thought I was going to set my dog on him. Artemis was desperately afraid he would try again. If he had come knocking at her window, he would never have fooled her into thinking he was you and meekly going with him.'

'That is right,' Hieronymus agreed.

'Instead he kept well hidden and watched,' I went on. 'He saw Goert Shyvers approach the house, and then he saw him ride away again, and Artemis was with him. He followed, and in a high-banked lane to the north of Plymouth, he struck. He killed Goert and abducted Artemis.'

The Dutchman dropped his head.

Perhaps I should not have spoken so bluntly, knowing as I now did that this latest victim had also been related to him, but I was deeply concerned about Artemis and sick of his evasions and his subterfuge.

'This brutal man Kytson is the last,' I went on. 'The final one alive out of the four men sent by the EIC and the VOC to track down the *Leopard* and . . .' And what? Take her cargo, of course, bring it secretly to England and do what Edwyn and Hieronymus were planning to do, which presumably was to hide it safely away, keep it dry and well protected, and wait till the demand grew to the maximum and the price right along with it.

When I didn't go on, Hieronymus said, 'These wealthy and powerful men of trade are ruthless, Doctor Taverner. They wish to overrun the islands of the Eastern Seas and exploit them for their own profit. They are forced to acknowledge each other's presence, and competition between them will only become more intense. Anyone else who has ambitions to take a slice of the islands' bounteous gifts for himself will not be tolerated.'

Will not be tolerated.

I thought about that. Thought about a ship heavily loaded with a cargo from the East, the men who had hidden her away on a small and distant island fully aware that the high value of what they had in their hold was increasing at an almost unimaginable rate . . .

I raised my mug of ale to drink an ironic toast to the man sitting before me, but realized I had already drained it. I turned to catch the tapster's eye and order a refill for us both – Hieronymus's mug was also empty – but, noticing what I was doing once again he forestalled me, leaping up with the two mugs in his hand.

I sat deep in thought, absently watching him over by the beer barrels. He leaned forward, presumably speaking to the tapster, and then a crowd of half a dozen men pushed into the room and briefly hid Hieronymus from view. As soon as they'd passed he came hurrying back, and put my full mug on the table in front of me.

'Your health!' he said, raising his own and taking a long draught. I did the same. It occurred to me that this must be a new barrel, for the ale tasted slightly different from the last mug. I was going to ask, but Hieronymus was saying something about deciding how we were going to start hunting for Artemis and her vicious captor. Muttering something in reply, I drank again.

* * *

Hieronymus Petrarcus believed he had mastered the art of observing people at close quarters without their notice. Usually he did not question his skill; usually he did not have to. This country doctor, however, was a challenge. At least once (and in all honesty more than once) he had come out with a remark so unexpected that Hieronymus had been momentarily distracted. Such as when he'd abruptly stated with such utter certainty that Hieronymus was Ned Warham's partner. As if someone had told him. Such had been the conviction in his tone that Hieronymus had wondered if he had somehow revealed the fact and forgotten he'd done so . . .

But the dangerous moment had passed. Hieronymus had picked up Taverner's probing curiosity, and also his fear for Artemis's safety. Which was not surprising, Hieronymus reflected as he stood waiting for the mugs to be refilled, for this country doctor it was who, with his household, had rescued the wretched woman from her attempt to kill herself, taken her in and nursed her to recovery.

No, he mused. This Gabriel Taverner was not a bad man.

And it surely must be assumed that he was a good doctor.

Hieronymus said a brief, silent and fervent prayer that this assumption was correct.

Ned, he thought. Oh, Ned.

He was fully prepared. He always went prepared; given the life he led, it was a wise precaution. Watching intently, his eyes everywhere, he waited. When the crowd of men came pushing and shoving up behind him, impatient to have their own mugs of ale in their hands, he took one final glance to make sure there were at least two of them between him and the table where he and Taverner were sitting.

Then, hands moving swiftly and surely, he acted.

He returned to the table, carefully put down the mugs, raised his own, said, 'Your health!', took a long drink and watched as his companion did the same. Saw an expression cross Taverner's face; one of doubt, for suspicion was surely too strong a word. Quickly he began speaking, aiming only to distract the doctor, saying with the earnestness of simulated anxiety that they must plan how to search for Artemis and rescue her from whatever vicious treatment Kytson had in mind.

The doctor was looking puzzled now. He shook his head a few times, put a hand up to his face. He seemed to be trying to focus on his fingers and was clearly failing.

'Are you unwell, Doctor Taverner?' Hieronymus asked, leaning forward with a solicitous frown. 'It is a little airless in here, with so many thirsty men crowding in on us.'

'It . . . I . . .' Taverner had gone pale, and sweat was standing out on his forehead.

It is indeed as swift-acting as I was told it was, Hieronymus reflected.

Putting down his mug, he stood up, offered his arm to Taverner and said gently, 'Let me help you outside. The cold air will refresh you, I am sure.'

Taverner tried to stand, but fell heavily against Hieronymus. 'Steady!' the Dutchman said, laughing. 'The ale is strong today,' he remarked to a young man standing behind him, who, observing what he was trying to do, came to his aid, going to Taverner's other side and getting a shoulder under his armpit. The doctor was a big man, tall and powerfully built, and Hieronymus was grateful for the help, not at all sure that he'd have managed the tricky manoeuvre between people, tables and benches on his own. With Taverner now an all but inert and very heavy weight between them, he and the young man forced a path between the tight-pressed crowd to the door, which someone opened for them with an exaggerated bow to quite a lot of laughter and a few jeers.

'Manage him now, can you?' the young man said, already turning away and clearly anxious to return to his ale.

'Yes, thank you, and I am grateful for your assistance,' Hieronymus said, smiling.

The young man nodded, dived back into the inn and closed the door.

Hieronymus draped Taverner's arm over his shoulder, and then, half-carrying him, half-dragging him, chattering away as if the doctor was merely drunk instead of rapidly falling into deep unconsciousness, covered the few feet of open ground and hurriedly turned into the dark little alley that led to an inlet.

He glanced behind him. Nobody was watching.

Then he dived off down the alley.

SIXTEEN

I opened my eyes.

My first thought was, a*h, yes, I know where I am.*

But the thought melted away almost before I'd registered it.

And now I could make no sense of the small, dark space where I found myself.

I wasn't even sure that I was awake. My dreams had been vivid and overpowering, full of images from my past, my present, as well as from some strange nightmare place that resembled nothing I'd ever seen before . . .

I had no idea where I was.

I tried to think back to what I last remembered, but, again, memories of real things were wound up within images of enormous waves, sea monsters, horribly distorted faces that were neither human nor animal, and a weird, conical island made out of black rock that spat jets of brilliant orange flames out of its summit.

Dismissing the totally unbelievable – not without considerable effort – I managed to recall I'd been in a tavern on the quay, with a man who I knew to be Dutch – although I had no idea how I knew this – and the Dutchman and I had been about to work out how we were going to find Artemis and get her away from the man I now knew was called Rogeus Kytson, because he was a brutal killer who would give her no mercy.

Artemis!

Oh, God, she was a real enough memory.

I tried to sit up – I was lying on a narrow bed, with a rough blanket over me – but long before I was upright I started seeing black spots in front of my eyes, so I quickly lay down again. My mind was fuddled and confused, and I was having trouble remembering what had happened in the tavern. We'd been drinking, and Hieronymus had just brought refills to the table, and I'd realized the tapster must have broached a new barrel because the taste was subtly altered.

Fuddled though I was, nevertheless I knew what had happened. Knew what the Dutchman had done. He'd slipped a drug in my ale – I saw again that group of men who had briefly hidden him from my view – and he must have manhandled me outside once it began to take effect.

I wondered what he'd given me.

I know of many substances that induce sleep, and indeed I use quite a lot of them myself. I usually limit my use to the milder ones; the strong ones – those that acted as quickly and as devastatingly as this one had done – carried too many attendant risks for them to be employed in all but desperate cases.

I tried to think about very potent soporifics, but my brain didn't respond. I think I briefly slipped into unconsciousness again. Back into the realm of violently colourful dreams and nightmares.

Next time I opened my eyes my first thought was that I was extremely thirsty. I looked around, and saw that there was a leather-bound water flask on the floor beside me. I didn't even stop to wonder if it too was drugged.

It was the right decision, I thought a little later. I had detected no alien taste, although the water had been very slightly brackish, and I was not sensing a further onset of drowsiness.

Hieronymus – Hieronymus Petrarcus: his full name had just popped into my head – clearly didn't want me to die of thirst. Assuming it had been he who had quietly slipped into the room and left the water, which seemed highly likely. I very much hoped he didn't want me to die of anything else, either.

I had been thinking about soporifics, hadn't I?

Chamomile, dill, motherwort, corn poppy, valerian. They all induced sleep, but they were mild.

Mandragora was a powerful narcotic, but it had to be gathered from beneath the gallows and when you had a black dog with you if it was to be really effective. Or so it was said. Judging by how deeply unconscious I had been, if it was mandragora that Hieronymus Petrarcus had meted out, he must have followed the arcane instructions to the letter.

Papaver somniferum. The opium poppy.

If I was right about Hieronymus and he was indeed Edwyn Warham's partner, then he too had voyaged to the East, and it was not at all unreasonable to assume he had encountered the opium poppy in his travels. If so, then I hoped very much he knew enough about it to have administered the right dosage, because . . .

Suddenly I realized how vulnerable I had been, and still was; totally dependent on a stranger's medical skill, and on him being aware just how much he could give a man of my height and weight to make him fall asleep but ensure he would not fail to wake up again.

Briefly panic took me over, and I felt cold sweat on my body as the black spots reappeared in front of my eyes. Then I thought, but I *did* wake up again, and I felt slightly better.

I closed my eyes – the black spots were disconcerting – and, to distract my thoughts, tried to work out where I was. There was something very familiar about my surroundings, but whenever I tried to probe in my memory to determine what it was, it seemed that something stopped me. I almost had the sense that my mind was protecting me from some awful knowledge that a part of me felt I wasn't able to face . . .

But that was absurd.

I wished it wasn't so hard to concentrate. I wished I could keep my mind where I wanted it to be and not keep slipping away into this half-sleep which was crammed with fantastical images so that I couldn't tell what was real and what was some lingering after-effect of whatever Hieronymus had put in my ale.

Eyes still firmly closed, I went through what my other senses were telling me. Smell: tar, saltiness on the air, old sweat and mould. Well, Plymouth was a port, everything smelt of tar and salt, so that was not much help. The bed I was lying on – a very hard bed, I now noticed – had undoubtedly been used by many other people, which accounted for the stench of sweat. And mould tended to accumulate wherever men and women shut themselves up in small rooms such as this one, windows tightly fastened so that not a zephyr of fresh air could get in to freshen it.

Window.

I didn't recall seeing a window. I risked opening one eye to check. No window. A low, narrow door, which I was quite sure I'd find locked if I got up and checked.

I wasn't ready to get up yet.

A small, windowless room that smelt of poverty, over-crowding and the sea.

What about the sense of hearing? Eyes closed again, I tried to ignore the loud pumping of my alarmed and drugged heart to listen.

Seagulls. The slap of water. A creaking sound. The first two, once again, were ubiquitous in a port. The third was . . .

My mind contorted and shied away again as I tried to identify it.

Touch: I reached out with my left hand to feel the wall behind the mean little bed. It was made of wood planking, and it was curved.

The gulls. The water. The sloping wooden wall.

Oh, no. Surely I was wrong. I must be, I *had* to be.

Realizing I would get no further unless I opened my eyes, I did so.

The room did indeed have wooden walls. A wooden floor. The wood consisted of planking, and I'd been right about the curve in the wall behind the bed.

I thought about the creaking sound again.

And about the strange familiarity of wherever it was that Hieronymus had brought me.

I knew, of course. I reckoned I'd probably known all along, since that first half-awake instant, but, drugged, deeply diso-rientated, struggling against the realization, I hadn't been willing to accept it.

And, besides, if I was right then I should not be feeling as I did. I was far from well: I kept sensing that I was wandering off into a dream world, and at times there seemed to be a mist floating between me and reality. And those black dots and spots still bobbed across my vision, but I thought they were lessening now. There was a gentle trembling in my limbs. My body ached.

But I didn't feel sick. I wasn't vertiginous, and the terrible nausea – which on a nightmare of a voyage I would never forget had made me wish I was dead – was utterly absent.

There was nothing to be glad about; nothing whatever to make me want to sing for joy. I had been given a powerful soporific and abducted, for a purpose I could not begin to guess at, and now I was being taken to an unknown destination.

But despite all of that, I was so happy.

Because the symptoms that had forced me to give up the life I loved and adopt the quiet round of a country doctor had not come back.

Despite the fact that I was at sea.

The flood of joy gave me the strength finally to sit up.

I felt as bad as I'd expected to. The dream-like mist filled my vision, and the black spots joined up into one big black curtain that blotted out everything else. As I sat there waiting for the curtain to dissipate, a rapid series of those vividly-coloured images danced across it.

Finally they stopped, and the blackness faded.

I waited, took another few slow sips of water, then stood up.

It was now to my advantage that the room – the cabin, of course it was a cabin – was so small, because I could move round it while steadying myself with a hand to the hull behind the bunk, the bulkhead opposite and the door.

I had no hope that the door would open when I tried it.

But it did.

I peered out into the small, dark space beyond. There was a second door opposite, and a ladder led up to my right. I went up it – very carefully, for the black spots were back with a vengeance – and put my hand to the hatch cover at the top.

That was locked. Bolted, probably, or else weighed down with something heavy. Either way, I could not shift it.

I went back down the ladder. I tried the door to the second cabin, which like the one I'd been put in was not locked. I went inside. It was much the same as mine, but crammed with a jumble of ropes, barrels and sundry junk. There was a damp, stinking blanket rolled up on the bunk. I stood gazing at it.

I'd noticed something – some small change in the surroundings that my mind had subconsciously registered – and I
waited for the fog still trying to flood my head to clear a little
and allow me to think.

There was a cold little draught on my right cheek.

I tried to orientate myself. I was facing forward – the
ship's motion left no doubt about that – so my right was
starboard.

So far, so good.

The cabin I'd been in was airless, but this one clearly was
not. Moving over to the planking that formed the hull, I opened
my hands and felt all over it. And after quite a long time I
found the source of the cold air.

It was about shoulder height, and as I bent to take in deep
breaths, the chilly saltiness rapidly began to clear my head. I
took my time – it felt so good to be coming back to myself
– and then I put my eye to the gap. It was small, only about
the size of my thumbnail, and, given the dim light, would
probably have been largely invisible if it had not revealed itself
by the draught.

I put my eye to it.

Nothing to see but open sea.

The day was fading into dusk, and darkness was rapidly
growing. What light there was came from behind me, from
the ship's port side, and soon encroaching night would blank
it out, the descent into obscurity hastened by the banks of fog
that were building up. Then I would be—

'Idiot,' I said aloud, adding a few more colourful descrip-
tions of my bone-headed slow-wittedness. Forcing my brain
to work was like wading shin-deep through mud, but I
persevered.

If the day was ending and what light there was came from
the west, then the craft on which I was imprisoned must be
sailing north. We'd set out from Plymouth – surely that at
least was hard fact – so, unless sufficient time had passed for
the ship to have gone all round Cornwall and be heading up
into the Irish Sea, we were sailing somewhere that we couldn't
possibly be sailing, since north from Plymouth there was
land . . .

I tried to calculate how long I'd been unconscious. Surely not long enough to have sailed round to the Irish Sea, for, to put it crudely, although now I realized I needed to pass water, the urge did not seem to be great enough for a night and a whole day to have gone by.

Understanding came so slowly that I'd begun to fear it never would.

It was morning, not evening. The sun was rising, not setting.

And whichever direction we were going, it certainly wasn't north. South? East? The mental effort was exhausting, and the more I tried to work it out, the more confused I became.

I returned to the cabin I'd been put in and sat down on the bunk. I was still weak, and even that small amount of activity had exhausted me. I tried to remember what time Hieronymus and I had been in the tavern, and the best of my reckoning told me it was late morning.

Dawn in February was between seven and eight hours after midnight. Which meant I'd been unconscious for at least nineteen or twenty hours. During which time – assuming Hieronymus Petrarcus had been eager to get on his way and leave Plymouth far behind – with a favourable wind we could have sailed as much as sixty or even a hundred nautical miles. I tried to think where our position might now be. Somewhere off Brittany?

And, far more crucially, where were we bound?

St Helena, a voice in my head replied.

As to why were we going there, I could only surmise that Hieronymus somehow knew that Rogeus Kytson was bound the same way. That he had forced Artemis to reveal some crucial clue and had found passage on a southbound ship. Or perhaps he'd already arranged the means of getting away by sea from Plymouth, and his vessel had been all ready and waiting only for the two passengers and a destination?

It sounded flimsy and unlikely. But in my confused, still-drowsy state, it was the best I could think of.

St Helena. I was on a ship bound for St Helena.

And while half of me railed furiously at my fate, the other half was shouting with delight.

I stood up again, for the need to empty my bladder was turning from moderate to acute. I strode back to the ladder, went up it and began thumping on the underside of the hatch cover. 'Hieronymus!' I yelled. 'Let me out, you devil! You—'

Holding on to the top rung of the ladder with both hands, I leaned sideways and got my shoulder to the hatch, shoving upwards with all the strength I could muster. Abruptly it gave and I went after it, the upper part of my body landing heavily on the deck.

And Hieronymus Petrarcus said brightly, '*Goedemorgen*, Doctor Taverner!' He looked down at me, smiling. 'There was no need for force, for, as you will have perceived, as soon as I heard you call out, I slid back the bolts.'

I crawled out of the hatch, resting for a moment to recover my breath. Then I raised my head and looked around.

We were aboard a small single-sailed boat, about the size of a pinnace or a balinger. Small though she was, Hieronymus was not handling her alone: three lads stood behind him, staring at me as if they'd just seen an apparition. A fourth was steering the craft, fully occupied with his task and obviously concentrating hard as he peered into the patches of fog that were gathering ahead of us. Hieronymus turned and said a few words to them – in Dutch, I noted, which effectively prevented me from understanding what he was saying – and while he did so I obeyed the demands of my body.

He waited till I had finished, then he said, 'How do you feel? Do you wish to eat?'

I did. I was very hungry. I nodded, and he spoke again to the smallest of the lads, who hurried aft. Feeling no need to make polite conversation with this man who had abducted me, I let my eyes run all around the horizon, trying fairly halfheartedly to find some clue as to our location. A vessel of this small size would probably sail close to the shore when possible, but even if I spotted the coast of Brittany, I didn't think I would recognize any telling details that happened to be visible. And there was the fog to contend with too.

Intermittently I could indeed make out the line of the shore, off to port. I was aware of Hieronymus watching me, but he did not speak. Presently the lad returned, and wordlessly shoved a hunk of bread at me, bisected to contain a thick slice of ham. I took it with a nod, then, hunger driving out any notion of good manners, wolfed it down before anybody could change their mind and take it away again. When I'd finished, the lad handed me a mug of weak and fairly acid ale.

I had been studying the shore while I ate.

Once again I was experiencing that odd sense that there was something very obvious staring at me which I ought to have noticed. I looked up towards the waxing light.

The rising sun was very nearly straight ahead. Sailing south, it should have been to port. It wasn't. We weren't sailing south but north-north-east.

But we couldn't be.

I swallowed the last mouthful of ale and spun round to face Hieronymus.

'If we're heading for St Helena, we're going the wrong way,' I said bluntly.

'St Helena,' he said musingly. 'A remote little island, only recently becoming known to sailors, and as yet only a few.'

'Yes I know,' I said testily.

He nodded. 'Of course. A man such as you, Gabriel – if I may?'

I nodded my assent. Really, it didn't matter what he called me.

'A man such as you,' he resumed, 'is learned, curious, undoubtedly possessed of a fine study whose shelves are full of books and charts and maps, and, for sure, strives always to understand the puzzles that life casts before him.'

'Yes, I do,' I replied hotly, 'and what is wrong with that?'

'Nothing! But striving often does not lead you to discover the truth, eh?'

'Perhaps not, although—'

Then I lost my temper. Here I was, removed by force from my own place in the world by this bloody Dutchman – drugged, shut in a stuffy cabin for a day and a night – and he had the gall to suggest the truth had a habit of frequently evading me.

'I know what you're doing!' I shouted furiously. 'You're on this blasted Rogeus Kytson's trail! You have guessed he has abducted Artemis, you fear she has unwittingly given away some fact that has revealed the *Leopard*'s hiding place, and you believe the only option is to go after him!' Even as I was shouting at him, it struck me that Artemis could well have known a lot more than she pretended to; hadn't she just revealed a subtle cleverness in leaving that broken strap and buckle where she'd be pretty sure I'd find them? 'You're a fool if you believe you'll succeed,' I added, 'for the vessel you have commandeered is little more than a coaster, and if you think she is adequate for the seas of the South Atlantic, you're wrong!'

He waited to see if I'd finished. Then he said calmly, 'Three mistakes in one utterance, my friend. I was right, I venture to suggest, concerning you and your pursuit of the truth. I did not commandeer this vessel. She is the *Maartje . . .*' He paused, shooting me a narrow-eyed look. 'Mary, I think, in your tongue? It was my grandmother's name, and a legacy she left to me permitted the purchase of the little craft I named after her. So, that is the first error. The second is that I do not know whether Rogeus Kytson has Artemis Brownyng in his power, nor do I very much care. Whilst I should be as regretful as any other man to learn that a young woman had been mistreated by a brutal thug such as Kytson, she is not my concern and we are not, I assure you, on some gallant mission to rescue her from Kytson's clutches. Finally, we are not bound for St Helena, which, as you correctly pointed out – yes, yes, one fact was quite right! – would be a hazardous venture in a craft such as the *Maartje*.'

I couldn't make my mind work fast enough to absorb all that he had just revealed. The confusion was back, returning forcefully as I tried to grapple with all that I had failed to understand.

Hieronymus was watching me closely, a sympathetic smile on his handsome face. 'I fear I may have exceeded the dose,' he said apologetically. 'You are a big man, Gabriel, tall and heavy, and it was better to risk too much than too little.' I could have argued with that, but he had taken hold of my arm and was guiding me to the hatch, now covered once more, where he urged me to sit down.

I hated to admit it, but I felt much better sitting down. I stared up at him.

'You bastard,' I said softly.

He nodded, dropping his gaze. He muttered something: *I had no choice*, I thought he said.

Then he met my eyes again and murmured, 'I should perhaps explain.'

Several replies occurred to me, but I simply said, 'You should.'

He was silent for a few moments, gazing out at the sea. Then he said, 'You have seen the map, of course. And you discovered that it depicted the outline of St Helena's northwest coast. That was clever.'

It had been Celia and Jonathan who had discovered what the map depicted. At the thought of them wondering with increasing anxiety where I was and what had happened to me – wondering if I was in peril or already dead – I felt like crying out in anguish. Either that or driving my fist into Hieronymus Petrarcus's blandly smiling face. 'Yes,' I said.

He nodded slowly. 'It was a device deliberately created to mislead, I am afraid. Drawn to faithfully resemble a stretch of that remote and distant island's coastline, in the hope that someone on the trail would leap to the conclusion that such a location would be the perfect hiding place for a missing ship and her cargo.' His eyebrows went up in feigned surprise. 'Someone like you, Doctor Taverner!'

I shook my head violently, slapping my hand to the side of it, for the black spots had returned, fuddling my wits at the very time I badly needed the power of cogent thought. But it seemed to be proving evasive.

Hieronymus waited courteously to see if I was going to speak, and when I didn't, he said, 'A very careful plan was devised to ensure that the map fell into the hands of Malin Piltbone. I will not bore you with the details, other than to say it was a simple matter of planting someone in the right place and encouraging Piltbone to believe he had been very clever in succeeding in stealing the very item we wished him to possess. The two agents of the VOC were already close on his trail, and they took the chance when for once Piltbone and

Rogeus Kytson were not together to assail him, intending only
the theft of the map. But Pieter Rutger hit him too hard.' He
turned and gave me a little bow. 'As you, of course, being the
physician who examined the body, already know. Goert
Shyvers extracted the map from Piltbone's secret pocket before
they disposed of the body; an understandable precaution, given
where they dumped him.' He gave me an apologetic smile. 'I
am sorry that the distasteful task of washing him down should
have fallen to you and your colleagues. However, Malin
Piltbone was not a good man – the very opposite, in fact – and
it was to indicate their deep contempt and disgust that my two
countrymen dealt with him as they did.'

And I remembered the street woman called Kat with red-
gold hair in the tavern on Plymouth quay; the one who had
come off worse in her encounter with Malin Piltbone.
Speaking of the manner of his death, she'd observed that
when you've killed a man, you don't waste time dragging
the corpse down a tiny alley and depositing it in a cesspit.
That's like a comment, and not a kindly one, she'd added.
That's personal, that is.

'And then Rogeus Kytson murdered Pieter Rutger,'
Hieronymus went on, his voice full of sorrow. 'It was a
frightful death. To behead a man . . .' He turned away, but
not before I had glimpsed his face. 'Goert was devastated,
naturally. Not only because he had lost his kinsman and his
partner in such a terrible manner, but because from that
moment on he was never free of the fear that Kytson would
kill him too.'

With total justification, I thought, since that was exactly
what had happened.

'Goert's fear made him impulsive,' Hieronymus went on.
'He believed that the danger would lessen – perhaps even to
nothing – if he no longer possessed the map. Accordingly he
decided to make a rough sketch of the map, purely as an aide-
memoire, as it is said in French, after which he ridded himself
of the original.'

'He sold it to Jacobus Schuer,' I finished for him.

He gazed at me thoughtfully. 'Which you know because,
of course, Jacobus Schuer also feared to keep the map and

passed it on to the first person who came asking about it. Why, do you imagine, was he so alarmed?'

'He was more than alarmed, he was frightened to death,' I replied. 'He was as covetous of the *Leopard*'s cargo as every other interested party in this cruel, ruthless business, but I imagine he had come to the conclusion that whatever wealth might fall into his lap was not worth dying for.'

Hieronymus nodded slowly. 'Perhaps. Probably,' he said. 'For my part, I suspect that the manservant, Gulworthy – a sinister figure, did you not think? – was far more involved than is usual in the case of a wealthy old man's servant. I wonder if he recognized that Goert Shyvers was of the VOC, and thus understood the map's importance? Perhaps it was he who told Jacobus Schuer exactly how Goert's companion died, so that Jacobus could hardly wait to give it to you when you and your companion, the coroner's man, presented yourselves before him.'

I stared at him.

Was there *anything* he didn't know? Had he managed to watch all of us as we went about our business, always concealed, always absorbing every move, every fact, and putting the picture together with what was clearly a very sharp and intelligent mind?

He was still speaking, and I cut off the line of thought to hear what he said.

'. . . this Gulworthy had his eyes on the bigger picture, perhaps. Observing that agents of both the EIC and the VOC were hunting for the map, he would calculate that it must be worth a great deal, and perhaps sold the information to whoever would pay?' He shook his head. 'It is of no importance. The map was, as I told you, created purely to mislead. To make those who thought they were so clever in having obtained it believe something that was not true. That was so far from being true, I might say—' a wide smile spread across his face '—that it is all but risible.'

'*Risible*?' I echoed hotly. 'Believe me, I see nothing whatsoever to laugh at in what you are doing!'

But he was still smiling. 'It is a work of art, is it not? The design, the colours, the calligraphy? That clever use of three different tongues for the words inscribes in that beautiful hand? *The Island* in English. *Nieuwe Stad* in Dutch. And *chaw in*—' Abruptly he stopped. The smile vanished. 'But I think we must leave that, for now.'

The youth at the tiller called out to him, and there was urgency – even apprehension – in his voice. With a polite bow to me, Hieronymus went back to speak to him. There was a conversation – quite a long one – and the lad pointed several times, mostly ahead.

I followed the line of his arm.

I'd had my back to our direction of travel. I'd been so intent on what Hieronymus Petrarcus was saying as I sat there on the hatch that I'd barely taken my eyes off him.

Now I looked ahead. And also to port and starboard.

The intensity of the fog had grown.

Now we seemed to be moving through a thick, moist white cloud. I realized with surprise – and a certain amount of apprehension – that I did not know exactly when it had started to envelop us. The wind had dropped, so that there was little movement in the air. Hieronymus took the lad's place at the tiller, and the boy and the other three took out oars. The soft noise of splashing was the only sound; even the sea birds had fallen silent.

Suddenly there was land to starboard. I had an impression of a rocky shore, with a wooded slope rising steeply immediately beyond. The ship moved to port. Then, as is the way with fog, abruptly there was a clear patch to port. Briefly, before the mist closed in again, I spotted a long tongue of low-lying land curving out into the sea, and what looked like a fort defended by strong walls.

Where in God's name *were* we?

I tried to stare through the billowing fog to see if I could make out more details, but all too soon the thick white blanket had enfolded us once more. Such sea frets were common, of course, and there was nothing particularly alarming about this one.

Unless it was a supernatural mist, called down by this Dutchman with his strange abilities to take us through the veil into another world . . .

I had no idea where that weird thought had come from. Such a fancy had no place in a rational man's mind, so I dismissed it.

And on we went, slowly now, through that white cloud.

SEVENTEEN

I became aware of a change in the quality of the sound; the soft noise of splashing as the four lads plied the oars was suddenly different. Louder, certainly, and it seemed to possess the nature of an echo.

I stared so hard into the mist all around us that my eyes stung and the black spots returned. I shut my eyes and rubbed them. When I looked again, the mist appeared to have thinned. Hieronymus said something to his lads, his voice soft, the tone steady and confident. It was, I admit, reassuring to realize that he appeared to know what he was doing.

I turned back to staring out into the mist.

Then, alarmingly, it was suddenly torn open like a soft white curtain being pulled back. Large holes appeared, and through them I saw land. And it was very close: there were low mudflats either side of us, and I glimpsed further soft, muddy ground stretching away to right and left, riven with dozens of little streams and channels. Beyond the mudflats was a line of trees.

We were making our slow and careful way up a small inlet.

It was tidal. I was sure of that. The tide was rising, moreover; the lads were not having to pull hard on the oars now, since the incoming sea was doing most of the work for them. Hieronymus stood in the bows, an oar in his hand, occasionally using it to correct our line and once or twice calling out quietly to one of the lads to do the same.

I stayed where I was.

I had absolutely no idea where we were. Nor of what we were doing there: Hieronymus had been ruthless in his correction of my misapprehension that we were chasing after Rogeus Kytson and poor Artemis and were on our way to St Helena, but he had given no clue to where it was we *were* going.

And where, it was rapidly becoming clear, we seemed to have arrived.

We had come to a virtual stop. We were bobbing a little on

the incoming tide as it flowed rapidly into the inlet, but making little forward progress.

Hieronymus came over to me. 'Now, Gabriel my friend, we wait,' he said. 'It will not be a long wait, but we cannot progress until the water performs her twice-daily miracle.' He smiled, gave his polite little nod of the head, and returned to his post in the bows.

It seemed we needed greater depth to progress. As I thought about that, once more trying to work out where we were, it struck me that Hieronymus and his company knew this place. Knew it well enough to understand the tides, to calculate with a fair degree of accuracy how long it would be before we could go on. And Hieronymus's estimate was indeed accurate: quite soon there was a rushing sound – as if the rising water had just achieved the height to overcome a bank or a levee – and we were moving forward in its flow.

The creek turned a slow bend. Hieronymus's instructions came swiftly now, the lads quick to respond – again, it was clear that this was a drill they had performed before, so that they were economical and efficient in their actions – and the *Maartje* made her smooth and stately presence up the inlet and around the curve of the bend . . .

. . . and then the banks on either side of us opened out and we were in a basin. A tidal pool, only accessible at high water.

Slowly I stood up. I let my gaze go all the way round the pool's edge. More mudflats, that line of trees and shrubs beyond, offering concealment. And not a sign of human presence.

Apart, that is, from the large sea-going vessel that stood at anchor right in the middle of the pool, where no doubt the water was deep enough to keep her afloat even at low tide.

There were men aboard her, young for the most part, lining her port side, which was facing us as we approached. A little apart, standing on the raised area of deck to the stern, was an older man. He was quite short, stockily built, broad-shouldered, and he held his hands away from his body as if constantly watching for some threat that would make him draw a blade. His hair was light brown and cut very close to his skull, he was clean-shaven, and his blue eyes were fixed on me.

Hieronymus raised a hand in greeting, and several men waved back. The older man merely gave a minuscule nod.

The ship looked fast. She was long and lean, with a low profile. Her sails were neatly furled. She appeared to be immaculate: her crew might be stuck here with her in her hiding place, but they had not been idle. As well as keeping her clean, her company had also obviously been carrying out repairs, and I could see several places where new timber had been patched into her planking.

If I was right, then the need for repairs was understandable. She had sailed a very long way. Her voyage could have begun either in an English port or a Dutch one. I was convinced, however, that she had set sail from Plymouth, for it was Plymouth where those who were hunting her down had congregated; Plymouth where Artemis Brownyng had eventually stumbled in her growing despair as she searched for her lover. And the voyage had taken this ship and her company to the other side of the world. To the Eastern Sea and the islands dotted across it.

My mind filled with images . . . volcanic islands made of black rock. Huge and devastating waves that bore weak and flimsy vessels deep down through vortexes to the ocean floor. Men and women who spoke in alien tongues and who looked so different from the fair, pale men who ventured so far in their little wooden ships that they might have come from a different planet.

And this beautiful, elegant and battle-worn vessel tucked away in her secret pool had been there and seen it all. Her voyage had achieved its goal – for why else would she be hiding here? – and even as she waited for whatever came next, she was being readied for the next time.

I did not yet know what exactly I should call her; which version of her name was the right one.

But, *Leopard* or *Luipaard*, what I did know was that I had found Edwyn Warham's ship.

And deep within me I felt a stab of longing to experience her delights for myself.

Hieronymus was back at the tiller, talking quietly to the lad. He and his crew were skilled at this, I reflected, taking in the ease with which the smaller ship drew alongside the bigger one, their hulls finally meeting with the gentlest of touches. A rope ladder appeared over the *Leopard*'s side, and another of the lads went to catch it.

I strode over to it, and instantly Hieronymus was beside me. 'Be careful,' he warned. 'You are still suffering from the after-effects of the draught. You should perhaps—'

I turned to glare at him. 'I do not need your advice,' I said roughly.

Climbing up the ladder, however, I discovered – annoyingly – that he was right. As I neared the top, all at once my head began to spin and I needed all my strength to cling on and avoid tumbling into the narrow gap between the vessels.

Members of the *Leopard*'s company hurried forward to help me, but I shoved them away. Hieronymus was coming up right behind me, and I did not want him to witness me being held up by two of his men. As he clambered over the rail, I said, 'Warham's here, no doubt, and so perhaps now you will—'

But he touched my arm and said, 'No. Ned is not here.'

It was the first time he'd mentioned Edwyn's name. The first confirmation he'd given that he knew him.

'Then why in hell have you brought me here?' I demanded.

One of the lads was now coming up the ladder. He was light and agile, scaling the swaying rungs like a monkey. It was just as well, since he was climbing one-handed.

In his other hand he clutched a very familiar object.

My medical bag.

I leaned on the rail and bellowed at him, 'What the *fuck* are you doing with that?' Before he could answer – he looked too fearful to say anything meaningful – Hieronymus touched my arm again and said quietly, 'I apologise, Gabriel. It was necessary.'

'But how did you get hold of it? Where did you find it?'

He smiled. 'You are a man of habit, Doctor. When you visit Plymouth, you leave your big black horse always at one of the same few taverns. Unless you are on urgent professional business, you leave your bag with your horse. It is not unknown for some messenger to be sent to fetch it, and the ostlers are used to handing it over without question at the mention of your name.'

He was right. It was something I frequently did.

I was struck once more by how closely he had been watching me. And for some time, it seemed, because—

Then I thought – and I blamed the drug for my slow wits – if he has arranged for my doctor's bag to come with me, there must be someone who needs my attentions.

'Take me to him,' I said resignedly. 'He's below, I assume?'

A look of profound relief flooded Hieronymus's face. Briefly he closed his eyes. Opening them again, he said, 'Thank you, Gabriel.' I guessed he was thanking me for my acquiescence; for the instant implied agreement to do what he had planned for me. *It is what physicians do*, I could have told him. *We take an oath, and most of us honour it.*

But he was speaking again, his hand on my arm now a grip as he led me across to the landward side of the *Leopard*. 'I must prevail upon your forbearance a while longer, I am afraid,' he was saying. 'You have endured the voyage by sea, and now there is a short way on foot, and then a ride of some five miles. The horses are waiting – please, follow me.'

Down a makeshift plank on to the shore of the creek. Along a muddy path that wound along beside it for perhaps a quarter of a mile. Then we emerged from under a tunnel of bare-branched trees and I found myself standing beside a track. To the right I thought I could make out some tumbledown dwellings, and further away there seemed to be what looked like the ruins of quite a sizeable settlement. We were approaching a solitary stone-built structure, quite large, with a flight of wooden steps leading to its door. The planks of the door gaped open, several of the steps were missing. Right in front of us there was an open-fronted shack, a water barrel, sacks of fodder, and, in the care of a middle-aged man with watchful eyes and a knife in his belt, a pair of short-legged and sturdy-looking ponies.

'Not as fine as your big black horse, Gabriel,' Hieronymus said with a smile, 'but experience tells me they are adequate. Which would you like?' he added courteously.

I took the nearer one, a bay with a long, thick hank of mane hanging over its brow. I mounted, lengthened the stirrup leathers, reached down and tightened the girth, and wordlessly took my bag from the lad who'd carried it from the creek. Hieronymus swung himself up on to the other pony, and with a few inaudible words to the middle-aged man, nudged his heels into its flanks and we were off.

The track was narrow, and I rode behind him. He made no attempt to turn round and talk to me, which was fine because it gave me space to try to work out where we were.

My obsession with St Helena had made me think we must have sailed south or southwest from Plymouth. I'd been wrong; I knew that now. I had emerged from the state of deep unconsciousness into which Hieronymus's wretched draught had plunged me with not much idea of how long we'd been sailing: it was pure guesswork that it had been a day and a night, and it could well have been more.

Which meant that now we could be almost anywhere.

I remembered that swift glimpse I'd had of a steep shoreline on the right and a fort to the left. My best guess was that it had been the mouth of whatever estuary led to that winding creek and the hidden pool where the *Leopard* lay in hiding. However, since the glimpse had been far too brief for me to spot any recognisable features, that information was pretty useless.

I looked around me to see if the landscape and the countryside gave any clues. The salt marsh and the muddy, winding paths of the creek were behind us now, and we were riding through woodland, grassland and some patches of heath. The track was overgrown and clearly little used. Recalling the derelict cottages, the old ruined stone building and the distant vestiges of an abandoned village or town, I concluded that this had once been a prosperous little community, a bustling port, until the creek had begun to silt up and the business of the place had moved elsewhere.

I looked up into the sky. The mist had gone now, and the sky was clear. We were travelling due south, I judged, and it appeared to be around midday.

Presently we began to climb. And went on climbing, the path at times doubling back to accommodate the steepest sections. Just as I was thinking I'd have to give my labouring mount a break and get off and walk, we reached the summit. We were on a long ridge of land, stretching away to the east and the west, and the sea opened up to the south. I was just thinking that I ought to be able to recognize where we were, when Hieronymus plunged ahead into the wooded descent on the far side and the view was abruptly cut off by the thickly-growing trees and the angle that the path took through the folds of the land.

I cursed softly.

Presently the steepness of the slope lessened. Hieronymus was riding faster now, increasing the pace, urging his mount on. I caught a glimpse of his face as we rounded a bend in the track. He was frowning deeply and was clearly anxious, and he was muttering to himself in his own tongue.

Noticing that I was staring at him, he forced a smile and said, 'Not far now!'

And, quite soon after that, we clambered down off the lower slopes of the ridge, picked up a lane running along its foot and turned sharply to the left. The lane rounded a bend, another one, then there was a small church to the right, an open green beyond it, and a narrow valley leading up to the left, cutting into the hillside we had just come down. Hurrying, kicking his pony to a fast trot, Hieronymus clattered off up the turning to the left. I was right behind him.

Before us, hunkering down in the valley with the ridge rising up protectively at its back, was a house. It was a beautiful house; a rich man's house, sheltered from the road by a single-storey structure through which a graceful arch gave access to what lay hidden beyond. The house was constructed out of grey stone, the roof of thick, reddish tiles, and it was made up of a tall, three-storey structure that faced us as we rode towards it and a second, lower wing that jutted out at the far end and sat at a right-angle. To the left of the courtyard there was a pair of sturdy, well-built barns, with another similar pair just visible behind them.

A grey-haired man had come out to meet us as we rode through the arch, and now he hastened to take the ponies. Hieronymus asked him an urgent question, his voice too low for me to overhear, and the man shook his head worriedly as he answered. Hieronymus's already anxious expression now became agonized, and momentarily he closed his eyes. I had the impression he was praying. I unfastened my bag from behind the pony's saddle and said firmly, 'I believe you owe me many words of explanation, Hieronymus, as well as a profound apology and some idea of where we are. But that must wait, for I judge from your face and your demeanour that the condition of the patient you have brought me to tend has not improved in your absence.' It was my turn to take hold of his arm, and I did so, leading him towards the house. He shot me a quick, grateful glance, and we increased our pace.

We approached the porch. The wide doorway was enclosed in a decorative stone surround, and a coat of arms rose importantly at the apex of the arch.

Hieronymus had his hand raised to knock on the door even as we approached, but someone must have been watching out for us, because it opened before we got there.

A tall, spare man stood at the top of the short flight of steps. He was dressed in sombre black, with very fine white linen visible at his collar and cuffs. His thick, shoulder-length hair was grey, as was the neatly-trimmed beard. His lean face was tanned and lined, his eyes clear grey-blue, and something about him suggested strongly he was, or had been, a sailor. Not some lowly member of a ship's company, however; his bearing, not to mention the richness of his garments and his fine leather boots, gave the lie to that. This man had been in command; he had probably owned the ship, and in all likelihood, the entire fleet as well.

He barely glanced at Hieronymus, his light eyes flicking to me as soon as he had given my companion a curt nod. 'You are the physician?' he demanded.

'I am.'

'Come.'

He spun round and led the way across a chequerboard-tiled hall, its walls lined with rich, carved oak furniture: a couple of chests, a narrow sideboard, several chairs. Hurrying, he set off up the beautifully-carved staircase, not even turning to check that Hieronymus and I were following. Even after such a short acquaintance, I had the impression that he was the sort of man who never had to.

We were on an upper hallway now; a gallery, in fact, wide and running the length of the house, with windows along one side and doors opening off the other.

I could smell my patient even before the tall man opened the last door.

I pushed him out of the way and strode into the room.

A man lay on the big tester bed that jutted out halfway along the right-hand wall. He was naked to the waist, his lower half clad in thin breeches. He had thrown off the bedding, which was rumpled up beneath and around him. He was talking – a jumble of meaningless words – and his face and torso gleamed with sweat. He stank of it, and also of urine, faeces and vomit.

I turned to the tall man, catching sight of Hieronymus's pale, horrified face as I did so.

'Could you not have done better for the poor man?' I demanded icily. 'Have you nobody who could have washed him? Found him clean linen? Changed the bedding?' Leaning closer, my face up against his, I added, 'Would it have been beneath you to do it yourself?'

His expression was a warning of the furious words he was preparing to hurl back at me, but I wasn't going to give him the chance. 'I need hot water, and a great deal of it. Bandages, towels, fresh sheets and blankets that aren't stinking and soiled with bodily waste,' I said. 'Arrange it, if you please, and then get out of my sight.'

Hieronymus gave a gasp, and the tall man got as far as 'How *dare* you—' when I cut him off.

'You want me to save his life, I imagine, since you've had me brought here?' I said in a suppressed shout.

'I—'

'Never mind. Go.'

And I turned my back on him and approached the man in the bed.

Then, as often seems to happen when a patient is very seriously ill, it seemed as if an invisible screen had cocooned us and shut us off. Although I was aware of Hieronymus, sidling into the room behind me, in those first moments it was just the sick man and me.

He was in the thirties, I guessed, dark-eyed and, I thought, dark-haired, although the long, thick hair was so dirty with sweat and grease that it was hard to tell. He was well-built, broad in the shoulder and, I reckoned, above average height. He was extremely thin, to the point of emaciation; it was clearly a long time since his body had been able to absorb any nourishment.

There was a jug of water and a mug beside the bed. His eyes were on it, pleading.

The blasted man in whose house he lay hadn't even seen to it that the sick man drank.

He was too weak to hold the cup, so I slid a hand in under his shoulders and fed the water to him. 'Slowly,' I said softly. 'It will come straight back up if you rush.'

Sip by slow sip, I gave him a cupful, then another.

Then I laid him down again on the sweat-matted pillow.

He had closed his eyes, exhausted, and I took advantage of the moment to examine him.

I'd guessed from the stench that what ailed him was some grave wound that had begun to suppurate. His face, head, chest, arms and belly were uninjured – I sent up a prayer of gratitude that he had not been injured in the guts – and so were his groin, thighs and buttocks.

The wound was in his left leg, just below and behind the knee in the flesh and muscle of the calf. It was a slice of a wound; as if someone had held the blade at an angle, which was lucky for the man – if anything about his condition could be described as lucky – since a wound driving straight down into the back of the leg would have gone in so deep that he could have lost his lower leg at best and bled to death at worst. Nevertheless, the wound was grave and the man was seriously sick.

I rolled up my sleeves and set about trying to save him.

Some time later I straightened up, put a hand to my aching back and looked down at my patient.

He was deeply asleep.

As soon as I had started on my ministrations he had screamed out in agony, and even Hieronymus and I together could not hold him still. I had taken the considerable risk of giving him a small measure of poppy; in his weakened state, it might have proved fatal, but if I didn't help him, he'd probably die anyway. As soon as it had begun to take effect, rapidly I had got to work with the first pail of hot water and cleaned out the wound. The stink had been awful; glancing at Hieronymus, still right beside me, I had wondered briefly why he did not retreat to a far corner, or even out of the room, but then I saw his expression.

And I thought I probably knew.

I worked on, washing, cutting, ridding the margins of the wound of the rotting matter until I was back to clean, healthy flesh. The smell of lavender began to compete with the stench of the sick man; some time ago I had experimented with Judyth's practice of including lavender oil in the water she used to bathe open wounds and found – to my admitted surprise – that it worked as well as she said it did.

Judyth.

For a very brief moment she was there with me, bending over the patient, her soft breath warm on my skin.

Then I forced myself to concentrate again.

When the wound was as clean as I could make it, I stitched it up. Then I placed a soft pad of clean linen on it, bound it up and, with Hieronymus's help, removed the last of the sick man's garments and washed him; we were now on the third pail of hot water. Very gently we rolled him to one side, and Hieronymus held him still while I ripped away the filthy bedding. We replaced it with the clean sheets that someone had left in a neat pile outside the door, then dressed the patient in a fine and clearly costly linen nightgown. I instructed Hieronymus to arrange four plump cushions, two under the patient's left thigh and two under his ankle, so that when we very gently laid the injured leg down, the wound was not bearing any weight.

Then we had covered him with the clean bedding.

I stood with my knuckles massaging my lower back.

Hieronymus was beside me. It was some time since he had spoken, and now he said softly, 'Will he live?'

'I hope so,' I replied. 'The infection is severe, but I do not think it has yet begun to run right through his body. He needs water – a lot of water – and good food. And, of course, sleep.'

'All of which he will be given,' said a voice from behind us.

I turned, and the tall grey-haired man stood in the doorway.

'Your generosity was very nearly too late,' I said, regarding him steadily. 'Much longer, and he would have been beyond help.'

'And now?' The question was sharp and urgent.

I shrugged. 'I have done what I can.'

I was still absently kneading my lower back, and, apparently noticing, the tall man said, nodding towards the man in the bed, 'If he can be left in Hieronymus's care for a while, perhaps you would agree to come and sit in comfort downstairs and accept some refreshment.'

The sitting in comfort was more appealing than food and drink just then, so I picked up my jerkin and, with a quick instruction to Hieronymus to fetch me as soon as the patient began to stir, followed the tall man along the gallery and down the stairs. He led the way into what appeared to be a study, with elegant furnishings and a blazing fire, and courteously indicated a chair beside the hearth, sitting down in the one opposite.

'Refreshments have been arranged,' he said, 'and—'

'Before you proceed with your polite hospitality,' I interrupted, 'I have one or two questions for you.' I had many more than that, but two would do to begin with. 'Am I right in thinking the man upstairs is Edwyn Warham?'

'You are.'

'And it is you who financed the voyage of the *Leopard* and the purchase of her precious cargo?'

For there had to be such a person; Hieronymus Petrarcus and Ned Warham were too young to have had the sort of money for such a venture. Now, as I stared at the man who had sent the *Leopard* and her company off on their great gamble, I realized I'd known of his existence all along.

He seemed to be waiting while I followed my thought to its conclusion. Then he said quietly, 'It was.'

He waited.

I was thinking quickly, trying to wade through the welter of things I needed to know and work out what was most important.

But then the tall man spoke. 'When you say precious cargo . . .' he said, and raised his eyebrows in enquiry.

'Nutmegs,' I replied. I might well have imagined it, but when I did not mention any other commodity, I thought he smiled very briefly. 'Yes, I know about the nutmegs. Artemis Brownyng gave me a small bag of them, and—' I stopped. 'You know who she is?'

He sighed. 'Oh, yes.' He eyed me closely. 'She is still alive?'

'Yes, although–yes.' I wasn't going to tell him that she had been abducted by Rogeus Kytson until he'd told me a great deal more concerning what *I* wanted to know.

He was shaking his head. 'I tried to stop Ned,' he said musingly. 'She was just one more young woman, and he has had so many.'

I waited, but he did not go on. So, remembering my opening remark, I said, 'And who are you?'

He looked at me for several moments, his eyes narrowed. Eventually he said, 'Walter Haverleigh.'

EIGHTEEN

Y es.

As I registered the fact of this powerful, self-possessed, elegant man's identity, many small half-registered pieces of information fell in a new pattern.

'Your *Leopard* is a beautiful ship,' I said.

'She is. In fact her name is the *Luipaard*, but the minor confusion created by her being known by both her Dutch and English names has not been discouraged.'

'And it is you who sent Edwyn Warham and Hieronymus Petrarcus on their voyage to the Eastern Seas.'

'Indeed,' he agreed. Then, leaning forward in his eagerness, a new brilliance in the clear blue-grey eyes, he said, 'Have you been there, Doctor Taverner? Have you seen the wonders for yourself? They speak of islands appearing and disappearing as if by mighty magic, you know, and I have read the work of one profoundly Christian captain who, witnessing a colossal eruption and then observing the new land that miraculously appeared when the fire and the smoke and steam had finally dissipated, believed that he was witnessing the predictions in the Book of Revelations before his very own eyes.'

'The Book of Revelations?' I thought I understood, but it was a long time since I had read the words.

'"I saw a new heaven and a new earth"', Walter Haverleigh intoned, '"for the first heaven and the first earth had passed away." And then, of course,' he went on, 'such cataclysmic activity in the crust of the earth opens huge rifts in the deep seabed, water pours in, gigantic walls of water rise up to crash down upon the land, leaving a temporary void and so creating the colourful, emotive image with which the quotation continues.' He looked enquiringly at me.

'"And there was no more sea",' I said.

'Quite so,' he agreed approvingly. 'And so the tales and the legends spread and multiply, Doctor, and in time become accepted as truths. Sea dragons, ancient Japanese myths of ships disappearing into holes in the sea.' He was looking intently at me. 'The Devil's Triangle. Now I read from your face when I asked that you have not sailed the Eastern Seas, but I imagine you have experience of that other mystical, mysterious area on the edge of the Caribbean Sea, in the vicinity of those stormy, enchanted islands where devils and witches abide?'

'I have sailed in those waters,' I replied neutrally.

'Perhaps, then it would interest you to know that, if you were to take down the globe which I am quite sure you possess, tucked away on a shelf in your study, and puncture it in two places, one in the middle of the Devil's Triangle in the Eastern Seas, the other in the Caribbean, and thread a length of narrow dowelling through both, you would discover them to be directly opposite one another.'

I had many experiences of the strange area of the ocean in the Caribbean that he referred to. We had been there on the *Falco*. I did not want to dwell on my memories of the huge and terrifying powers that could be unleashed in those dark blue waters.

'It is possible to link an infinite number of opposite locations in the world by the method you describe,' I said. 'Are we, then, to ascribe such magic and fear-inducing mystery to every last pair?'

He went on staring at me for a moment, then his face creased in a wide, bright smile and he burst out laughing. 'Ah, I might have guessed!' he said through the merriment. 'A man of science is not susceptible to the fancy-induced terrors of normal men, is he, Doctor?' Then, abruptly straight-faced again, he added, 'Neither am I, I should tell you. However, the perpetration of these tales of great peril – with a subtle amount of exaggeration wherever possible – serves well the purpose of men such as I who fight for a share of the trade opportunities rapidly opening out, for—'

'It discourages less foolhardy men from looking in the regions where your agents made their discovery,' I said.

'Foolhardy,' he mused. 'I prefer to say bold, or courageous.

But in essence you are right, of course. They do not understand, you see, they believe that—'

But I'd heard enough.

'Does it not disturb you, Master Haverleigh, to sit here discussing these admittedly absorbing matters when a young woman is in very great peril?' I interrupted.

He did not answer straight away, and I sensed that it was taking some effort to pull his mind away from the deep fascination of the Eastern Seas and the magical islands found there. His mobile face expressionless now, he said quietly, 'Artemis Brownyng. Yes.' Another pause, and then: 'When I asked just now if she was still alive, you said she was and then you were about to add something else.' He looked enquiringly at me but I did not answer. He shook his head. 'I *told* Ned that to involve himself with her so profoundly was precipitous; that he would be far wiser to wait until – to wait.'

'He didn't listen. Artemis is with child,' I said bluntly.

'How far advanced is she?' he demanded.

'Six, seven months. It is Edwyn's child, conceived before he set out.'

'And she is in your care?'

'She was.' I studied him for a few moments. Then, angered by him, repelled by his indifference to Artemis's suffering and impatient with myself for my caution when her life was in danger, I told him the whole story.

His face fell as detail followed detail. When I had finished, he said, 'Forgive me for what I perceive you interpret as my callousness, Doctor. The young woman has endured much, and I share your fear at what she may now be experiencing. But I do not believe that her life is in danger, for it seems to me that this Kytson brute must surely keep her alive if he is to force me to exchange her life for the *Luipaard*'s cargo.'

There was a faintly dismissive tone to his final words, as if he found the very idea that he would bow to such pressure laughably unlikely. Watching him closely, my fears for Artemis rapidly increased.

It was not, however, the moment to share my apprehension with him.

'I wish I shared your optimism,' I said neutrally.

He smiled briefly, but it was not in the least amusing. Then he got up and, excusing himself, left the room. I heard a muttered conversation – two, three other men spoke in addition to Walter Haverleigh – and then he returned and resumed his seat.

'You do not approve of me, Doctor Taverner,' he said.

Taken aback, I considered my reply. 'It is not for me to approve or disapprove,' I began. I thought he muttered something – *it might prove to be* – but I did not take it in. 'I believe you may well put profit above human well-being, not to say human life, but in this world you are not alone in that.'

'Thank you for your honesty,' he murmured. Then, the hungry eagerness back in his face, he said, 'They wish to have it all, you know, the London Company and the VOC; to carve up the riches of the East purely for themselves. Just as in the very recent past the great Catholic nations, the Spanish and the Portuguese, decided it was their right to divide the globe and her riches between them, now it is the merchants who do the same thing. Who attempt to, I should say, for there are independently-minded men who have the means and the ability to prevent this monopoly of the financial giants.'

'Men such as you.'

He inclined his head. 'Men such as I,' he agreed. 'I took the gamble, Doctor. I invested in my two young men and the raw sailors who have now been turned into a highly efficient ship's company. And, Doctor, I found the *Luipaard*. You have seen her. Do you not agree that she is a jewel among craft, with the speed, the agility, the strength and the courage of the magnificent creature for which she is named?'

I remembered the surge of hungry desire that had assailed me when I first glimpsed the beautiful ship in her hiding place. She'd been like a tiger in a cage – a leopard in a cage – and I wanted to be with her when she broke out.

But I kept those thoughts to myself. Turning away from Walter Haverleigh's acute and penetrating eyes, I merely said, 'Yes. I agree.' Before he could demand a more honest reply, I added, 'But we were speaking of Artemis Brownyng, Master Haverleigh. Twice now you have implied that you do not approve of Edwyn Warham's close association with her. I very much hope this will not stop you making every effort to save her.'

He stared at me, and I wondered if he felt I had insulted him. Not that I cared; if he did, let him.

But eventually he sighed, then said, 'Perhaps, in all honesty, without you to prick my conscience I should have been tempted to make a token effort and not much more. However, Ned loves her, Doctor. He has told me more than once – a rather boring number of times, in fact, so that I weary of the repetition – that he would only be making the one voyage on the *Luipaard*, that whatever he makes as his share of the profits will suffice for what he wants. Which seems to be to marry the young woman and retire to enjoy his wealth in some modest home whose maintenance will not cost more than he manages to save from the voyage to the East. And, of course, it appears that offspring will begin to appear rather sooner than he perhaps planned . . .'

He stopped, his eyes wide, as if further details of Ned Warham's future were too awful to contemplate.

'It is what many men aim for,' I said quietly.

He did not hear, or if he did he chose not to reply. 'Were it left up to Hieronymus to rescue the young woman, now, it would be a very different matter.' He shot a glance at me, eyebrows raised.

'Yes, I know,' I replied. 'Hieronymus loves Edwyn.'

Haverleigh nodded. 'He does. The love is sincere and profound. He – Hieronymus – could scarcely bear to tear himself away, and I only persuaded him by convincing him that he had no choice, for with Ned so badly wounded, he alone was left. Plus, of course,' he added casually, 'I pointed out to him that bringing a physician back with him was the only hope he had of saving Ned's life.'

The very tone of his voice was the clearest indicator of Walter Haverleigh's priorities: the fulfilment of his carefully-laid plan first, the saving of a human life a poor second.

Then an echo of something else he had just said rang in my head: *he could scarcely bear to tear himself away*. For the mission to Plymouth, of course.

More obfuscation melted away. I was thinking hard. There

was one question I still had to ask, but I reckoned I already knew the answer.

'The *Luipaard* sailed from Plymouth, didn't she?'

'She did.' He was smiling, an approving expression on his face.

'And so Plymouth was the home port to which it would reasonably be expected that she would return.'

'Yes, and—'

But I was into my stride and I didn't want to stop. 'And so someone – Hieronymus, of course – had to go there, to Plymouth, and lay a false trail.' I heard Hieronymus's voice in my memory: *It was a device deliberately created to mislead.* 'He – you, Edwyn, all of you – knew all along where the *Luipaard* would be hiding. But nobody else could be allowed to know, and so an elaborate deception was set up. A map of a credible alternative hiding place, which was drawn like an enticing scent before Malin Piltbone, who got hold of it only to die because Pieter Rutger hit him too hard when he relieved him of it. Then he too died—' despite my efforts not to, I saw again that decapitated body– '—as did his companion, Goert Schuer. And now the only one left from this quartet of determined and ruthless men is Rogeus Kytson, the worst of them all, and he has Artemis in his power.' I held Walter Haverleigh's eyes. 'I hope it was worth it.'

He did not answer for some moments. He did not look away; it was as if he was silently saying, *Yes, I acknowledge that men have died, that a young woman is in peril. But such is life.*

I wondered – not for the first time – why he was treating me with such courtesy. More than once I had come so close to insulting him that other men might have challenged me to take back the remark or defend it with my sword. Walter Haverleigh, however – who nobody but an imbecile could possibly take for a coward – accepted it.

Why?

Mentally I shook off the thought; there were graver matters to address.

'We should consider the possibility that—' I began.

But just then there was a clatter of feet on the stairs, the door was pushed open and Hieronymus appeared in the doorway. His face was flushed, there were beads of sweat on his forehead, and his eyes were very bright.

'Doctor Taverner!' he cried, rushing over to me and clutching my shoulder. 'He's stirring! Ned's stirring, he's twisting and turning, he wants to get out of bed but he mustn't, so you must come!'

I stood up, shoved Hieronymus aside and raced across the hall and up the stairs to the room where I'd left Edwyn Warham.

I could see at a glance that Edwyn was already much better. He was propped up on several pillows, he was staring at the door as I entered and as he saw me, his expression lightened and he smiled.

'Thank you, Doctor Taverner,' he said. 'I believe you saved my life.'

'I don't think so,' I replied bluntly. 'The wound was quite severe, but the infection seemed to have been limited to the area immediately surrounding it. You have been bathed, put in a clean nightgown and between fresh sheets, you have drunk a lot of water—' I had noticed the almost-empty carafe by the bed '—and your wound has been cleaned out, stitched and the leg propped up. Those are the reasons why you are feeling better.'

But I might as well not have spoken, for he was still looking at me out of admiring eyes. 'Hieronymus was quite right to trust you,' he said. 'He—'

I crouched down beside the bed. 'I must look at your leg,' I said, and he nodded. He gritted his teeth while I prodded the wound and felt the flesh around it, and when I glanced at him he had paled. 'I've finished,' I said, covering him up again. 'How did this happen?' I indicated his leg. 'Who attacked you, and where?'

He grinned. 'Nobody. I fell.'

'You *fell*?' But that long, slicing cut had surely been done with a very sharp weapon.

'As to where, right here. Well, in the inlet where the *Luipaard* lies hidden. Ambroos Leyn – he's the captain – told us we shouldn't start on the spirits, but Hieronymus and I were too overwhelmed by our success to listen, and we thought we knew better. We'd managed to negotiate the tricky passage into that pool – well, Captain Leyn had – and we reckoned a measure or two wouldn't hurt. But it was several more than two, and I started doing this stupid celebratory dance and I slipped and fell heavily, right on to the bottle I'd had in my hand.' He made a rueful face. 'It broke. Apart from the waste of good brandy, it stung like hell fire when it got into the cut.'

Another of Judyth's practices slipped into my mind: her insistence on cleaning the tools of her trade in very hot water after use. In the absence of water or the means to bring it to the boil, she had occasionally cleansed her blades with spirits.

I wondered if this accidental cleaning of Edwyn's cut was what had saved him from the deadly post-wound suppuration that so often took a man's life . . .

With an effort, I stopped pondering that and, glaring down at Edwyn, said, 'I think it's high time you told me where we are. Where *you*—' I turned to bestow the glare on Hieronymus, who was standing right behind me '—brought me, after you drugged my ale and manhandled me on board the *Maartje*.'

It was Edwyn who answered. 'Yes, Doctor, you have every right to be told. Fetch my pack,' he said to Hieronymus, waving a hand towards the door.

I noticed that he didn't bother to add a *please*. Hieronymus hurried to obey, picking up a well-worn leather bag from beside the door and putting on the bed. Edwyn unfastened it and withdrew a folder, from which he took a piece of heavy parchment.

'Here we are, Doctor,' he said. He pointed.

At first I thought he was showing me another version of the map with which I was already far too familiar. There was the same jutting headland bisected by the river estuary, and, over to the southwest, another, smaller promontory, with the winding passage of a many-branched creek cutting through it.

'But that's St Helena!' I protested.

Then I looked at what was written on the map. The same word *chaw* appeared, well inland from the branching inlet. But where the original map had said *Nieuwe Stad,* now there was a single word: *Newtown*. And the title written at the top of this map did not say *The Island*; it said *Vectis*.

I had been told in the course of some long-ago history lesson that Vectis was the Roman name for the Isle of Wight. It had probably been called several different names by earlier inhabitants, for it was very likely that this place had been occupied since people first lived in Britain. Even the most dull-witted of them would have recognized the value of an island that stood right in the mouth of the waterway leading up into one of the finest natural harbours in northwest Europe.

It took me some time to work out how Edwyn and Hieronymus had done it. I knew why, of course: they had a very valuable cargo to hide, and they wanted to send those searching for it – and undoubtedly intending to relieve them of it – off in quite the wrong direction.

I looked up from the map. At Edwyn; at Hieronymus. Both faces wore the same expression, combined of glee and apprehension; they were, it seemed, hoping I'd accept their cleverness with a congratulatory smile while fearing I'd lose my temper and thump them both.

Reflecting on how thoroughly I'd been duped, I admit it was not an easy decision.

'Well done,' I said with a grin. 'Which of you was the artist?'

'Me!' Edwyn said proudly. 'I drew the sketches, although he—' he jerked his head towards Hieronymus '—found the charts and the maps for me to copy.'

'And are the two islands really so similar?'

His smile widened. 'I may have exaggerated some of the salient features. Just a little.'

I let the silence extend until Hieronymus's smile began to fade. Then I said quietly, 'Why did you need me? Why could you, Hieronymus, or this Captain Leyn you mentioned, or even the man downstairs whose house I imagine this is, not have gone to fetch some local physician to tend you, Edwyn?'

He glanced at Hieronymus. Then he said quietly, 'Because Walter would not have permitted *some local physician* through the gates. There is far too much at stake to risk loose talk and lively rumours, and besides, Walter wants—'

'Ned,' Hieronymus said gently.

Ned glanced at him, then back at me. 'Hieronymus had to find someone we could trust,' he resumed. I had the clear sense that this wasn't what he'd been about to say. 'He realized very quickly that he could trust you—'

'How?' I interrupted.

'Because of Artemis,' Hieronymus said. 'That coroner's man was the one who dragged her out of the water, but it was you who took her in and nursed her back to health.' His expression was earnest. 'It was you who kept her secret, when you could have denounced her as a suicide.'

And, as my sister had pointed out what seemed a very long time ago, Artemis didn't die. She wasn't a suicide.

'I believed you would not refuse to help us, Gabriel, and I was right,' Hieronymus went on. 'You did all you could for Artemis. And I – we needed you, to help Ned. We were so afraid for him!' The anguish in his voice was very clear. 'We believed that if he did not receive a doctor's care very soon – *your* care – then rapidly he would die.'

'Why did you not simply ask for my help?' I said softly.

'Because I did not believe you would come.'

'Of course I would have done!' I protested.

Neither of them responded.

As the silence extended, I wondered if that was true. I'd only just met Hieronymus when he slipped the drug into my ale. He might have already made up his mind he could trust me, but would I have trusted him? Enough for me to have agreed to sail off with him to an unknown destination?

I might have done, I reflected. But that was because of another factor: one that Hieronymus could not have known about. One that meant that if he or anyone else had said, *Please, Doctor, come with me because a man has been badly injured and needs your care, and my boat is waiting to take us to him*, I would have refused. I might not have liked it, for I honour my doctor's oath and it was alien to the rules by which I live my life to turn away from the sick and the injured. But not even for those principles would I have agreed to go anywhere on a boat.

I hadn't been given the choice. As Hieronymus's drug had worn off, I had awoken to find myself at sea.

With not one single adverse effect.

And only I, of all of us in that big house – on that whole island – knew what that meant.

I had believed that my life at sea – the life I had loved – was over. Dead and gone.

And now I was adjusting to the amazing, joyous fact that it wasn't.

Far from punching Hieronymus and Ned for their scheming, for Hieronymus's treatment of me, I should be going down on my knees to thank them.

And the surge of memories of my former life that had besieged me over the last few days had made me so hungry to go back to sea that I was finding it hard to stay still.

NINETEEN

There was a sudden noise from below. It sounded like wheels on hard ground, and a horse's hooves.

Hieronymus was on his feet in an instant, moving swiftly to the window. I went to join him. The window overlooked the front of the house, and the curve of the path leading down from the track. As we watched, a tall figure emerged from the porch, beneath us and over to the right, striding down the stone-slabbed path to where a small wooden cart drawn by a single horse was advancing towards the house.

'Sir Walter has gone out to see who it is,' Hieronymus said softly.

Sir Walter, I thought. Not only a man of wealth, then, but of some importance. Some influence, perhaps . . .

A man in a heavy, hooded cloak sat on the bench at the front of the cart. As Hieronymus and I watched, he drew the horse to a standstill. Sir Walter said something – a greeting, I thought – but the man did not answer.

And my initial wariness quickly grew to something more alarming.

'We must go down,' I said urgently to Hieronymus, and he nodded. We moved to the door, and I took in the fact that he was carrying a long-bladed knife at his belt. Noticing the direction of my brief glance, he said, 'Take Ned's,' and pointed to a sword in a scabbard propped behind the door. As I slung its belt around my hips, Ned said, 'What is it? Where are you going?' straight away adding, 'I'm coming too!' and already pushing back the bedding.

'You are not.' I was beside him even as he did so, pushing him none too gently back against the pillows. 'You may be feeling better but you are still very weak. If you come down with us, someone will have to catch you when you faint, and that someone will probably be me. Stay here!' I commanded.

He slumped back into the bed. Looking at him, I guessed

even that brief attempt to rise had made him feel light-headed.

Then I followed Hieronymus out of the room.

Down the stairs. Across the hall. The inner door standing open, the porch door ajar. We went outside, moving forward to stand either side of Sir Walter. He acknowledged our presence with a brief nod.

'I do not like the look of this fellow,' he muttered.

The driver of the cart was climbing down, although not, I thought, at Sir Walter's invitation. He came towards us. He had a strange way of moving: as if he was a predator, keeping his actions smooth, steady; giving the impression that he was creeping along the ground.

He raised his head. His hood was still up, casting his features into shadow. But there was no mistaking that dark, heavy beard that densely covered the lower half of his pale face. He raised his head and stared at us. His eyes were deep beneath the heavy brows, and as profoundly dark as his hair.

'Sir Walter Haverleigh,' he said, making a bow. 'And you, I believe, are Hieronymus Petrarcus?' Hieronymus nodded. 'And I have the pleasure of meeting at last Doctor Gabriel Taverner of Rosewyke.' Another bow.

'Who are you?' Sir Walter asked coolly. 'I recognize neither you nor your horse and cart.'

The man glanced over his shoulder at the cart. 'My name is Rogeus Kytson, of the Company of Merchants of London trading in the East Indies, if we are to be formal. And the horse and cart are not mine, Sir Walter. A hired conveyance, picked up at Yarmouth when we left the ferry from Lymington.'

'We?' Sir Walter demanded.

Kytson gave a sinister smile. He had a long knife in his hand – I had not noticed him reach for it or remove it from wherever he had hidden it – and even from where I stood, I could see the comfortable familiarity with which he handled it.

He is a killer, I thought. *He has beheaded a man; smashed the skull of another.*

Kytson strolled round to the rear of the cart. He picked up

the edge of the heavy canvas covering whatever was loaded on it, beckoning to us. 'Please, come and see!' he said, grinning.

As we moved to join him, Hieronymus and Sir Walter to his right, I to his left, he threw back the canvas, and the two heavy blankets beneath it. Artemis Brownyng lay on her side, amid a load of well-stuffed sacks. Her head was facing the rear of the cart, resting on one of the sacks. Her hands were bound behind her back, her ankles tightly roped, and both wrists and ankles were securely fastened to staples set in the side of the cart. Kytson had tied a thick knot in a length of cloth and pushed it in her mouth, pulling the cloth tight behind her head. 'She kicks,' he said, gazing dispassionately at her. 'And she bites.'

Her bodice was torn, and one shoulder was exposed. The cloth of her gown was pulled tight across her body. Positioned as she was, the bulge of her belly stood out in sharp relief. Hieronymus gasped; Sir Walter made an instinctive lunge towards the cart. But, moving so fast that his movements were all but invisible, Kytson had shoved the sack supporting Artemis's head down under her upper back so that her neck now lay across it, exposing her bare throat. And Kytson had his knife in his hand, the bright blade pressed to her flesh. '*Stand back,*' he said, his voice hard.

'What have you done to her?' Sir Walter cried. 'It is February, you devil – would you have her freeze to death on this wretched cart?'

Kytson appeared to consider the question. 'She has been covered until this moment by the blankets,' he said calmly. 'I do not believe she will die of cold.'

Artemis was watching us, her eyes wide. She was trembling with terror.

'Did you follow us?' Hieronymus asked, his voice hoarse.

'I did not need to sail after the *Maartje,*' Kytson replied. 'I knew where you were going.'

'How?' Hieronymus's single word was almost a howl.

Kytson considered the question. 'I–ah–*persuaded* Jacobus Schuer to tell me.'

'But he did not know!' Hieronymus cried.

Kytson smiled. 'He did not reveal to anyone that he knew, but I assure you he did. He is an antiquarian, is he not?' He did not wait for assent. 'He has in his possession countless maps, and he is, I would wager, better equipped than any man in Plymouth – perhaps in the whole of Devon – to study the maps and charts of the world, make the appropriate comparisons and reach the right conclusion. He is dead, by the way,' he added casually. 'The persuasion was perhaps a little heavy-handed.'

Whatever he had done to the antiquarian did not bear thinking about. 'You took Mistress Brownyng from the man with whom she rode away from my house,' I said. 'And somehow you managed to get her on board a vessel in Plymouth, and—'

Kytson waved the hand not holding the knife. 'It is a minor matter, to bring on unconsciousness with the right potion, Doctor Taverner, as I am quite sure you know. Thus was I able to carry the lady on board the boat, and, of course, a bag of coins put in the hands of the vessel's master effectively discouraged questions about my mysterious sacking-wrapped load. I kept her concealed on the voyage, and she was amenable to my orders.' He glanced down at her, his face expressionless. 'It is surprisingly easy to quell the rebellious spirit of the bravest of women, I have found, when you threaten her life and her unborn child's life with a very sharp knife. We proceeded by sea up the coast to Lymington, after which there was a short hop over to Yarmouth, where we transferred to the conveyance you now see before you. The sacks are full of corn, incidentally. In case you were wondering.'

'What do you want?' Sir Walter said icily. 'What would you have me do, in exchange for Mistress Brownyng's life?'

'I want your cargo, of course, Sir Walter!' Kytson exclaimed. 'I want the enormous load of nutmegs your two young adventurers brought back from Neira.' He frowned, feigning doubt. 'I should perhaps say that those I represent – that aforementioned London Company – want the cargo, and I would, except that it would be a lie.' He looked in turn at Sir Walter and Hieronymus, one eyebrow quirked, a half-smile on his face. 'As a pair of independently-minded merchants such as you would no doubt agree, there is no reason why the big concerns should monopolise the bounty that those wonderful eastern islands give so freely. Not when men such as ourselves are more than capable of taking our share!'

He had been smiling – beaming – but abruptly his expression changed.

Now he looked like the brutal killer he was.

'The lady for the cargo, gentlemen,' he said, so quietly that he was barely audible. Once again moving with that sinister reptilian speed, he had the blade to Artemis's throat, the edge cutting the flesh and producing a line of tiny bead-like drops of blood.

'Let us discuss your proposal in the manner of civilized men,' Sir Water said stiffly. 'I am a reasonable man, and—'

Before I could shout out my fury that he had not instantly agreed with Kytson's terms – even if only to play for time – his smooth words were abruptly cut off.

There was a roar, a sudden violent flurry of movement as something large and white cannoned into Kytson from the other side of the cart, a dreadful crack as a skull hit the hard ground and a long, moaning 'Aaaaagh!'

Kytson was down.

He had fallen on his face, and it was the front of his skull that had met the ground. I very much hoped the impact had killed him.

Edwyn Warham lay quite still across Kytson's inert body. He was no longer groaning. His extreme pallor suggested that, just as I had predicted, violent exertion after being injured and lying in bed for so long had made him pass out.

Hieronymus sank down beside Edwyn. Sir Walter had picked up Kytson's dropped knife and was crouching warily over him, watching, presumably, to see if he was going to get up.

I could have told him he was wasting his time.

But I was already tending to Artemis. Before releasing her, I pulled up the blankets, warming her, covering her. I drew my knife and cut through the ropes, then untied the cloth and pulled it out of her mouth. Then I gathered her up, drew the blankets more tightly around her and held her to me. After a moment she said hoarsely, 'I am all right. He did not harm me.'

I said a brief prayer of thanks. Then, sensing that gentleness and sympathy would undermine her resolve not to show weakness, I said, 'My household and I saved you from the effects of near-drowning, Mistress Brownyng. I was not prepared to see you give up your life just yet.'

And, brave woman that she was, she even managed a short laugh.

Between us, Sir Walter, Hieronymus and I bore Edwyn and Artemis back inside the house. Edwyn had regained consciousness after the brief faint, and he fought me for who carried Artemis; he was wild with a mixture of fury and fear, and he did not want to see any man put hands on her. But he was too weak to fight with any effect, and he was clearly in a lot of pain from the wound in his leg. Artemis told him quite firmly to accept that his part in the day's activities was over – an understatement if ever there was one – and to allow Hieronymus and Sir Walter to help him away.

'I can walk!' Artemis protested as I went to pick her up.

I smiled at her. 'Go on, then. I'll be here to catch you.'

She managed five paces, then her legs failed and she slumped against me. I carried her the rest of the way.

Back upstairs, I examined Edwyn's leg, fearful that his exertions had torn the stitches. But they had held; he needed nothing other than more of what he'd been treated with already: rest, food, drink. Artemis accepted my ministrations; my main anxiety, like hers, was that harm might have come to her child, but as I put my hands on her belly, both she and I felt the little flutters of movement.

'Rest,' I said to her. 'Sit there beside your young man—' Sir Walter had summoned two of his servants to bring a huge, well-upholstered chair '—and look after each other.' I helped her to sit down, putting cushions behind her back, and Edwyn turned to her, opening his arms. She gave a soft gasp, and threw herself against him. I waited only to hear him say, 'Oh, my love, I'm sorry, so sorry,' even as she was demanding to know how his leg had been wounded and if he was in pain. Then I crept out of the room and closed the door firmly behind me.

*   *   *

I went down to find Sir Walter.

He was in his study. I sensed he had been waiting for me. 'How are they?' he asked.

'Neither has taken harm from this morning's events,' I replied. 'Both of them need rest, which they will find much easier now that they have been reunited. They will be renewing their protestations of love even as we speak, and no doubt Edwyn will say they must be married as soon as possible, Artemis will agree, and he'll promise never to leave her again.'

Sir Walter gave a rueful smile. 'I am forced to agree with you, despite my former reservations. They have remained constant to one another, and I expect Ned will gladly give up pursuing excitement on the other side of the world and settle down to whatever role I can find for him here. He and Artemis will be wealthy, by and by, once the cargo is sold, as indeed will everyone who works for me.' He paused, and I noticed that he was watching me closely. 'But I shall be missing one very efficient and capable member of my ship's company – indeed, of my venture in the Eastern Seas in general – next time the *Luipaard* sails.'

'I imagine you will.' I had still been thinking about Edwyn and Artemis, and it took a moment for what he had just said to register. 'You plan a second voyage?'

'Of course!' he said, clearly surprised. 'I have several very capacious barns out there full to bursting with – with a very valuable cargo. The *Luipaard* will return to Neira for more of the same, and in due course bring it back to England. Here, in fact, to Cheverstone.'

'This is your house?'

'It is. Cheverstone Manor has been in my family for several generations.'

He was a man of wealth and position, I reflected. He was surely not in need of the vast profit he expected to make on the cargo stowed away in his barns. But that, I have often observed, is the way of very rich men: they do not stop to pause; to ask themselves, *do I need to go on making more and more money? I have a fine house, land, a well-run estate and a highly efficient household, and the means to*

*purchase any and every single material object that takes my
fancy. Have I not got enough?*

Having enough, it seems, is a concept that simply never
occurs to them. Not for nothing is avarice listed as one of the
seven deadly sins.

He was watching me, the pale eyes narrowed, a slight smile
on his handsome face. I wondered if he guessed what I was
thinking. I didn't care if he did.

After quite a long silence, he said. 'Would you like to see
the cargo?'

Would I? I knew what nutmegs looked like, I still had the
bag of them that Artemis had given me. I was tired, relaxed
and comfortable in my chair by the fire, and I was pretty sure
that when presently refreshments were brought, as undoubtedly
they would be, the food and drink would be of the best.

Yet there was something in Sir Walter's expression; some
new tension in him, as if it mattered very much that I should
agree to his suggestion.

'Very well.'

He led the way out of the house and round to the first pair of
barns. Three men materialised from the shadows as we
approached. All were armed. Sir Walter spoke to the oldest of
them, the man nodded, then produced a bunch of keys on a big
iron hoop and opened the barn door. Not the main pair of doors
– they were heavily barred and padlocked – but a smaller door
set into the left-hand one, of the type known as a Judas door.

Sir Walter stepped inside, and I followed.

The smell of nutmegs almost took the breath away.

The *Luipaard*'s cargo filled the vast space, arrayed on
wooden racks that rose right up into the roof. It would have
been vulgar to ask what sort of profit Sir Walter expected to
make on the contents of this barn and the one next door, so I
didn't. However, given what I had already learned, and adding
in the fact that the market price of nutmeg appeared to be
rising daily, I calculated that the man standing beside me,
contemplating the heavily-loaded racks with a smile of quiet
satisfaction, would soon be able to buy the throne of England
if he so chose.

He had turned to me; I felt his eyes on me. 'Have you seen enough, Doctor Taverner?' he asked courteously.

'Oh, yes.'

He led the way outside, and there was the rattle of keys and chains as the door was fastened again. I began to move away in the direction of the house, but Sir Walter said very softly, 'There is more.'

I didn't want to see more. I didn't know if taking his visitors to look inside his barns was something Sir Walter often did, or if I was being given special treatment. Again, I didn't care; I had had enough of being forced into the guise of awestruck, envious witness to this man's wealth. Especially since I was neither awestruck nor envious.

'More nutmegs? I asked blandly.

He smiled. 'Come and see.'

The path to the second pair of barns was narrow, bordered by high walls on either side. There was a locked gate at the outer end, and four more guards were waiting to receive us at the door to the first of the pair.

Whatever was stored away here was clearly not shown to many people.

Again, the Judas gate was opened; only by enough of a gap to admit Sir Walter and me. Then it was closed behind us.

More wooden racks, more goods stacked high. Not in sacks this time, but in chests made of some sort of thin, light wood. Each one was lidded, the lids sealed. But even such care for the contents had not stopped the fragrance of whatever the chests contained from spreading through the barn.

I tried and failed to identify it. It was a very appealing scent: fresh, a little spicy, something herbal about it . . .

'What is it?' For some reason I found myself whispering.

'It is a herb that they use widely in the East,' Sir Walter replied. 'They have known of it for centuries. It is a mild stimulant, it raises the spirits, and – and this is the crucial benefit in these terrible plague-ridden times – it is believed to be a magical health-giving elixir.'

'I do not believe there is any such thing,' I said.

'*You* do not, Doctor Taverner, *I* do not,' he replied, 'but what is important is that very many people do. Merchants venturing into the East have frequently observed how indigenous gangs of labouring men do better drinking a brew containing this herb than those drinking water. Some of these merchants recorded their observations, and others – your friend Hieronymus Petrarcus for one – developed the desire to see for themselves.' He paused, watching me, and I sensed he was weighing up how much more he was going to reveal to me. 'People *like* this drink, Doctor. They like it for its own sake; one could even propose, I believe, that it is slightly addictive. That alone makes it worthwhile to transport it back to England. If we consider that were its reputation as a heal-all to be quietly spread among the population of London, where plague is rife and people will try anything, no matter the cost, if they are made to believe it will protect them, then we must surely agree that the concept of a *good* profit should be changed to an *outstanding* profit.'

'For a herb that you and I both know affords no more protection against the plague than a mug of ale?' I protested.

He put his head on one side. 'We cannot say we *know* that,' he said softly.

I didn't answer.

After a brief pause he spoke again. 'In the East they call it *chaw*.' he said. 'Or, in some dialects, *chai*.'

Then, standing in his dimly-lit, airy, fragrant barn, he told me why he'd taken me out there.

TWENTY

The next day, Hieronymus and I went out to the *Luipaard*, descended on to the *Maartje*, still moored alongside, and he and his lads took me back to Plymouth.

It was very different from the outward journey. Then the weather had been misty and cold and the sea fairly calm, with what wind there was coming from the southwest and helping us on our way. Now it was still cold, but the wind had changed and now came from the north, at times with great force. The sea was rough, the lads had to fight the wind and the driving rain, and I found to my ongoing delight that even these far more challenging conditions did not bring back my awful nausea and vertigo.

We arrived in Plymouth late in the day. I picked up my bag and went ashore, leaving Hieronymus frowning over the long lists of supplies that Sir Walter had handed to us before we left Cheverstone.

Hal was still where I had left him.

I went first to see Theo.

When he had finished shouting at me for having disappeared for days on end with not a word of explanation and then telling me how delighted he was to see me safe and sound, I made my report.

We already knew the name of the first victim; the man found in the cesspit ditch. Now, thanks to Hieronymus's account, I was able to provide names for the beheaded man and the one whose skull was bashed in: Pieter Rutger and Goert Shyvers. I was also able to tell Theo that I knew who had murdered them.

'There has been a further death, I understand,' I went on.

'Jacobus Schuer. The antiquarian fellow, yes. Found beaten to death in his study. Brutal.' He shook his head in sorrow.

'The same man killed him. His name was Rogeus Kytson, he was an agent of the London Company – a rogue agent, for I hope very much they are not all like him.'

'You said his name *was*,' Theo said sharply.

'Yes. He's dead too.'

And, trying to keep to the main narrative in the face of Theo's questions, I told him everything that had happened.

When I'd done that, I told him about Sir Walter Haverleigh's barns. And what was hidden away inside them.

And I revealed what he had proposed to me.

Theo didn't speak for quite a long time. Watching him intently while hoping he didn't notice, I saw several emotions cross his face. At one point he put up his hand and covered his eyes. Finally he looked up at me and said gruffly, 'You'll leave a great many people needing care.'

'There are other physicians,' I replied. 'Plymouth abounds with ship's surgeons. There's a retired doctor in Buckland who may well agree to take on some of the minor cases.' I hadn't seen Josiah Thorn for a while, but last time I'd visited we had gone fishing and he said he was frequently bored, which suggested he would be amenable to the idea of returning to medical practice. 'Also, I have a colleague who is looking for a new venture.' Jasper Hart, my Symposium friend, had not said as much, but I had definitely sensed his restlessness with his present London life. 'I might be able to persuade him to act in my stead for a while.'

'You'd come back, then?' Theo said.

'I–I don't know.'

'Well, that's honest,' he muttered. There was a long silence, which I found I did not know how to break.

Then he sighed heavily and said, 'Gabe, it seems to me you've already made up your mind, and if that's the case, there's not much point in me adding any more. Save to say you'd better come back, because I'll bloody well miss you.'

His voice broke on the words, and then he was on his feet, round his desk and giving me a bear hug that made my bones creak.

I went to see Judyth. She was in her little still room behind the house.

When I told her where I had been and, far more vitally, where I was going, an expression crossed her face, but too swiftly for me to interpret it. Then she smiled a twisted sort of smile and said softly, 'I knew there was something. You've been so restless. And in addition you—'

But she cut off the words.

I wanted to ask her how she felt. Whether she understood, or was about to plead with me to change my mind. I don't know if I wanted her to try; I have no idea what I'd have done if she did. But women like Judyth Penwarden don't plead.

In the end, simply standing in her sweet-smelling, secure and comfortable little room staring down into her silvery eyes became too much. For both of us, probably; for me, certainly. With a farewell that was far too abrupt, I left her and rode home.

I found Celia in her chair beside the fire in the library.

On hearing what I was about to do, she responded with the full range of objections I'd anticipated. It took me some time to convince her that I was over whatever malfunction in my head had caused the awful nausea, and to counter all her other sound arguments against what I was proposing to do. Then she became very angry, and finally she gave way to the distress that I'd thought I might have seen in Judyth.

'But I thought you *liked* it here!' Celia cried at one point, when fury had turned into tears of pain and she was well on the way back to anger. 'I thought you were *happy*!'

'I do! I am!' I was kneeling on the floor at her feet and now I took hold of her hands. 'These past years of living at Rosewyke with you have been among the happiest times! But—' I stopped.

Slowly, she nodded. 'But,' she echoed very softly.

And then she didn't say any more.

It did not take my strong and pragmatic sister very long to get over the shock. Perceiving, no doubt, just what Theo had seen – that I'd already made up my mind – after a while she got to her feet, drawing me up with her, and put her arms round me. 'You will face considerable opposition when you tell our parents,' she remarked. 'Mother believes she has her sailor boy home for good, as I'm sure you know. But it's your decision, Gabe, and I will support you.'

'Thank you,' I said. Then, after a moment, I began to ask her something, then stopped.

'Go on,' she said. She looked up, meeting my eyes. 'Judyth?' she asked quietly.

'Yes. She–er–she made no objection. I thought–I'd wondered if—' Once again I stopped.

'She knew, I think,' Celia said after a moment. She broke away from our embrace, sitting down again, and I did the same. 'She had noticed your failure to–er–to increase the level of intimacy in your friendship, following that little private supper you shared before Christmas. She sensed how restless you were, and she thought it might be because you might be thinking of–well, of doing exactly what you are doing.' She managed a smile.

So Judyth too was perceptive. It was no surprise, but as I took on what Celia had said, I wished very much that Judyth had told me what was on her mind. But then I thought, would it have made any difference? and instantly answered my own question: no, it wouldn't.

No wonder Judyth had kept her distance.

Finally I rode down to Tavy St Luke's.

It was almost dark by then, but Hal and I knew the way. I was tying my horse's reins to the post behind the priest's house long before I was ready . . .

Jonathan was the closest to me of all of them. He was like my brother, and, striding up the path to the door, I recognized that friendship and liking had turned into love. As I prepared to break my news to him and face the immediate future without his kind, compassionate presence in it, I knew that I'd left him till last because this was going to be the hardest.

He did not speak for some time when I'd finished.

Finally I said, 'What do you think? Please tell me, Jonathan. Your silence is starting to worry me.'

He turned. He looked . . . I couldn't tell. Then he smiled. 'It means a great deal to me that my opinion matters, Gabe.

There is nothing sinister in the delay, I assure you; I was thinking.'

'And?'

'It seems to me that when you left your life as a ship's surgeon, it was because you had no choice. It was forced upon you. Because of this, there has perhaps always been a part of you that has carried a profound resentment. You have made a success of life here. You have worked hard, you have made friends, there are very many people who would now be dead were it not for you. But I have often sensed that a part of you wanted to return to the old life.'

'I thought it was impossible,' I muttered.

'Yes, I understand that. Now you know it *is* possible.' He paused, then said softly, 'And that changes everything.'

'Then I go with your blessing?'

'Of course. I will pray for you. And,' he added – and that enigmatic expression was back – 'I shall pray for your safe return.'

'I—' But I could not go on.

'If you do return, my dear friend,' Jonathan's quiet voice filled the difficult silence, 'if you do eventually decide that life on land is the right life for you, next time it will not be because it has been forced upon you. It will be because you have chosen it.'

And now, little more than a month later – Walter Haverleigh is not a man who brooks unnecessary delay – here I was on the Plymouth quayside, waiting for Hieronymus Petrarcus to collect me in the *Maartje* and take me to join the *Luipaard*. She would have been furnished with everything necessary for her long voyage, and in my own quarters I knew I would find the crates of medical supplies that I myself had purchased – with Walter's money – when Hieronymus and I returned to Plymouth from Cheverstone.

It had not taken very much for Walter Haverleigh to persuade me to take up the role of ship's surgeon on the *Luipaard*'s next voyage to the Eastern Seas. Given my state of mind immediately before he asked me, the rapidity with which I agreed might have surprised him. But it didn't surprise me.

It transpired that Ned Warham's accident, although it happened when the ship was back in the creek at Newtown, was not the first medical emergency of the voyage. The urgent need for a surgeon had been painfully felt on too many occasions, and when some of these accidents and sicknesses were described to me, I knew I could have saved at least some of the lives that had been lost. Now that the first cargoes were safely stored at Cheverstone and profits were assured, it was clear that Walter felt confident in expending more capital on the fitting-out of his beautiful ship, including providing his company with an extremely well-equipped physician.

I stood and stared out to where the *Maartje* was approaching. Hieronymus saw me, and raised an arm in greeting. I returned the gesture.

I turned and looked along the quay, then back at the buildings and the rooftops of Plymouth rising up in their ranks behind. Beyond were the fields, the moorland, the Tamar estuary and the Tavy, winding its way up into the green and wooded country where I had lived these past four years; where I had expected to live out my quiet country physician's life.

But I thought you liked it here! my sister had cried. *I thought you were happy!*

She was right: I did like the Rosewyke life, and it had indeed made me happy. For a moment I allowed the pain of departure to flood through me, picturing the faces of the people I loved and who I knew quite well I would miss deeply.

The *Maartje* was close now, and, bending down, I picked up my old familiar leather bag.

Firmly closing off the thoughts of home, I braced my shoulders and prepared to face my future.